THE WORLD'S CLASSICS

VATHEK

WILLIAM BECKFORD was born, probably in London, in 1760. On the death of his father, a famous Lord Mayor of London, in 1770 he inherited an immense fortune. At the age of nineteen he left for a tour of Holland, Germany, Italy, and France and over the next forty years he was often away from England, at times in order to escape scandal. In 1783 he married, and in the following year he became the Member of Parliament for Wells. In 1786, soon after the birth of a second child, his wife died. Beckford spent large sums in collecting works of art and curios and in the building and extravagant decoration of his mansion, Fonthill Abbey. He died in 1844 from a severe attack of influenza.

Beckford was eccentric, extravagant, and of undoubted intellectual ability. *Vathek*, first written in French at the age of twenty-one, was translated under his supervision and published in England in 1786. His other books include *Dreams, Waking Thoughts, and Incidents* (1783, revised 1834) and *Recollections of an Excursion to the Monasteries of Alcobaça and Batalka* (1835).

ROGER LONSDALE is Fellow and Tutor in English at Balliol College, Oxford. His published work includes *Dr Charles Burney: a Literary Biography* (1965) and an edition of *The Poems of Gray, Collins and Goldsmith* (1969). He is currently engaged on a *New Oxford Book of Eighteenth-Century Verse*.

THE WORLD'S CLASSICS

===

WILLIAM BECKFORD
Vathek

===

Edited with an Introduction by
ROGER LONSDALE

Oxford New York
OXFORD UNIVERSITY PRESS
1983

Oxford University Press, Walton Street, Oxford OX2 6DP

London Glasgow New York Toronto
Delhi Bombay Calcutta Madras Karachi
Kuala Lumpur Singapore Hong Kong Tokyo
Nairobi Dar es Salaam Cape Town
Melbourne Auckland

and associates in
Beirut Berlin Ibadan Mexico City Nicosia

Introduction, Notes, Bibliography, and Chronology
© Oxford University Press 1970, 1983

This edition first published 1970 by Oxford University Press
First issued, with revisions, as a World's Classics paperback 1983

British Library Cataloguing in Publication Data
Beckford, William
Vathek.—(The world's classics)
I. Title II. Lonsdale, Roger
823'.7[F] PR6091.V/
ISBN 0-19-281645-4

Printed in Great Britain by
Hazell Watson & Viney Limited
Aylesbury, Bucks

CONTENTS

INTRODUCTION

I

THE long and extravagant career of the author of *Vathek* would surely have impressed Samuel Johnson as a notable and sustained illustration of what his Imlac had called (in his own very different 'oriental' tale) 'that hunger of imagination which preys incessantly upon life'. The son of a famous radical Member of Parliament for the City of London (and twice its Lord Mayor), inheriting at the age of nine his father's huge income from his West Indian plantations, 'England's wealthiest son' (as Byron called him) was to be driven from England in his early twenties after a scandal over an adolescent boy, to wander restlessly round Europe for a number of years, to return to virtual ostracism by respectable society, to become a celebrated and fastidious collector of books and paintings, to publish some brilliant travel books, and to build at prodigious expense the most famous if least substantial of his monuments, the huge Gothic edifice known as Fonthill Abbey, which was to collapse three years after Beckford sold it in 1822 for £300,000. Beckford himself survived until 1844.

Inevitably *Vathek*, written in French in 1782 when Beckford was twenty-one, has often been considered as merely one more manifestation of a brilliant but baffling personality. The story of its origins and publication is a bizarre episode almost as strange as the tale itself; and the difficulty of attaching any clear meaning or satiric purpose to *Vathek* has also tended to force its readers back on the author himself for enlightenment. What is known about the boy after the early death of his father can easily come to seem a preparation for *Vathek*. There is plenty of evidence of the rapid growth of his escapist longings for the exotic and beautiful, especially the oriental. John Lettice, his tutor, had to force him at the age of thirteen to burn a 'splendid heap of oriental drawings etc.', but Beckford's appetite for such reading matter as the *Arabian Nights* and its imitators, for the more substantial imaginative literature which he read voraciously, as well as for any works concerned with the sadistic exploits of famous despots of all ages, remained irrepressible. An important influence on the boy was Alexander Cozens, his Russian-born and widely travelled drawing-master, who encouraged Beckford's exotic interests and who became the recipient of a remarkable series of rhapsodic letters in his pupil's adolescence and early manhood. An influence of a different sort may be attributed to his possessive and autocratic mother, with her Calvinistic leanings: *Vathek* itself, both in its defiant, over-insistent, sometimes childish ridicule of all religion, and in the unexpected power and conviction with which the Caliph's final damnation is represented, may embody a complex reaction to her.

Beckford soon became an author. In Switzerland in 1777 he wrote *The Long Story* (published in 1930 as *The Vision*), an extraordinary if somewhat indigestible achievement for a seventeen-year-old boy, compounded of spectacular Alpine scenery, Beckford's apparent interest in some local occultist philosophers, and his own unusually powerful and fertile imagination. Other tales, still largely unpublished, followed his return to England in 1778, and between 1780 and 1783 he worked spasmodically on translations from the Arabic manuscripts which had belonged to Edward Wortley Montagu (now in the Bodleian Library). His own additions to these tales (discussed at length by Professor Parreaux)[1] reveal the characteristic alternation in Beckford of moods of longing for secluded, prelapsarian innocence and the indulgence of sexual and sadistic fantasy.

The young Beckford was always claiming for himself an amoral, childish innocence: 'I am like one of those plants which bloom in a sequestered crevice of the rocks, and which but few are destined to discover', he wrote at the age of twenty.[2] In April 1781 he wrote to Lady Hamilton: 'I fear I shall never be . . . good for anything in this world, but composing airs, building towers, forming gardens, collecting old Japan, and writing a journey to China or the moon.'[3] In October 1781 he pleaded with the Countess Rosenberg: 'Don't call me *illustre ami* and *homme unique*. I'm still in my cradle! Spare the delicacy of my infantile ears. Leave me to scamper on verdant banks—all too ready, alas, to crumble, but rainbow-tinted and flower-strewn.'[4] Inevitably the escapist was in constant danger of collision with the real world. His hostess in Naples during his Grand Tour in 1780-1, Lady Hamilton, horrified to learn of a homosexual entanglement in Venice, pursued him with well-intentioned advice: 'infamy, *eternal infamy* (my Soul freezes when I write the word) attends the giving way to the soft alluring of a criminal passion.'[5] Back in England,

[1] See Bibliography, p. xxxix.
[2] Lewis Melville, *William Beckford*, p. 92.
[3] Ibid., p. 105.
[4] Boyd Alexander, *England's Wealthiest Son*, p. 14.
[5] Chapman, *Beckford*, p. 78.

Beckford found his family and friends concerned about his conduct and planning an illustrious political career for him. Ignoring such expectations and the conventions of English society for as long as possible, Beckford was before long involved in two complex relationships. By the summer of 1781 Louisa Beckford, the wife of his cousin Peter, was in love with him and, by the following autumn, Beckford himself was passionately attracted to William Courtenay, the thirteen-year-old son of Lord Courtenay.

The later months of 1781 were therefore a curiously intense period in Beckford's life, marked by emotional entanglements and a confrontation between his own irresponsible longings and the responsibilities carried by his wealth and social position. Mid-September 1781 brought celebrations at Fonthill of almost oriental magnificence to mark his coming of age. But the event which has always seemed most closely related to the conception of *Vathek* was the houseparty at the old Fonthill House at the following Christmas, to which Louisa Beckford and her sisters, some boys under their tutor Samuel Henley, William Courtenay, Alexander Cozens, and other guests were invited. Music was performed by famous singers, and the contribution of Philip de Loutherbourg, who had designed scenery, lighting and other theatrical effects for Garrick at Drury Lane, is also evident in Beckford's own, no doubt exaggerated, memories of this occasion, contained in a note dated 9 December 1838:

Immured we were 'au pied de la lettre' for three days following—doors and windows so strictly closed that neither common day light nor common place visitors could get in or even peep in—care worn visages were ordered to keep aloof—no sunk-in mouths or furroughed foreheads were permitted to meet our

eye. Our société was extremely youthful and lovely to look upon.
. . . The solid Egyptian Hall looked as if hewn out of a living
rock—the line of apartments and apparently endless passages
extending from it on either side were all vaulted—an intermin-
able stair case, which when you looked down it—appeared as
deep as the well in the pyramid—and when you looked up—
was lost in vapour, led to suites of stately apartments gleaming
with marble pavements—as polished as glass—and gawdy ceil-
ings. . . . Through all these suites—through all these galleries
—did we roam and wander—too often hand in hand—strains
of music swelling forth at intervals. . . . Sometimes a chaunt
was heard—issuing, no one could devine from whence—innocent affecting sounds—that stole into the heart with a bewitching languour and melted the most beloved the most susceptible
of my fair companions into tears. Delightful indeed were these
romantic wanderings—delightful the straying about this little
interior world of exclusive happiness surrounded by lovely
beings, in all the freshness of their early bloom, so fitted to
enjoy it. Here, nothing was dull or vapid—here, nothing
ressembled in the least the common forms and usages, the 'train-
train' and routine of fashionable existence—all was essence—
the slightest approach to sameness was here untolerated—
monotony of every kind was banished. Even the uniform
splendour of gilded roofs—was partially obscured by the vapour
of wood aloes ascending in wreaths from cassolettes placed low
on the silken carpets in porcelain salvers of the richest japan.
The delirium of delight into which our young and fervid bosoms
were cast by such a combination of seductive influences may be
conceived but too easily. Even at this long, sad distance from
these days and nights of exquisite refinements, chilled by age,
still more by the coarse unpoetic tenor of the present dis-
enchanting period—I still feel warmed and irradiated by the
recollections of that strange, necromantic light which Loutherbourg had thrown over what absolutely appeared a realm of
Fairy, or rather, perhaps, a Demon Temple deep beneath the
earth set apart for tremendous mysteries—and yet how soft,

how genial was this quiet light. Whilst the wretched world
without lay dark, and bleak, and howling, whilst the storm was
raging against our massive walls and the snow drifting in clouds,
the very air of summer seemed playing around us—the choir of
low-toned melodious voices continued to sooth our ear, and
that every sense might in turn receive its blandishment tables
covered with delicious viands and fragrant flowers—glided
forth, by the aid of mechanism at stated intervals, from the
richly draped, and amply curtained recesses of the enchanted
precincts. The glowing haze investing every object, the mystic
look, the vastness, the intricacy of this vaulted labyrinth
occasioned so bewildering an effect that it became impossible
for any one to define—at the moment—where he stood, where
he had been, or to whither he was wandering—such was the
confusion—the perplexity so many illuminated storys of infinitely varied apartments gave rise to. It was, in short, the
realization of romance in its most extravagant intensity. No
wonder such scenery inspired the description of the Halls of
Eblis.[1]

II

Beckford later stated more than once that *Vathek* was
written in immediate response to the imaginative and
emotional stimulation of the events at Fonthill at Christmas 1781. After the description just quoted, he added:
'I composed *Vathek* immediately upon my return to town
thoroughly embued with all that passed at Fonthill during
this voluptuous festival.' After a similar account, he noted
again: 'I wrote V immediately upon my return to London
at the close of this romantic villegiatura.'[2] Since he was
back in London by January 1782, the date of composition
might seem to be unambiguously established. Elsewhere

---

[1] Oliver, *Beckford*, pp. 89-91.
[2] Chapman, *Beckford*, p. 102.

he noted that 'The fit I laboured under when I wrote Vathek lasted two days and a night.—W.B.'[1] Slightly longer was allowed in an account recorded by Cyrus Redding, according to whom Beckford stated: 'You will hardly credit how closely I could apply myself to study when young. I wrote "Vathek" in the French, as it now stands, at twenty-two [sic] years of age. It cost me three days and two nights of labour.'[2]

If the first draft of Vathek in French was written with unusual rapidity, it seems clear that Beckford then spent some months writing a full version. His unpublished 'Histoire de Darianoc' was written in obvious haste in cryptic, fragmentary and ungrammatical French, in contrast with the fair copy of the opening pages which also survives. The possibility that Vathek was drafted in a similar manner seems to have been confirmed by Professor Parreaux's recent discovery of a fragmentary draft of passages which occur towards the end of the tale.[3] The first dated reference to Vathek is in a letter to Henley on 1 May 1782: 'The Tale of the Caliph Vathec goes on surprisingly.'[4] At about the same time, it may be assumed, Beckford told Henley: 'My Caliph advances in his journey to Persepolis, alias Istekar; but want of time, I believe, will force me to stop his immediate proceedings.' But by 15 May 1782, when he left for the Continent, Vathek was almost certainly complete. His friend Lady Craven had read it by 29 May and

[1] In his copy of Stanhope's Greece in 1823-24 (1825), listed in the catalogue of the Third Portion of the sale of the Hamilton Palace Libraries, 1883, p. 155.

[2] Fifty Years' Recollections, Literary and Personal (1858), iii. 89.

[3] Beckford, pp. 529-32.

[4] Unless otherwise indicated the Beckford-Henley correspondence is quoted from The Collection of Autograph Letters and Historical Documents formed by Alfred Morrison (Second Series, 1882-1893), vol. i (1893), pp. 182-200; and Lewis Melville, William Beckford (1910), pp. 126-39 (mainly Henley's letters).

thought it 'very fine, horribly fine'.[1] At about the same time
Beckford wrote to her: 'quel Calife—pardonnez ma vanité;
j'avoue que je suis un peu fier de son voyage — je l'ai même
damné avec assez de magnificence'.[2] Further revision
lay ahead in the various French and English editions,
but *Vathek* was basically conceived and written between
January and mid-May 1782.

From this point an increasingly significant figure in the
history of *Vathek* is the Revd. Samuel Henley, formerly a
professor at William and Mary College in Virginia, who
had returned to a career as schoolmaster and private tutor
after the American Revolution. Henley's scholarly interest
in oriental literature inspired Beckford's confidence and
he came to rely heavily on the older man's willingness to
assist his literary enterprises. Henley was not, however,
meant at first to be the translator of *Vathek* into English.
On 15 September 1782 Beckford's tutor, John Lettice,
began a translation which breaks off less than half-way
through, a clumsy, literal version which nevertheless use-
fully indicates the nature of the French text at this early
stage. But Beckford turned eventually to the more accomplished Henley. Writing from Geneva on 18 November
1783, Beckford referred to Henley's agreement to translate
Vathek, 'the only production of mine which I am not
ashamed of, or with which I am not disgusted'. He also
promised to 'bring you some Caliphs not unworthy to
succeed your beloved *Vathec*'—a reference to his progress
with the 'Episodes', the additional tales which he planned
to add to *Vathek* shortly before the final catastrophe.
Working on the 'Episodes' in Paris, London, and at

[1] Oliver, *Beckford*, p. 100.
[2] Chapman, *Beckford*, p. 134.

Fonthill, he inquired regularly about the translation of *Vathek*: 'I suppose by this time you are deep in the halls of damnation, hear the melancholy voice of Eblis in the dead of night, & catch moonlight glimpses of Nouronihar. I long eagerly to read your translation' (19 May 1784).

In June 1784 Henley promised a complete transcript of the translation, but it was apparently not until early 1785 that Beckford began to see it. The intervening scandal over William Courtenay had no doubt distracted him. In a letter of about 26 February 1785 he wrote to Henley: 'Your translation had all the spirit of the Caliphs & their daemons. I long for the continuation.' On 21 March he wrote even more warmly in a passage which may be quoted as some indication of his approval of the English translation:

You make me proud of *Vathec*. The blaze just at present is so overpowering that I can see no faults; but you may depend upon my hunting diligently after them.

Pray send the continuation . . . the original when first born scarce gave me so much rapture as y^r translation.

Were I well & in spirits I should run wild among my rocks and forests, telling stones, trees & labourers how gloriously you have succeeded. My imagination is again on fire.

Beckford later made some changes to the translation and his letters with Henley discuss the handling of specific episodes in the novel and material for the annotation which it had been decided Henley should provide. Beckford's superior knowledge is always evident, as he advises the sometimes puzzled Henley about various scholarly sources for oriental material; but it was undoubtedly Henley who wrote most of the extremely elaborate notes which were to appear in 1786. Such was Henley's zeal that in late April or early May 1785 (misdated 13 April 1786 in the *Morrison Catalogue*) Beckford had to restrain him:

> Upon my word you pay *Vathec* much more attention than he deserves, & do you not think we shall usher him too pompously into the world with a dissertation on his parts & machinery? Notes are certainly necessary, & the diss[ertation] I myself should very much approve, but fear the world might imagine I fancied myself the author, not of an Arabian tale, but an Epic poem.

Beckford also urged on Henley 'a light, easy style, that *Misses*, &c., may not be scared—for, after all, a poor Arabian story teller can only venture to say *Virginibus Puerisque canto*'. Significantly, Henley's enthusiasm was becoming proprietorial.

In July 1785 Beckford submitted to family pressure and left for Switzerland, leaving the English translation of *Vathek* with Henley. He was still working on the 'Episodes' and on 9 February 1786 wrote to Henley to stress unambiguously that *Vathek* was not to be published without them. He expected they would take about a year to complete. Henley had perhaps been pressing for the separate publication of the tale for which he had laboured so hard but Beckford was firm: 'The anticipation of so principal a tale as that of the Caliph would be tearing the proudest feather from my turban.' He planned to publish the complete French text first, to be followed by Henley's annotated English version, which Beckford assured him, 'I doubt not, will be received with the honors due to so valuable a morsel of *orientalism*.' Beckford wrote again on 1 August 1786. He was awaiting the manuscript of Henley's 'notes & illustrations' to *Vathek*, but the death of his wife had depressed him and he had not completed the

'Episodes'. There was no hope of *Vathek*'s publication
during the coming winter. He again emphasized: 'I
would not have him on any account come forth without
his companions.'

Such instructions were already futile, as Beckford soon
learned, for Henley's English translation had in fact been
published in London on 7 June 1786. Whether or not we
believe Henley's later claim that he had not received Beckford's letters forbidding publication, it is possible to feel
some sympathy for his desire to see his labours in print. In
a letter to Beckford's legal adviser, Thomas Wildman, on
23 October 1786,[1] Henley defended his action on the
grounds of Beckford's enthusiasm for his translation,
especially in contrast to his disapproval of Lettice's earlier
attempt. Beckford 'not only supervised and corrected my
manuscript, but retained the variations and additions I had
made'. Even so, Henley was clearly dishonest: just how
dishonest is indicated by an inscription in a copy of his
translation in the Bibliothèque Nationale: 'From the
Author/Rev^d S Henley.' Beckford's name was not mentioned in this translation, Henley's ambiguous preface
implying that the work was a translation from a genuine
Arabic original. Henley's proprietorial attitude was revealed
again when he replied to the suggestion by the antiquary
Stephen Weston (*Gentleman's Magazine*, lvii (Jan. 1787),
55) that the tale had been 'composed as a text for the purpose of giving to the publick the information contained in
the notes'. Henley's reply in February 1787 (p. 120) does
nothing to suggest that the work was not a translation from
the Arabic or that it was not the entire concern of one man,
the editor himself.

[1] Melville, pp. 137-9.

Beckford, who was in Lausanne, retaliated as best he could. Until recently an ingenious hypothesis has been accepted according to which Beckford was forced to commission a clumsy retranslation of Henley's English into French, and that this was the text printed at Lausanne in late November or early December 1786 (with 1787 on the title-page). Professor Parreaux's careful investigation finally disposed of this theory in 1960. The Lausanne text undoubtedly represents Beckford's own French text, from a manuscript which he must have had with him, in a slightly earlier state than that translated by Henley. Before publication this text was corrected by Jean David Levade, according to his own statement. None of Henley's notes appear in this edition and Beckford's authorship is established in the prefatory note. At the end of June 1787 an extensively revised version of the French text, in which sentences were made shorter and less complex and the style generally was lightened, was published at Paris (a second issue can be dated 4 September 1787). The evidence suggests that this edition was supervised by François Verdeil, Beckford's doctor who was accompanying him on his travels. The revision was no doubt basically Beckford's own but Verdeil's advice may have been important: at the same time Verdeil was probably responsible for the many errors and defects of this edition, especially in the notes, a selection from Henley's edition now being translated for the first time.

III

While the publication of *Vathek* ended in confusion and disappointment for Beckford, it is not true to say, as do Chapman, Parreaux, and other writers, that the publication of his youthful masterpiece passed virtually unnoticed in England. Indeed, since it is central to Professor Parreaux's argument that Beckford was in revolt against the social and literary conventions of his time, which were unsympathetic to his genius, the actual reception of the tale is worth summarizing.[1]

Vathek was in fact reviewed at length, and on the whole enthusiastically, in at least five of the leading literary journals. No reviewer took seriously Henley's claim that the tale was a translation from the Arabic, but its literary affiliations were readily apparent. The *Monthly Review* in May 1787 (lxxvi. 450) stated calmly enough that *Vathek* 'preserves the peculiar character of the Arabian Tale, which is not only to overstep nature and probability, but even to pass beyond the verge of possibility, and suppose things, which cannot be for a moment conceived'. It was 'written with spirit, fancy, and humour, and will afford much entertainment to those who are fond of this kind of reading'. The notes, 'which are of a character entirely different from that of the work', contained 'many learned quotations, elegant criticisms, and judicious remarks'. The *Critical Review* in July 1786 (lxii. 37–42) had speculated, as did other reviews, about the nature of our pleasure in the supernatural. It went on to detect in *Vathek* 'the acute turns of modern composition, so easily learned in the school of Voltaire', but thought that it was told with 'elegance and spirit'. Its moral was praised as applicable to 'every climate and religion'. The only criticism of the notes was that they were 'too short'.

---

[1] Cf. Parreaux, *Beckford*, p. 333: 'En 1786, les conditions psychologiques nécessaires au succès de *Vathek*, que les changements historiques allaient favoriser, n'étaient pas encore prêtes. Aussi en 1786, *Vathek* passa-t-il presque inaperçu.'

The *European Magazine* in August 1786 (x. 102-4), after congratulating the author on his knowledge of eastern customs and his handling of 'the marvellous', praised *Vathek* for its superiority to genuine Arabian Tales in that it inculcated 'a moral of the greatest importance': i.e. the fate of those who pursue unlawful and immoral pleasures. The ending was acclaimed as 'picturesque description, which more than borders on the sublime'. This writer also suspected that the tale was of French origin and again praised the notes. Henry Maty's *A New Review* in June and July 1786 (ix. 410-12, x. 33-9) could not have been more enthusiastic: 'it is not often that works of real genius appear. Whenever, therefore, a literary comet visits our hemisphere, it becomes a duty in us to point it out. As a phenomenon of this sort we regard the history of Vathek.' The moral, character portrayal and impressive knowledge of the manners and customs of the East were praised and the 'sublime' was once more adduced: 'A machinery, not only new, but wild and sublime, seizes on the mind, and pervades the whole composition.' In summary, 'the author, in the diversities of writing, appears to display at pleasure the caustick quickness of Voltaire; the easy sportiveness of Ariosto; the sombrous grotesque of Dante; and the terrific greatness of Milton'. The reviewer hoped that a favourable reception would encourage the author 'to publish the whole suite of Tales to which Vathek belongs'.

The *English Review* in September 1786 (viii. 180-4) was alone in questioning Beckford's 'moral', which the other reviewers gratefully accepted at face value. This writer first praised the tale for its characters ('strongly marked, though carried beyond nature'), its suitably 'wild and improbable' incidents, its use of the supernatural ('solemn and awful, though sometimes horrid'), and the 'bold and shocking' catastrophe. The ending was once more 'striking, and sometimes sublime'. In objecting to the moral, however, this reviewer was pointing—even if clumsily, more sensitively than his colleagues—to the personal implications of the tale for Beckford: 'Indolence and childishness are represented as the source of happiness; while ambition and the desire of knowledge, so laudable and meritorious when properly directed, are painted in odious colours, and punished as crimes.'

In spite of the praise of the reviewers, the evidence suggests that *Vathek* did not at first sell particularly well (the 1809 edition consists of the unsold sheets of the 1786 edition). In any case, such praise as it received was inevitably soured for Beckford, if it ever reached him as he travelled on the Continent, by the unpleasant circumstances of its publication. A certain 'A. V.' paid Beckford a curious compliment by contributing a long versification in couplets of the conclusion of the tale to the *Gentleman's Magazine* between January and March 1790 (lx. 69-70, 163-5, 258-9), in the belief that it was 'a subject more adapted to Poetry than to Prose'. But now that his authorship was known, interest in the novel tended all too easily to turn to gossip about Beckford's character. Thus, Mrs. Thrale-Piozzi wrote in her journal on 3 January 1791:

I have been reading Vathek, 'tis a mad Book to be sure, and written by a mad Author, yet there is a sublimity about it— particularly towards the Conclusion.

Mr Beckford's *favourite Propensity* is all along visible I think; particularly in the luscious Descriptions given of Gulchenrouz . . .[1]

---

[1] *Thraliana*, ed. K. C. Balderston (1940), ii. 799; cf. ii. 969, n. 2.

Yet, in one way or another, *Vathek* was soon exerting a definite influence on the next literary generation. Henley's voluminous notes were quarried by such writers as Isaac D'Israeli (*Romances*, 1799) and John Hamilton Reynolds (*Sofie, An Eastern Tale*, 1814), and the oriental fantasies of such poets as Southey, Moore, Landor and Barry Cornwall are also indebted to the tale itself. Novelists in whose work, to a greater or lesser extent, the influence of *Vathek* has been detected, include Benjamin Disraeli (*Alroy*, 1833), Hawthorne (*The Scarlet Letter*, 1850), and Meredith (*The Shaving of Shagpat*, 1855). Beckford's most enthusiastic admirer among the Romantics was Byron, who referred warmly to *Vathek* in the final note to *The Giaour* (1813) and on other occasions imitated a passage from it and mentioned Beckford himself in his poetry. Byron's recorded conversation bears further testimony to his admiration. A colourful series of later admirers, including Poe, Mallarmé and Swinburne, sustained interest in Beckford's minor masterpiece; and its popularity is sufficiently indicated by the number of editions in the later nineteenth century. More recently, the appearance of unpublished material has helped to increase interest in his life and writings. The 'Episodes' intended for *Vathek* were translated into English in 1912; *The Long Story* was published (as *The Vision*) in 1930; and a number of translations from Arabic, still unpublished, were described in full for the first time as recently as 1960 by Professor Parreaux. Beckford's correspondence and journals are still being published, his scope and achievement as a collector reassessed, and, with the appearance of each mass of new material, his puzzling character re-examined.

IV

The fascination of Beckford's inscrutable personality and the difficulty of relating *Vathek* securely to contemporary literary conventions have resulted in a great deal of discussion of the novel as a manifestation merely of the author's own psyche. Ultimately, this approach may be justified, but various comments made by the early reviewers, as they tried to find their bearings with this strange tale, can provide guidance in the purely literary consideration of *Vathek*. Most of the reviewers, while refusing to believe that *Vathek* was a genuine Arabian tale, had no difficulty in relating it to the *Arabian Nights*, first translated into English early in the century. Here was the precedent for wild, extravagant, and sometimes savage, incidents, supernatural agencies, and exotic settings. The eighteenth-century reader to some extent rationalized his delight in the *Arabian Nights* by telling himself that it was also instructive as a genuine depiction of Eastern manners and Eastern genius. If this was not true of the numerous European imitations of the *Arabian Nights* which had subsequently appeared in France and England, it is clear that *Vathek* impressed its reviewers as markedly superior to the usual 'oriental' imitation. The author's apparently detailed knowledge of Eastern manners and customs, his careful attention to local colour and to what Byron was to praise as the 'costume' of the tale, had no precedent in English. Henley's elaborate annotation undoubtedly reinforced this impression; but this was a different matter from Beckford's own ability to combine an imaginative entry into the East with detailed, even if second-hand, knowledge of its life and literature. (Cf. *A New Review*, cited above: 'Perpetual references to the opinions and doctrines of the Orientals are every where interwoven with the incidents of the narrative. Traits of nature are discernible, in every page, through the veil of associations and habits dissimilar from our own.')

Equally heartening, of course, to several of the reviewers was the 'moral' framework of Beckford's tale, which seemed to justify its more bizarre and grotesque incidents. Such didacticism, inevitably of a more simple-minded character, had been an especial feature of English 'oriental' tales and earlier writers had more than once similarly described the punishment of unrestrained longings and aspirations, sometimes reinforced, as were Vathek's, by defiance of Mahomet. But the contrast between *Vathek* and what had preceded it can be easily emphasized by reference to another literary work with the same title, the existence of which seems to have been hitherto unnoticed. This long-forgotten *Vathek* was a comedy written in French by the Countess de Genlis and translated into English in her *Theatre of Education* by Thomas Holcroft in 1781, only a year before Beckford's *Vathek* was written. This sentimental, sententious, humourless and didactic drama on the education of the young Vathek makes clear the chasm between what could so perfunctorily pass for 'oriental' literature at this period and Beckford's ability to start from Vathek as an actual historical personage as described in d'Herbelot's *Bibliothèque Orientale* (1697) and create around him a world which had its own imaginative intensity and coherence. Beckford certainly exploited what the *Arabian Nights* guaranteed: an escape into an exotic, voluptuous, sometimes cruel world of fantasy. Yet his treatment of 'oriental' elements went beyond the traditional in several ways: at times he burlesques the world he describes and its literary conventions

and at times he indulges in fantasy more potent and evo-
catively sensual than had yet appeared in the English
'oriental' imitations. In addition, *Vathek* looks ahead in
its awareness of the genuine oriental scholarship which
was beginning to appear through such scholars as Sir
William Jones, for example, and which would eventually
inhibit the purely fanciful 'oriental' fiction which had been
popular for so long.

To its first reviewers *Vathek* seemed an admirable imitation of the genuine Arabian tale, revealing 'picturesque'
and 'sublime' descriptive powers of an unusual kind, while
the extravagances proper to the form were counter-
balanced by an emphatic moral and a convincing knowledge
of the East. If there was little to relate it to the numerous
earlier English oriental tales, there was nothing in *Vathek*
which obliged the reviewers to connect it with contemporary 'Gothic' tendencies in the novel. Although later
literary historians have frequently resorted to the assertion
that such a relationship exists, it is not easy to see that
Vathek sets out to exploit the imaginative terror, the suspense or psychological shock tactics which were entering
the English novel at about this time (the most powerful
contributions to the kind were yet to appear, in the novels
of Mrs. Radcliffe and M. G. Lewis). Potential melodrama
and horror are almost invariably undermined and deflated
by Beckford's detached, urbane, and often comic tone.
When Nouronihar pursues a strange light up a mountain
and hears mysterious voices promising her infinite riches,
if she will desert Gulchenrouz for Vathek, we may seem to
be close to the 'Gothic'; but even here Beckford is less
concerned to exploit the 'terrific' possibilities of the scene
than to expound the choice facing Nouronihar. When

Carathis and her companions visit a cemetery and its ghouls, the result is ludicrously grotesque comedy. The final scenes of the tale are serious enough, but the sudden sombre power and sustained intensity of this vision of damnation transcend anything achieved by the Gothicists.

More instructive is the suspicion of the early reviewers that *Vathek* was of French origin. While the English version of the tale approved by Beckford has its own authority, it is significant that he did choose to write it in French (which he wrote and spoke with unusual facility)—a fact which only emphasizes that his real kinship is with such French writers of ironic oriental tales as Anthony Hamilton and Voltaire. Two reviewers detected in *Vathek* the 'acute turns' and 'caustick quickness' of Voltaire and parallels and similarities can be detected, although Beckford's often gratuitous comedy does not ultimately seem very close to Voltaire's purposeful, penetrating, rational irony. The real clue may be found in what Voltaire himself told the young Beckford: 'Je dois tout à votre oncle, le comte Antoine Hamilton.' Anthony Hamilton was indeed an ancestor (if not an uncle) of Beckford, but the literary kinship with the ironic pseudo-oriental tales which Hamilton wrote early in the century, supposedly to satirize the vogue for the *Arabian Nights* and their imitators at the French court, is even more striking. On 25 April 1782, while *Vathek* was being completed, Beckford wrote to Henley: 'By the bye, my Arabian tales go on prodigiously, & I think Count Hamilton will smile upon me when we are introduced to each other in paradice.' Beckford had a natural affinity with Hamilton's witty, ironic tone, his far-fetched and ludicrous episodes, his fondness for grotesque humour, his juxtapositions of the magnificent and commonplace, his alternation of evocative and farcical, even brutal, episodes, and his derisive subversion of conventional expectations, in such tales as *Fleur d'Epine* and *Les Quatres Facardins*. Many of Beckford's stylistic effects, his fondness for zeugma and bathos, the frequent deflationary touches at the end of paragraphs, the ludicrous hyperboles, as well as much of the comic tone as a whole, can be related more closely to Hamilton than to any earlier fiction.

The influence of Hamilton's opportunistic and casual burlesques perhaps made it inevitable that the tone of *Vathek* would not be consistent and the tale itself not very clearly unified. But beneath Beckford's elegant, urbane and lucid prose (not unsuccessfully imitated in Henley's slightly more ponderous English), ambiguity and even uncertainty of a different kind can often be detected. If Beckford enjoyed burlesquing the conventions and incidents of the traditional oriental tale and various features of the oriental world itself, the comic exaggeration cannot conceal strong elements of private fantasy. Brutal farce, perverse and gratuitous derision of the aged and pious, grotesque comedy centred around Carathis, childish sarcasm and cynical irony are strangely mingled with an imaginative sympathy with Vathek's sensual and intellectual aspirations, with Nouronihar's longings, and with Gulchenrouz's amoral innocence. Vathek himself is handled in a number of different ways in the tale: unrestrained in the indulgence of his senses and appetites, restless, impatient, and insatiably curious, his self-importance is frequently comic, his childish exasperation and fury that of a buffoon. He can be flung like a sack of dates over the shoulder of one of his Ethiopian women, or appear a majestic and 'noble' lover to Nouronihar, can be stung by bees in revenge for his desecration of Rocnabad or approach a tragic defiance in his impiety and acceptance of his evil fate, when warned to repent by the Good Genius.

·Beckford wavers between identification with the magnificent pursuit of forbidden knowledge (treated seriously in *The Long Story* in 1777) and self-conscious, Hamiltonian detachment from Vathek's predicament, just as some of his descriptions of scenes of oriental magnificence are strangely interrupted by bawdy farce. And just as the tone at times seems unsteady and distractingly variable, the tale's 'moral' is itself ambiguous. It is not enough simply to regard the supposed lesson—that the indulgence of unrestrained appetites and the pursuit of forbidden knowledge will be punished by Heaven—as a perfunctory gesture or parody. Admittedly, most of the original reviewers accepted it at face value and only one of them pointed out the ⌐ her aspect of the 'lesson', the recommendation of Gulchenrouz's dubious, amoral, childish 'innocence' as some kind of good in itself. The official moral framework is in practice constantly subverted by the conduct of the tale, for Beckford clearly enjoys Vathek's constant excesses and crimes against the pious and sacred. But his final vision of the lonely damned ultimately succeeds in fusing Beckford's sense of his own predicament with the ostensible message of his story.

Perhaps no more definite meaning should be sought for in *Vathek* than is suggested by its role as a vehicle for the imaginative projection of private fantasy and emotional turmoil, which the obtrusive comic tone and polished style essay to keep under some kind of control. Enough has already been said in biographical terms about the origins of the tale, although it may be repeated that Beckford himself explicitly related it to the events and setting at the old Fonthill House, especially the great 'Egyptian Hall', at Christmas 1781. Indeed, he was prepared to admit later that real persons were portrayed in his story, and commentators have not hesitated to descry aspects of his parents and other members of his circle, including William Courtenay and Louisa Beckford, in its characters. Such literal interpretation, whatever its limitations, is perhaps preferable to Professor Parreaux's elaborate expansion of the meaning of *Vathek* to the point where it becomes a myth of aristocratic defiance of bourgeois morality in the England of the Industrial Revolution. If Beckford did come to dislike intensely the changing world into which he survived (he did not die until 1844), most of the embittered statements to illustrate that dislike have to be found at a later period than *Vathek*. At the age of twenty-one, Beckford was still 'basically too irresponsible to write a convincing myth of the doomed future of irresponsibility'.[1] Most of his defiance is directed against narrower and more immediate threats to his own self-indulgence: family disapproval of his extravagant aestheticism and irresponsibility, his mother's Methodistical rigour, the expectation that he embark on a purposeful political career. Combined or alternating with such defiance, which often seems childish or gratuitous, is the troubled fantasy which enters the story with Nouronihar and Gulchenrouz, in which Beckford appears to identify variously with the perplexities, frustrations and longings of all three of his main characters. From this point on, the comic tone is less assured, something close to a genuine apprehension of unhappiness can

---

[1] 'The Mask of Beckford', *Times Literary Supplement*, 10 Feb. 1961, p. 82.

be felt, and most of the grotesque comedy is transferred to
Carathis.

Beckford's elegant, ironic prose may in itself go some of
the way to draw into a workable unity the various elements
of youthful irresponsibility, self-indulgent fantasy, occult
speculation and fastidious orientalism. Yet it is only in
the final pages of *Vathek* that Beckford's nervousness at
being caught taking his own story seriously disappears.
This vision of damnation in the Halls of the melancholy
Eblis, himself so striking and acceptable a recreation of
Milton's newly fallen Satan, attains a conviction and unexpected tragic power (in part the 'sublimity' unanimously
recognized by the early reviewers), which will always leave
the reader with the impression that he has been reading a
greater book than has in fact been the case. It remains a
remarkable achievement for so youthful an author, a partial manifestation at least of powers which were never to
be fully revealed in any of the preoccupations of his long
and lonely life: fascinating and yet unsatisfying, hardly
more substantial than the fastidiously assembled and now
dispersed collections of paintings and books, or the fallen
tower of Fonthill Abbey itself.

The young Beckford had always envisaged some grand
or dramatic fate for himself. At the age of seventeen he
had asked: 'What will be my Life? what misfortunes lurk in
wait for me? what Glory?'[1] He wrote a partial answer in
his journal some ten years later: 'How tired I am of keeping a mask on my countenance. How tight it sticks—it
makes me sore.' That mask came to present to the world
defensive pride, elaborate self-indulgence, and, at last,
cold cynicism. *Vathek*, described by Marcel May as 'songe

[1] Melville, p. 32.

et confession d'un Gulchenrouz, récit magnifique et puéril d'un enfant de génie qui ne voulut point grandir', had offered one glimpse, and not an entirely illuminating one, behind the mask. Perhaps Swinburne, writing on 9 June 1876 to another significant admirer of *Vathek*, Stéphane Mallarmé, best described the tantalizing talent of the tale and, bringing us back as ever to its author, the sad predicament of the Caliph of Fonthill:

Etre millionnaire et vouloir être poète et ne l'être qu'à moitié, — se sentir quelque chose comme du génie, qui n'est après tout et ne sera jamais qu'un à peu près, — réussir presque à trouver le chemin de l'artiste créateur, puis retomber sur ses richesses, cela doit faire de la vie d'un poète manqué quelque chose de plus triste que la salle d'Eblis.[1]

[1] *The Swinburne Letters*, ed. Cecil Y. Lang, 6 vols., New Haven, 1959-62, vi. 276-7.

NOTE ON THE TEXT

THE problems presented by the text of *Vathek* are probably unique. Beckford himself wrote the work in French in 1782, from which year dates Lettice's incomplete manuscript translation into English. The text published at Lausanne late in 1786 evidently represents an intermediate stage in the development of the novel between the text translated by Lettice and that translated by Henley and published in London in June 1786. The Lausanne text was corrected by Jean David Levade; that published in Paris in 1787 was extensively revised, no doubt by Beckford himself, but with the assistance of François Verdeil. Beckford made about a hundred further changes to the French text when it was reprinted at London in 1815, in some cases returning to readings in the Lausanne edition.

Although the English translation published in 1786 was the work of Samuel Henley, Beckford read, corrected and praised it before publication and shared some responsibility for the elaborate annotation. The 1809 edition was merely a reissue of the unsold sheets of the 1786 edition with a new title-page. The text printed here is the 'Third Edition' of 1816, in which Beckford made several hundred changes, large and small, to Henley's translation. Rather unsystematically he adopted many, though by no means all, of the changes which he had made to the French text in 1787 and 1815. He also introduced changes which do not appear in any French text and, while he corrected some of the blunders in Henley's translation, he allowed (whether deliberately or not) other mistranslations to remain. (For Beckford's treatment of Henley's notes in 1816, see the introduction to the Explanatory Notes.) The 1823 edition, perhaps published in response to public interest in the sale of Fonthill, contained a few small changes, for which Beckford may not have been responsible.

The 1816 edition clearly contains the text which Beckford himself prepared for English readers. There are three issues of this edition, the most important feature of what is here called the first issue being an expanded version of the passage (on p. 116 of the present edition) concerning the narrators of the 'Episodes' in the Hall of Eblis, which Beckford must still have thought of publishing. The second issue omits the names and compresses the passage. Although Chapman states (*Bibliography*, p. 26) that these two issues are otherwise 'exactly similar', there are a few other changes. Since these are clearly corrections to the other issue, they are important as confirming that it is the second issue which embodies Beckford's final version. Twice 'funeral' is corrected to 'funereal' (p. 70, l. 7, p. 112, l. 8 in the present edition) and 'yourself' is corrected to 'thyself', as demanded by the grammar (p. 118, l. 24). The third issue is identical textually, merely adding the names of the booksellers, Taylor and Hessey, to that of Clarke on the title-page.

The extent of the corrections which Beckford made to the edition of 1816, together with his earlier approval of Henley's original translation, give this English text an

authority neglected by those who emphasize the fact that
Beckford wrote the work in French, or who read *Vathek*
in the modern translation of the French text of 1815 by
H. B. Grimsditch. The fact remains that no one text of
Vathek in either French or English can be absolutely
definitive.

  The text of the second issue of the 1816 edition of
Vathek has been reproduced here. In a few cases readings
from the editions of 1786 and 1823 have been preferred.
The sometimes inconsistent spelling has been preserved,
as has the heavy and idiosyncratic punctuation, which
evidently served an emphatic and rhythmic function.
Occasionally missing quotation marks have been supplied at the end of passages of direct speech.

SELECT BIBLIOGRAPHY

EDITIONS OF *VATHEK*

SOME account of the earliest editions has necessarily been given already in the Introduction and there is more detailed comment on their complex relationships in the Note on the Text. In Beckford's lifetime there were seven editions of the French text: 1786 (Lausanne, dated 1787), 1787 (Paris, two issues), 1791 (London, apparently the Lausanne edition with a cancel title), 1815 (London), 1819 (Paris; a retranslation of Henley's English version), [1828?] (London), and 1834 (London). The next French edition (Paris, 1876) contained Mallarmé's notable 'Préface' and there have been nine later editions of the French text, four of which reunite it with the 'Episodes': ed. Guy Chapman (2 vols., Cambridge, 1929); ed. J. B. Brunius (Paris, [1948]); ed. E. Giddey (Lausanne, 1962); and ed. M. Lévy (Paris, 1981). The 'Episodes' have been separately edited by R. J. Gemmett (1975). (For the 'Episodes', see the explanatory note to p. 116.)

Henley's original English translation (1786) was reissued with a cancel title-page in 1809, but with no other change to the unsold sheets. Beckford's own final revision of the text and notes appeared in 1816 as the 'Third Edition. Revised and Corrected' (there were three issues). It was followed by editions in 1823 (the 'Fourth', with a few very slight changes), 1832 ('Fifth Edition'), 1834 (as Vol. 41 of Bentley's Standard Novels, with Walpole's *The Castle of Otranto* and M. G. Lewis's translation of *The Bravo of Venice*). There were other editions in English in 1834 in Philadelphia (the first American edition had been in 1816), Baltimore, and Paris (as Vol. 59 of Baudry's Collection of Ancient and Modern British Novels and

Romances). The last edition in English before Beckford's death was in 1836. There were at least thirty-three further editions in English (sometimes with other works in one volume) before the end of the century and a further thirty have appeared since 1900. Of these editions those by Richard Garnett (1893; with Henley's notes) and H. B. Grimsditch (a new translation of the French text of 1815; Nonesuch Press, 1929, new editions, 1945, 1953, 1958) deserve mention. Recent editions include: 1930 (Everyman's Library, in *Shorter Novels of the Eighteenth Century*); 1931 (Modern Student's Library, New York, as *Three Eighteenth Century Romances*; reprinted 1963); 1966 (Four Square Books); 1970 (Oxford English Novels, ed. R. Lonsdale, with a selective collation of the English and French texts); 1972 (a facsimile of the English text of 1786 and the French texts of Lausanne and Paris, 1787, ed. R. J. Gemmett).

Vathek has appeared in German (1788, three different translations; later translations, 1842, 1907, 1921, 1924), Dutch (1837), Swedish (1927), and Italian (1946).

For a full list of editions of *Vathek* see R. J. Gemmett, 'An Annotated Checklist of the Works of William Beckford', *Papers of the Bibliographical Society of America*, lxi (1967), 243–58; and see also the 'Bibliographie Sommaire' in André Parreaux, *William Beckford* (Paris, 1960), pp. 543–6.

GENERAL WORKS ON BECKFORD

Boyd Alexander, *The Journal of William Beckford in Portugal and Spain, 1787–1788* (1954); *Life at Fonthill, 1807–1822* (1957), and *England's Wealthiest Son* (1962); John Britton, *Graphical and Literary Illustrations of Fonthill Abbey, Wiltshire* (1823); H. A. N. Brockman, *The Caliph of Fonthill* (1956); Guy Chapman, *A Bibliography of William Beckford of Fonthill* (1930), and *Beckford* (1937; revised edition 1952); Marc Chardonne, *Eblis ou L'Enfer de William Beckford* (Paris, 1967); *The Collection of Autograph Letters and Historical Documents Formed by Alfred*

Morrison (Second Series, 1882–1893), i (1893); M. P. Conant, *The Oriental Tale in England in the Eighteenth Century* (New York, 1908); A. B. Fothergill, *Beckford of Fonthill* (1979); R. J. Gemmett, *William Beckford* (Boston, 1977); H. B. Gottlieb, *William Beckford of Fonthill . . . A Brief Narrative and Catalogue of an Exhibition* (New Haven, 1960; but see the review by R. B. Metzdorf and L. S. T. Thompson in *Papers of the Bibliographical Society of America*, liv (1960), 131–5); Charlotte Lansdown, *Recollections of the Late Willism Beckford of Fonthill* (1893); J. Lees-Milne, *William Beckford* (1976); Fatma Moussa Mahmoud (ed.), *William Beckford . . . Bicentenary Essay* (*Cairo Studies in English*, 1960); Jean-Jacques Mayoux, 'La Damnation de Beckford', *English Miscellany*, xii (1961), 41–77; Lewis Melville (i.e. L. S. Benjamin), *The Life and Letters of William Beckford of Fonthill* (1910); J. W. Oliver, *The Life of William Beckford* (1932); André Parreaux, *Le Portugal dans l'Œuvre de William Beckford* (Paris, 1935), 'Beckford et Byron', *Études Anglaises*, viii (1955), 11–31, 113–32, 'Le Tombeau de Beckford par Stéphane Mallarmé, *Revue d'Histoire Littéraire de la France*, lv (1955), 327–38, 'Beckford et le Portugal', *Bulletin des Études Portugaises*, xxi (1958), 97–155, 'Beckford en Italie', *Revue de Littérature Comparée*, xxxiii (1959), 321–47, and *William Beckford, Auteur de Vathek (1760–1844): Étude de la création littéraire* (Paris, 1960; gives an exhaustive listing of works dealing with or mentioning Beckford, pp. 533–63); Cyrus Redding, *Memoirs of William Beckford of Fonthill* (2 vols., 1859); John Rutter, *Delineations of Fonthill and its Abbey* (1823) and other works on Fonthill; Sacheverell Sitwell, *Beckford and Beckfordism. An Essay* (1930); K. F. Thompson, 'Beckford, Byron and Henley', *Études Anglaises*, xiv (1961), 225–8 (and see A. Parreaux, ibid., pp. 228–9).

SPECIAL STUDIES OF *VATHEK*

J. K. Folsom, 'Beckford's *Vathek* and the Tradition of Oriental Satire', *Criticism*, vi (1964), 53–69; E. Giddey, 'La

Vision Créatrice de *Vathek* de Beckford', in *Mélanges Offerts à Monsieur Georges Bonnard* (Geneva, 1966), pp. 43–56; André Gide, Lucien Lavault, Lewis Melville, Valéry Larbaud, 'Le Dossier *Vathek*', *Nouvelle Revue Française*, ix (1913), 1944–50; K. W. Graham, 'Beckford's Adaptation of the Oriental Tale in *Vathek*', *Enlightenment Essays*, v (1974), 24–33, '*Vathek* in English and French', *Studies in Bibliography*, xxviii (1975), 153–66, 'Beckford's Design for The Episodes', *Papers of the Bibliographical Society of America*, lxxi (1977), 336–43, 'Implications of the Grotesque', *Tennessee Studies in Literature*, xxiii (1978), 61–74; Fatma Moussa Mahmoud, 'Beckford, *Vathek* and the Oriental Tale', in *William Beckford... Bicentenary Essay* (Cairo, 1960), pp. 63–121; Stéphane Mallarmé, 'Préface' to *Vathek* (Paris, 1876); Mahmoud Manzalaoui, 'Pseudo-Orientalism in Transition: The Age of *Vathek*', in *William Beckford... Bicentenary Essays* (Cairo, 1960), pp. 123–50; Marcel May, *La jeunesse de William Beckford et la genèse de son Vathek* (Paris, 1928); J. H. Rieger, '*Au pied de la Lettre*: Stylistic Uncertainty in *Vathek*', *Criticism*, iv (1962), 302–12; and K. F. Thompson, 'Henley's Share in *Vathek*', *Philological Quarterly*, xxxi (1952), 75–80.

A CHRONOLOGY OF
WILLIAM BECKFORD

―――――

VATHEK

Vathek, ninth Caliph[1] of the race of the Abassides, was
the son of Motassem, and the grandson of Haroun al
Raschid. From an early accession to the throne, and the
talents he possessed to adorn it, his subjects were induced
to expect that his reign would be long and happy. His
figure was pleasing and majestic; but when he was angry,
one of his eyes became so terrible,[2] that no person could
bear to behold it; and the wretch upon whom it was fixed,
instantly fell backward, and sometimes expired. For fear,
however, of depopulating his dominions and making his
palace desolate, he but rarely gave way to his anger.

Being much addicted to women and the pleasures of the
table, he sought by his affability, to produce agreeable
companions; and he succeeded the better as his generosity
was unbounded and his indulgencies unrestrained: for he
did not think, with the Caliph Omar Ben Abdalaziz[3] that
it was necessary to make a hell of this world to enjoy paradise in the next.

He surpassed in magnificence all his predecessors. The
palace of Alkoremi,[4] which his father, Motassem, had
erected on the hill of Pied Horses, and which commanded
the whole city of Samarah,[5] was, in his idea far too scanty:
he added, therefore, five wings, or rather other palaces,
which he destined for the particular gratification of each
of the senses.

In the first of these were tables continually covered with

the most exquisite dainties; which were supplied both by night and by day, according to their constant consumption; whilst the most delicious wines and the choicest cordials flowed forth from a hundred fountains that were never exhausted. This palace was called *The Eternal or unsatiating Banquet*.

The second was styled, *The Temple of Melody*, or *The Nectar of the Soul*. It was inhabited by the most skilful musicians and admired poets of the time; who not only displayed their talents within, but dispersing in bands without, caused every surrounding scene to reverberate their songs; which were continually varied in the most delightful succession.[1]

The palace named *The Delight of the Eyes*, or *The Support of Memory*, was one entire enchantment. Rarities, collected from every corner of the earth were there found in such profusion as to dazzle and confound, but for the order in which they were arranged. One gallery exhibited the pictures of the celebrated Mani,[2] and statues, that seemed to be alive. Here a well-managed perspective attracted the sight; there the magic of optics agreeably deceived it: whilst the naturalist on his part, exhibited in their several classes the various gifts that Heaven had bestowed on our globe. In a word, Vathek omitted nothing in this palace, that might gratify the curiosity of those who resorted to it, although he was not able to satisfy his own; for, of all men, he was the most curious.

The Palace of Perfumes, which was termed likewise *The Incentive to Pleasure*, consisted of various halls, where the different perfumes which the earth produces were kept perpetually burning in censers of gold. Flambeaux and aromatic lamps were here lighted in open day. But the too

powerful effects of this agreeable delirium might be allevi-
ated by descending into an immense garden, where an
assemblage of every fragrant flower diffused through the
air the purest odours.

The fifth palace, denominated *The Retreat of Mirth, or
the Dangerous*, was frequented by troops of young females
beautiful as the Houris,[1] and not less seducing; who never
failed to receive with caresses, all whom the Caliph allowed
to approach them, and enjoy a few hours of their company.

Notwithstanding the sensuality in which Vathek indulged, he experienced no abatement in the love of his
people, who thought that a sovereign giving himself up to
pleasure, was as able to govern, as one who declared himself
an enemy to it. But the unquiet and impetuous disposition
of the Caliph would not allow him to rest there. He had
studied so much for his amusement in the life-time of his
father, as to acquire a great deal of knowledge, though not
a sufficiency to satisfy himself; for he wished to know every
thing; even sciences that did not exist. He was fond of
engaging in disputes with the learned, but did not allow
them to push their opposition with warmth. He stopped
with presents the mouths of those whose mouths could be
stopped; whilst others, whom his liberality was unable to
subdue, he sent to prison to cool their blood; a remedy
that often succeeded.

Vathek discovered also a predilection for theological
controversy;[2] but it was not with the orthodox that he
usually held. By this means he induced the zealots to
oppose him, and then persecuted them in return; for he
resolved, at any rate, to have reason on his side.

The great prophet, Mahomet, whose vicars the caliphs
are, beheld with indignation from his abode in the seventh

heaven,[1] the irreligious conduct of such a vicegerent. 'Let us leave him to himself,' said he to the Genii,[2] who are always ready to receive his commands: 'let us see to what lengths his folly and impiety will carry him: if he run into excess, we shall know how to chastise him. Assist him, therefore, to complete the tower,[3] which, in imitation of Nimrod, he hath begun; not, like that great warrior, to escape being drowned, but from the insolent curiosity of penetrating the secrets of heaven:—he will not divine the fate that awaits him.'

The Genii obeyed; and, when the workmen had raised their structure a cubit in the day time, two cubits more were added in the night. The expedition, with which the fabric arose, was not a little flattering to the vanity of Vathek: he fancied, that even insensible matter shewed a forwardness to subserve his designs;[4] not considering, that the successes of the foolish and wicked form the first rod of their chastisement.

His pride arrived at its height, when having ascended, for the first time, the fifteen hundred stairs of his tower, he cast his eyes below, and beheld men not larger than pismires; mountains, than shells; and cities, than bee-hives. The idea, which such an elevation inspired of his own grandeur, completely bewildered him: he was almost ready to adore himself; till, lifting his eyes upward, he saw the stars as high above him as they appeared when he stood on the surface of the earth.[5] He consoled himself, however, for this intruding and unwelcome perception of his littleness, with the thought of being great in the eyes of others; and flattered himself that the light of his mind would extend beyond the reach of his sight, and extort from the stars the decrees of his destiny.

With this view, the inquisitive Prince passed most of his nights on the summit of his tower, till becoming an adept in the mysteries of astrology, he imagined that the planets had disclosed to him the most marvellous adventures, which were to be accomplished by an extraordinary personage, from a country altogether unknown. Prompted by motives of curiosity, he had always been courteous to strangers; but, from this instant, he redoubled his attention, and ordered it to be announced, by sound of trumpet through all the streets of Samarah, that no one of his subjects, on peril of his displeasure, should either lodge or detain a traveller, but forthwith bring him to the palace.

Not long after this proclamation, arrived in his metropolis a man so abominably hideous that the very guards, who arrested him, were forced to shut their eyes, as they led him along:[1] the Caliph himself appeared startled at so horrible a visage; but joy succeeded to this emotion of terror, when the stranger displayed to his view such rarities as he had never before seen,[2] and of which he had no conception.

In reality, nothing was ever so extraordinary as the merchandize this stranger produced: most of his curiosities, which were not less admirable for their workmanship than splendour, had, besides, their several virtues described on a parchment fastened to each. There were slippers, which, by spontaneous springs, enabled the feet to walk; knives, that cut without motion of the hand; sabres, that dealt the blow at the person they were wished to strike; and the whole enriched with gems, that were hitherto unknown.[3]

The sabres, especially, the blades of which, emitted a dazzling radiance, fixed, more than all the rest, the Caliph's

attention; who promised himself to decipher, at his leisure,
the uncouth characters engraven on their sides. Without,
therefore, demanding their price, he ordered all the coined
gold to be brought from his treasury, and commanded the
merchant to take what he pleased. The stranger obeyed,
took little, and remained silent.

Vathek, imagining that the merchant's taciturnity was
occasioned by the awe which his presence inspired, encouraged him to advance; and asked him, with an air of
condescension, who he was? whence he came? and where
he obtained such beautiful commodities? The man, or
rather monster, instead of making a reply, thrice rubbed
his forehead, which, as well as his body, was blacker than
ebony; four times clapped his paunch, the projection of
which was enormous; opened wide his huge eyes, which
glowed like firebrands; began to laugh with a hideous
noise, and discovered his long amber-coloured teeth, be-
streaked with green.

The Caliph, though a little startled, renewed his inquiries,
but without being able to procure a reply. At which, beginning to be ruffled, he exclaimed:—'Knowest thou, wretch,
who I am, and at whom thou art aiming thy gibes?'—Then,
addressing his guards,—'Have ye heard him speak?—is he
dumb?'—'He hath spoken,' they replied, 'but to no purpose.' 'Let him speak then again,' said Vathek, 'and tell me
who he is, from whence he came, and where he procured
these singular curiosities; or I swear, by the ass of Balaam,
that I will make him rue his pertinacity.'

This menace was accompanied by one of the Caliph's
angry and perilous glances, which the stranger sustained
without the slightest emotion; although his eyes were fixed
on the terrible eye of the Prince.

No words can describe the amazement of the courtiers, when they beheld this rude merchant withstand the encounter unshocked. They all fell prostrate with their faces on the ground, to avoid the risk of their lives; and would have continued in the same abject posture, had not the Caliph exclaimed in a furious tone—'Up, cowards! seize the miscreant! see that he be committed to prison, and guarded by the best of my soldiers! Let him, however, retain the money I gave him; it is not my intent to take from him his property; I only want him to speak.'

No sooner had he uttered these words, than the stranger was surrounded, pinioned and bound with strong fetters, and hurried away to the prison of the great tower; which was encompassed by seven empalements of iron bars, and armed with spikes in every direction, longer and sharper than spits.[1] The Caliph, nevertheless, remained in the most violent agitation. He sat down indeed to eat; but, of the three hundred dishes that were daily placed before him, he could taste of no more than thirty-two.

A diet, to which he had been so little accustomed, was sufficient of itself to prevent him from sleeping; what then must be its effect when joined to the anxiety that preyed upon his spirits? At the first glimpse of dawn he hastened to the prison, again to importune this intractable stranger; but the rage of Vathek exceeded all bounds on finding the prison empty; the grates burst asunder, and his guards lying lifeless around him. In the paroxism of his passion he fell furiously on the poor carcases, and kicked them till evening without intermission. His courtiers and vizirs exerted their efforts to soothe his extravagance; but, finding every expedient ineffectual, they all united in one vociferation— 'The Caliph is gone mad! the Caliph is out of his senses!'

This outcry, which soon resounded through the streets of Samarah, at length reached the ears of Carathis, his mother, who flew in the utmost consternation to try her ascendancy on the mind of her son. Her tears and caresses called off his attention; and he was prevailed upon, by her intreaties, to be brought back to the palace.

Carathis, apprehensive of leaving Vathek to himself, had him put to bed; and, seating herself by him, endeavoured by her conversation to appease and compose him. Nor could any one have attempted it with better success; for the Caliph not only loved her as a mother, but respected her as a person of superior genius. It was she who had induced him, being a Greek herself, to adopt the sciences and systems of her country which all good Mussulmans hold in such thorough abhorrence.

Judiciary astrology[1] was one of those sciences, in which Carathis was a perfect adept. She began, therefore, with reminding her son of the promise which the stars had made him; and intimated an intention of consulting them again. 'Alas!' said the Caliph as soon as he could speak, 'what a fool I have been! not for having bestowed forty thousand kicks on my guards, who so tamely submitted to death; but for never considering that this extraordinary man was the same that the planets had foretold; whom, instead of ill-treating, I should have conciliated by all the arts of persuasion.'

'The past,' said Carathis, 'cannot be recalled; but it behoves us to think of the future: perhaps, you may again see the object you so much regret: it is possible the inscriptions on the sabres will afford information. Eat, therefore, and take thy repose, my dear son. We will consider, tomorrow, in what manner to act.'

Vathek yielded to her counsel as well as he could, and arose in the morning with a mind more at ease. The sabres he commanded to be instantly brought; and, poring upon them, through a coloured glass,[1] that their glittering might not dazzle, he set himself in earnest to decipher the inscriptions; but his reiterated attempts were all of them nugatory: in vain did he beat his head, and bite his nails; not a letter of the whole was he able to ascertain. So unlucky a disappointment would have undone him again, had not Carathis, by good fortune, entered the apartment.

'Have patience, my son!' said she:—'you certainly are possessed of every important science; but the knowledge of languages is a trifle at best; and the accomplishment of none but a pedant. Issue a proclamation, that you will confer such rewards as become your greatness, upon any one that shall interpret what you do not understand, and what is beneath you to learn; you will soon find your curiosity gratified.'

'That may be,' said the Caliph; 'but, in the mean time, I shall be horribly disgusted by a crowd of smatterers, who will come to the trial as much for the pleasure of retailing their jargon, as from the hope of gaining the reward. To avoid this evil, it will be proper to add, that I will put every candidate to death, who shall fail to give satisfaction: for, thank Heaven! I have skill enough to distinguish, whether one translates or invents.'

'Of that I have no doubt,' replied Carathis; 'but, to put the ignorant to death is somewhat severe, and may be productive of dangerous effects. Content yourself with commanding their beards to be burnt:[2]—beards in a state, are not quite so essential as men.'

The Caliph submitted to the reasons of his mother; and,

sending for Morakanabad, his prime vizir, said,—'Let the
common criers proclaim, not only in Samarah, but through-
out every city in my empire, that whosoever will repair
hither and decipher certain characters which appear to be
inexplicable, shall experience that liberality for which I am
renowned; but, that all who fail upon trial shall have their
beards burnt off to the last hair. Let them add, also, that
I will bestow fifty beautiful slaves, and as many jars of
apricots from the Isle of Kirmith, upon any man that shall
bring me intelligence of the stranger.'

The subjects of the Caliph, like their sovereign, being
great admirers of women and apricots from Kirmith, felt
their mouths water at these promises, but were totally unable to gratify their hankering; for no one knew what had
become of the stranger.

As to the Caliph's other requisition, the result was different. The learned, the half learned, and those who were
neither, but fancied themselves equal to both, came boldly
to hazard their beards, and all shamefully lost them. The
exaction of these forfeitures, which found sufficient employment for the eunuchs, gave them such a smell of singed
hair, as greatly to disgust the ladies of the seraglio, and to
make it necessary that this new occupation of their guardians should be transferred to other hands.

At length, however, an old man presented himself,
whose beard was a cubit and a half longer than any that
had appeared before him. The officers of the palace whispered to each other, as they ushered him in—'What a pity,
oh! what a great pity that such a beard should be burnt!'
Even the Caliph, when he saw it, concurred with them
in opinion; but his concern was entirely needless. This
venerable personage read the characters with facility, and

explained them verbatim as follows: 'We were made where every thing is well made: we are the least of the wonders of a place where all is wonderful and deserving, the sight of the first potentate on earth.'

'You translate admirably!' cried Vathek; 'I know to what these marvellous characters allude. Let him receive as many robes of honour and thousands of sequins of gold as he hath spoken words. I am in some measure relieved from the perplexity that embarrassed me!' Vathek invited the old man to dine, and even to remain some days in the palace.

Unluckily for him, he accepted the offer; for the Caliph having ordered him next morning to be called, said—'Read again to me what you have read already; I cannot hear too often the promise that is made me—the completion of which I languish to obtain.' The old man forthwith put on his green spectacles, but they instantly dropped from his nose, on perceiving that the characters he had read the day preceding, had given place to others of different import. 'What ails you?' asked the Caliph; 'and why these symptoms of wonder?'—'Sovereign of the world!' replied the old man, 'these sabres hold another language to-day from that they yesterday held.'—'How say you?' returned Vathek:—'but it matters not; tell me, if you can, what they mean.'—'It is this, my lord,' rejoined the old man: 'Woe to the rash mortal who seeks to know that of which he should remain ignorant; and to undertake that which surpasseth his power!'—'And woe to thee!' cried the Caliph, in a burst of indignation, 'to-day thou art void of understanding: begone from my presence, they shall burn but the half of thy beard, because thou wert yesterday fortunate in guessing:—my gifts I never resume.' The old

man, wise enough to perceive he had luckily escaped,
considering the folly of disclosing so disgusting a truth,
immediately withdrew and appeared not again.

But it was not long before Vathek discovered abundant
reason to regret his precipitation; for, though he could
not decipher the characters himself, yet, by constantly
poring upon them, he plainly perceived that they every
day changed; and, unfortunately, no other candidate
offered to explain them. This perplexing occupation inflamed his blood, dazzled his sight, and brought on such
a giddiness and debility that he could hardly support himself. He failed not, however, though in so reduced a condition, to be often carried to his tower, as he flattered himself
that he might there read in the stars, which he went to
consult, something more congruous to his wishes; but in
this his hopes were deluded: for his eyes, dimmed by the
vapours of his head, began to subserve his curiosity so ill,
that he beheld nothing but a thick, dun cloud, which he
took for the most direful of omens.

Agitated with so much anxiety, Vathek entirely lost all
firmness; a fever seized him, and his appetite failed.
Instead of being one of the greatest eaters, he became as
distinguished for drinking. So insatiable was the thirst
which tormented him, that his mouth, like a funnel, was
always open to receive the various liquors that might be
poured into it, and especially cold water, which calmed him
more than any other.

This unhappy prince, being thus incapacitated for the
enjoyment of any pleasure, commanded the palaces of the
five senses to be shut up; forebore to appear in public,
either to display his magnificence, or administer justice,
and retired to the inmost apartment of his harem. As he

had ever been an excellent husband, his wives, over-whelmed with grief at his deplorable situation, incessantly supplied him with prayers for his health, and water for his thirst.

In the mean time the Princess Carathis, whose affliction no words can describe, instead of confining herself to sobbing and tears, was closetted daily with the vizir Morakanabad, to find out some cure, or mitigation, of the Caliph's disease. Under the persuasion that it was caused by enchantment, they turned over together, leaf by leaf, all the books of magic that might point out a remedy; and caused the horrible stranger, whom they accused as the enchanter, to be every where sought for, with the strictest diligence.

At the distance of a few miles from Samarah stood a high mountain, whose sides were swarded with wild thyme and basil, and its summit overspread with so delightful a plain, that it might have been taken for the Paradise destined for the faithful. Upon it grew a hundred thickets of eglantine and other fragrant shrubs; a hundred arbours of roses, entwined with jessamine and honey-suckle; as many clumps of orange trees, cedar, and citron; whose branches, interwoven with the palm, the pomegranate, and the vine, presented every luxury that could regale the eye or the taste. The ground was strewed with violets, hare-bells, and pansies; in the midst of which numerous tufts of jonquils, hyacinths, and carnations perfumed the air. Four foun-tains, not less clear than deep, and so abundant as to slake the thirst of ten armies, seemed purposely placed here, to make the scene more resemble the garden of Eden watered by four sacred rivers. Here, the nightingale sang the birth of the rose,[1] her well-beloved, and, at the same time,

lamented its short-lived beauty; whilst the dove deplored
the loss of more substantial pleasures; and the wakeful
lark hailed the rising light that re-animates the whole
creation. Here, more than any where, the mingled melodies
of birds expressed the various passions which inspired
them; and the exquisite fruits, which they pecked at pleasure, seemed to have given them a double energy.

To this mountain Vathek was sometimes brought, for
the sake of breathing a purer air; and, especially, to drink
at will of the four fountains. His attendants were his
mother, his wives, and some eunuchs, who assiduously
employed themselves in filling capacious bowls of rock
crystal, and emulously presenting them to him. But it frequently happened, that his avidity exceeded their zeal,
insomuch, that he would prostrate himself upon the ground
to lap the water, of which he could never have enough.

One day, when this unhappy Prince had been long lying
in so debasing a posture, a voice, hoarse but strong, thus
addressed him: 'Why dost thou assimilate thyself to a dog,
O Caliph, proud as thou art of thy dignity and power?' At
this apostrophe, he raised up his head, and beheld the
stranger that had caused him so much affliction. Inflamed
with anger at the sight, he exclaimed:—'Accursed Giaour!¹
what comest thou hither to do?—is it not enough to have
transformed a prince, remarkable for his agility, into a
water budget? Perceivest thou not, that I may perish by
drinking to excess, as well as by thirst?'

'Drink then this draught,' said the stranger, as he presented to him a phial of a red and yellow mixture: 'and, to
satiate the thirst of thy soul, as well as of thy body, know,
that I am an Indian; but, from a region of India, which is
wholly unknown.'

The Caliph, delighted to see his desires accomplished in part, and flattering himself with the hope of obtaining their entire fulfilment, without a moment's hesitation swallowed the potion, and instantaneously found his health restored, his thirst appeased, and his limbs as agile as ever. In the transports of his joy, Vathek leaped upon the neck of the frightful Indian, and kissed his horrid mouth and hollow cheeks, as though they had been the coral lips and the lilies and roses of his most beautiful wives.

Nor would these transports have ceased, had not the eloquence of Carathis repressed them. Having prevailed upon him to return to Samarah, she caused a herald to proclaim as loudly as possible—'The wonderful stranger hath appeared again; he hath healed the Caliph;—he hath spoken! he hath spoken!'

Forthwith, all the inhabitants of this vast city quitted their habitations, and ran together in crowds to see the procession of Vathek and the Indian, whom they now blessed as much as they had before execrated, incessantly shouting—'He hath healed our sovereign;—he hath spoken! he hath spoken!' Nor were these words forgotten in the public festivals, which were celebrated the same evening, to testify the general joy; for the poets applied them as a chorus to all the songs they composed on this interesting subject.

The Caliph, in the meanwhile, caused the palaces of the senses to be again set open; and, as he found himself naturally prompted to visit that of Taste in preference to the rest, immediately ordered a splendid entertainment, to which his great officers and favourite courtiers were all invited. The Indian, who was placed near the Prince, seemed to think that, as a proper acknowledgment of so

distinguished a privilege, he could neither eat, drink, nor
talk too much. The various dainties were no sooner served
up than they vanished, to the great mortification of Vathek,
who piqued himself on being the greatest eater alive; and,
at this time in particular, was blessed with an excellent
appetite.

The rest of the company looked round at each other in
amazement; but the Indian, without appearing to observe
it, quaffed large bumpers to the health of each of them;
sung in a style altogether extravagant; related stories, at
which he laughed immoderately; and poured forth ex-
temporaneous verses, which would not have been thought
bad, but for the strange grimaces with which they were
uttered. In a word, his loquacity was equal to that of a
hundred astrologers; he ate as much as a hundred porters,
and caroused in proportion.

The Caliph, notwithstanding the table had been thirty-
two times covered, found himself incommoded by the
voraciousness of his guest, who was now considerably
declined in the Prince's esteem. Vathek, however, being
unwilling to betray the chagrin he could hardly disguise,
said in a whisper to Bababalouk,[1] the chief of his eunuchs,
'You see how enormous his performances are in every way;
what would be the consequence should he get at my wives!
—Go! redouble your vigilance, and be sure look well to
my Circassians, who would be more to his taste than all of
the rest.'

The bird of the morning had thrice renewed his song,
when the hour of the Divan[2] was announced. Vathek,
in gratitude to his subjects, having promised to attend,
immediately arose from table, and repaired thither, lean-
ing upon his vizir who could scarcely support him: so

disordered was the poor Prince by the wine he had drunk,
and still more by the extravagant vagaries of his boisterous
guest.

The vizirs, the officers of the crown and of the law,
arranged themselves in a semicircle about their sovereign,
and preserved a respectful silence; whilst the Indian, who
looked as cool as if he had been fasting, sat down without
ceremony on one of the steps of the throne, laughing in his
sleeve at the indignation with which his temerity had filled
the spectators.

The Caliph, however, whose ideas were confused, and
whose head was embarrassed, went on administering justice
at haphazard; till at length the prime vizir,[1] perceiving his
situation, hit upon a sudden expedient to interrupt the
audience and rescue the honour of his master, to whom
he said in a whisper:—'My lord, the Princess Carathis,
who hath passed the night in consulting the planets, in-
forms you, that they portend you evil, and the danger is
urgent. Beware, lest this stranger, whom you have so
lavishly recompensed for his magical gewgaws, should
make some attempt on your life: his liquor, which at first
had the appearance of effecting your cure, may be no more
than a poison, the operation of which will be sudden.
—Slight not this surmise: ask him, at least, of what it was
compounded, whence he procured it; and mention the
sabres, which you seem to have forgotten.'

Vathek, to whom the insolent airs of the stranger became every moment less supportable, intimated to his
vizir, by a wink of acquiescence, that he would adopt his
advice; and, at once turning towards the Indian, said—
'Get up, and declare in full Divan of what drugs was compounded the liquor you enjoined me to take, for it is

suspected to be poison: give also, that explanation I have
so earnestly desired, concerning the sabres you sold me, and
thus shew your gratitude for the favours heaped on you.'

Having pronounced these words, in as moderate a tone
as he well could, he waited in silent expectation for an
answer. But the Indian, still keeping his seat, began to
renew his loud shouts of laughter, and exhibit the same
horrid grimaces he had shewn them before, without vouchsafing a word in reply. Vathek, no longer able to brook such
insolence, immediately kicked him from the steps; instantly descending, repeated his blow; and persisted, with
such assiduity, as incited all who were present to follow
his example. Every foot was up and aimed at the Indian,
and no sooner had any one given him a kick, than he felt
himself constrained to reiterate the stroke.

The stranger afforded them no small entertainment: for,
being both short and plump, he collected himself into a
ball, and rolled round on all sides, at the blows of his
assailants, who pressed after him, wherever he turned, with
an eagerness beyond conception, whilst their numbers
were every moment increasing. The ball indeed, in passing
from one apartment to another, drew every person after
it that came in its way; insomuch, that the whole palace
was thrown into confusion and resounded with a tremendous clamour. The women of the harem, amazed at the
uproar, flew to their blinds to discover the cause; but, no
sooner did they catch a glimpse of the ball, than, feeling
themselves unable to refrain, they broke from the clutches
of their eunuchs, who, to stop their flight, pinched them
till they bled; but, in vain: whilst themselves, though
trembling with terror at the escape of their charge, were as
incapable of resisting the attraction.

After having traversed the halls, galleries, chambers, kitchens, gardens, and stables of the palace, the Indian at last took his course through the courts; whilst the Caliph, pursuing him closer than the rest, bestowed as many kicks as he possibly could; yet, not without receiving now and then a few which his competitors, in their eagerness, designed for the ball.

Carathis, Morakanabad, and two or three old viziers, whose wisdom had hitherto withstood the attraction, wishing to prevent Vathek from exposing himself in the presence of his subjects, fell down on his way to impede the pursuit: but he, regardless of their obstruction, leaped over their heads, and went on as before. They then ordered the Muezins to call the people to prayers; both for the sake of getting them out of the way, and of endeavouring, by their petitions, to avert the calamity; but neither of these expedients was a whit more successful. The sight of this fatal ball was alone sufficient to draw after it every beholder. The Muezins themselves, though they saw it but at a distance, hastened down from their minarets,[1] and mixed with the crowd; which continued to increase in so surprising a manner, that scarce an inhabitant was left in Samarah, except the aged; the sick, confined to their beds; and infants at the breast, whose nurses could run more nimbly without them. Even Carathis, Morakanabad, and the rest, were all become of the party. The shrill screams of the females, who had broken from their apartments, and were unable to extricate themselves from the pressure of the crowd, together with those of the eunuchs jostling after them, and terrified lest their charge should escape from their sight; the execrations of husbands, urging forward and menacing each other; kicks given and received;

stumblings and overthrows at every step; in a word, the
confusion that universally prevailed, rendered Samarah
like a city taken by storm, and devoted to absolute plunder.
At last, the cursed Indian, who still preserved his rotundity
of figure, after passing through all the streets and public
places, and leaving them empty, rolled onwards to the
plain of Catoul, and entered the valley at the foot of the
mountain of the four fountains.

As a continual fall of water had excavated an immense
gulph in the valley whose opposite side was closed in by a
steep acclivity, the Caliph and his attendants were apprehensive, lest the ball should bound into the chasm, and,
to prevent it, redoubled their efforts, but in vain. The
Indian persevered in his onward direction; and, as had
been apprehended, glancing from the precipice with the
rapidity of lightning, was lost in the gulph below.

Vathek would have followed the perfidious Giaour, had
not an invisible agency arrested his progress. The multitude that pressed after him were at once checked in the
same manner, and a calm instantaneously ensued. They all
gazed at each other with an air of astonishment, and notwithstanding that the loss of veils and turbans, together
with torn habits, and dust blended with sweat, presented a
most laughable spectacle, yet there was not one smile to
be seen. On the contrary, all with looks of confusion and
sadness returned in silence to Samarah, and retired to their
inmost apartments, without ever reflecting, that they had
been impelled by an invisible power into the extravagance,
for which they reproached themselves: for it is but just
that men, who so often arrogate to their own merit the good
of which they are but instruments, should also attribute to
themselves absurdities which they could not prevent.

The Caliph was the only person who refused to leave the valley. He commanded his tents to be pitched there, and stationed himself on the very edge of the precipice, in spite of the representations of Carathis and Morakanabad, who pointed out the hazard of its brink giving way, and the vicinity to the magician, that had so cruelly tormented him. Vathek derided all their remonstrances; and, having ordered a thousand flambeaux to be lighted, and directed his attendants to proceed in lighting more, lay down on the slippery margin, and attempted, by the help of this artificial splendour, to look through that gloom, which all the fires of the empyrean had been insufficient to pervade. One while he fancied to himself voices arising from the depth of the gulph; at another, he seemed to distinguish the accents of the Indian; but all was no more than the hollow murmur of waters, and the din of the cataracts that rushed from steep to steep down the sides of the mountain.

Having passed the night in this cruel perturbation, the Caliph, at day-break, retired to his tent; where, without taking the least sustenance, he continued to doze till the dusk of evening began again to come on. He then resumed his vigils as before, and persevered in observing them for many nights together. At length, fatigued with so fruitless an employment, he sought relief from change. To this end, he sometimes paced with hasty strides across the plain; and, as he wildly gazed at the stars, reproached them with having deceived him; but, lo! on a sudden, the clear blue sky appeared streaked over with streams of blood, which reached from the valley even to the city of Samarah. As this awful phenomenon seemed to touch his tower, Vathek at first thought of repairing thither to view it more distinctly; but, feeling himself unable to advance, and being overcome with apprehension, he muffled up his face in the folds of his robe.

Terrifying as these prodigies were, this impression upon him was no more than momentary, and served only to stimulate his love of the marvellous. Instead, therefore, of returning to his palace, he persisted in the resolution of abiding where the Indian had vanished from his view. One night, however, while he was walking as usual on the plain, the moon and stars were eclipsed at once, and a total darkness ensued. The earth trembled beneath him, and a voice came forth, the voice of the Giaour, who, in accents more sonorous than thunder, thus addressed him: 'Wouldest thou devote thyself to me? adore the terrestrial influences, and abjure Mahomet? On these conditions I will bring thee to the Palace of Subterranean Fire. There shalt thou behold, in immense depositories, the treasures which the stars have promised thee; and which will be conferred by those intelligences, whom thou shalt thus render propitious. It was from thence I brought my sabres, and it is there that Soliman Ben Daoud[1] reposes, surrounded by the talismans that control the world.'

The astonished Caliph trembled as he answered, yet he answered in a style that shewed him to be no novice in preternatural adventures: 'Where art thou? be present to my eyes; dissipate the gloom that perplexes me, and of which I deem thee the cause. After the many flambeaux I have burnt to discover thee, thou mayest, at least, grant a glimpse of thy horrible visage.'—'Abjure then Mahomet!' replied the Indian, 'and promise me full proofs of thy sincerity: otherwise, thou shalt never behold me again.'

The unhappy Caliph, instigated by insatiable curiosity, lavished his promises in the utmost profusion. The sky immediately brightened; and, by the light of the planets, which seemed almost to blaze, Vathek beheld the earth open; and, at the extremity of a vast black chasm, a portal of ebony, before which stood the Indian, holding in his hand a golden key, which he sounded against the lock.

'How,' cried Vathek, 'can I descend to thee;—Come, take me, and instantly open the portal.'—'Not so fast,' replied the Indian, 'impatient Caliph!—Know that I am parched with thirst, and cannot open this door, till my thirst be thoroughly appeased; I require the blood of fifty children. Take them from among the most beautiful sons of thy viziers and great men; or, neither can my thirst nor thy curiosity be satisfied. Return to Samarah; procure for me this necessary libation; come back hither; throw it thyself into this chasm, and then shalt thou see!'

Having thus spoken, the Indian turned his back on the Caliph, who, incited by the suggestions of demons, resolved on the direful sacrifice.—He now pretended to have regained his tranquillity, and set out for Samarah amidst the acclamations of a people who still loved him, and forbore not to rejoice, when they believed him to have recovered his reason. So successfully did he conceal the emotion of his heart, that even Carathis and Morakanabad were equally deceived with the rest. Nothing was heard of but festivals and rejoicings. The fatal ball, which no tongue had hitherto ventured to mention, was brought on the tapis.[1] A general laugh went round, though many, still smarting under the hands of the surgeon, from the hurts received in that memorable adventure, had no great reason for mirth.

The prevalence of this gay humour was not a little grateful to Vathek, who perceived how much it conduced to his project. He put on the appearance of affability to every one; but especially to his vizirs, and the grandees of his court, whom he failed not to regale with a sumptuous banquet; during which, he insensibly directed the conversation to the children of his guests. Having asked, with a good-natured air, which of them were blessed with the handsomest boys, every father at once asserted the pretensions of his own; and the contest imperceptibly grew so warm, that nothing could have withholden them from coming to blows, but their profound reverence for the person of the Caliph. Under the pretence, therefore, of reconciling the disputants, Vathek took upon him to decide; and, with this view, commanded the boys to be brought.

It was not long before a troop of these poor children made their appearance, all equipped by their fond mothers with such ornaments, as might give the greatest relief to their beauty, or most advantageously display the graces of their age. But, whilst this brilliant assemblage attracted the eyes and hearts of every one besides, the Caliph scrutinized each, in his turn, with a malignant avidity that passed for attention, and selected from their number the fifty whom he judged the Giaour would prefer.

With an equal shew of kindness as before, he proposed to celebrate a festival on the plain, for the entertainment of his young favourites, who, he said, ought to rejoice still more than all, at the restoration of his health, on account of the favours he intended for them.

The Caliph's proposal was received with the greatest delight, and soon published through Samarah. Litters, camels, and horses were prepared. Women and children, old men and young, every one placed himself as he chose. The cavalcade set forward, attended by all the confectioners in the city and its precincts; the populace, following on foot, composed an amazing crowd, and occasioned no little noise. All was joy; nor did any one call to mind, what most of them had suffered, when they lately travelled the road they were now passing so gaily.

The evening was serene, the air refreshing, the sky clear, and the flowers exhaled their fragrance. The beams of the declining sun, whose mild splendour reposed on the summit of the mountain, shed a glow of ruddy light over its green declivity, and the white flocks sporting upon it. No sounds were heard, save the murmurs of the four fountains; and the reeds and voices of shepherds calling to each other from different eminences.[1]

The lovely innocents destined for the sacrifice, added not a little to the hilarity of the scene. They approached the plain full of sportiveness, some coursing butterflies, others culling flowers, or picking up the shining little pebbles that attracted their notice. At intervals they nimbly started from each other for the sake of being caught again, and mutually imparting a thousand caresses.

The dreadful chasm, at whose bottom the portal of ebony was placed, began to appear at a distance. It looked like a black streak that divided the plain. Morakanabad and his companions, took it for some work which the Caliph had ordered. Unhappy men! little did they surmise for what it was destined. Vathek unwilling that they should examine it too nearly, stopped the procession, and ordered a spacious circle to be formed on this side, at some distance from the accursed chasm. The body-guard of eunuchs was detached, to measure out the lists intended for the games; and prepare the rings for the arrows of the young archers. The fifty competitors were soon stripped, and

presented to the admiration of the spectators the supple-
ness and grace of their delicate limbs. Their eyes sparkled
with a joy, which those of their fond parents reflected.
Every one offered wishes for the little candidate nearest
his heart, and doubted not of his being victorious. A
breathless suspence awaited the contest of these amiable
and innocent victims.

The Caliph, availing himself of the first moment to
retire from the crowd, advanced towards the chasm; and
there heard, yet not without shuddering, the voice of the
Indian; who, gnashing his teeth, eagerly demanded:
'Where are they?—Where are they?—perceivest thou not
how my mouth waters?'—'Relentless Giaour!' answered
Vathek, with emotion; 'can nothing content thee but the
massacre of these lovely victims? Ah! wert thou to behold
their beauty, it must certainly move thy compassion.'—
'Perdition on thy compassion, babbler!' cried the Indian:
'give them me; instantly give them, or, my portal shall be
closed against thee for ever!'—'Not so loudly,' replied the
Caliph, blushing.—'I understand thee,' returned the Giaour
with the grin of an Ogre;[1] 'thou wantest no presence of
mind: I will, for a moment, forbear.'

During this exquisite dialogue, the games went forward
with all alacrity, and at length concluded, just as the twilight began to overcast the mountains. Vathek, who was
still standing on the edge of the chasm, called out, with all
his might:—'Let my fifty little favourites approach me,
separately; and let them come in the order of their success.
To the first, I will give my diamond bracelet; to the second,
my collar of emeralds; to the third, my aigret of rubies; to
the fourth, my girdle of topazes; and to the rest, each a part
of my dress, even down to my slippers.'

This declaration was received with reiterated acclamations; and all extolled the liberality of a prince, who would thus strip himself, for the amusement of his subjects, and the encouragement of the rising generation. The Caliph, in the meanwhile, undressed himself by degrees; and, raising his arm as high as he was able, made each of the prizes glitter in the air; but, whilst he delivered it, with one hand, to the child, who sprung forward to receive it; he, with the other, pushed the poor innocent into the gulph; where the Giaour, with a sullen muttering, incessantly repeated; 'more! more!'

This dreadful device was executed with so much dexterity, that the boy who was approaching him, remained unconscious of the fate of his forerunner; and, as to the spectators, the shades of evening, together with their distance, precluded them from perceiving any object distinctly. Vathek, having in this manner thrown in the last of the fifty; and, expecting that the Giaour, on receiving him, would have presented the key; already fancied himself, as great as Soliman, and, consequently, above being amenable for what he had done:—when, to his utter amazement, the chasm closed, and the ground became as entire as the rest of the plain.

No language could express his rage and despair. He execrated the perfidy of the Indian; loaded him with the most infamous invectives; and stamped with his foot, as resolving to be heard. He persisted in this till his strength failed him; and, then, fell on the earth like one void of sense. His vizirs and grandees, who were nearer than the rest, supposed him, at first, to be sitting on the grass, at play with their amiable children; but, at length, prompted by doubt, they advanced towards the spot, and found the

Caliph alone, who wildly demanded what they wanted?
'Our children! our children!' cried they. 'It is, assuredly,
pleasant,' said he, 'to make me accountable for accidents.
Your children, while at play, fell from the precipice, and
I should have experienced their fate, had I not suddenly
started back.'

At these words, the fathers of the fifty boys cried out
aloud; the mothers repeated their exclamations an octave
higher; whilst the rest, without knowing the cause, soon
drowned the voices of both, with still louder lamentations
of their own. 'Our Caliph,' said they, and the report soon
circulated, 'our Caliph has played us this trick, to gratify
his accursed Giaour. Let us punish him for perfidy! let
us avenge ourselves! let us avenge the blood of the innocent! let us throw this cruel prince into the gulph that is
near, and let his name be mentioned no more!'

At this rumour and these menaces, Carathis, full of
consternation, hastened to Morakanabad, and said: 'Vizir,
you have lost two beautiful boys, and must necessarily be
the most afflicted of fathers; but you are virtuous; save
your master.'—'I will brave every hazard,' replied the
vizir, 'to rescue him from his present danger; but, afterwards, will abandon him to his fate. Bababalouk,' continued
he, 'put yourself at the head of your eunuchs: disperse the
mob, and, if possible, bring back this unhappy prince to
his palace.' Bababalouk and his fraternity, felicitating each
other in a low voice on their having been spared the cares
as well as the honour of paternity, obeyed the mandate of
the vizir; who, seconding their exertions, to the utmost of
his power, at length, accomplished his generous enterprize;
and retired, as he resolved, to lament at his leisure.

No sooner had the Caliph re-entered his palace, than

Carathis commanded the doors to be fastened; but, perceiving the tumult to be still violent, and hearing the imprecations which resounded from all quarters, she said to her son: 'Whether the populace be right or wrong, it behoves you to provide for your safety; let us retire to your own apartment, and, from thence, through the subterranean passage, known only to ourselves, into your tower: there, with the assistance of the mutes[1] who never leave it, we may be able to make a powerful resistance. Bababalouk, supposing us to be still in the palace, will guard its avenues, for his own sake; and we shall soon find, without the counsels of that blubberer Morakanabad, what expedient may be the best to adopt.'

Vathek, without making the least reply, acquiesced in his mother's proposal, and repeated as he went: 'Nefarious Giaour! where art thou? hast thou not yet devoured those poor children? where are thy sabres? thy golden key? thy talismans?'—Carathis, who guessed from these interrogations a part of the truth, had no difficulty to apprehend, in getting at the whole as soon as he should be a little composed in his tower. This Princess was so far from being influenced by scruples, that she was as wicked, as woman could be; which is not saying a little; for the sex pique themselves on their superiority, in every competition. The recital of the Caliph, therefore, occasioned neither terror nor surprize to his mother: she felt no emotion but from the promises of the Giaour, and said to her son: 'This Giaour, it must be confessed, is somewhat sanguinary in his taste; but, the terrestrial powers are always terrible; nevertheless, what the one hath promised, and the others can confer, will prove a sufficient indemnification. No crimes should be thought too dear for such a reward:

forbear, then, to revile the Indian; you have not fulfilled
the conditions to which his services are annexed: for
instance; is not a sacrifice to the subterranean Genii required? and should we not be prepared to offer it as soon
as the tumult is subsided? This charge I will take on myself,
and have no doubt of succeeding, by means of your
treasures, which as there are now so many others in store,
may, without fear, be exhausted.' Accordingly, the Princess,
who possessed the most consummate skill in the art of
persuasion, went immediately back through the subterranean passage; and, presenting herself to the populace,
from a window of the palace, began to harangue them with
all the address of which she was mistress; whilst Bababalouk, showered money from both hands amongst the
crowd, who by these united means were soon appeased.
Every person retired to his home, and Carathis returned
to the tower.

Prayer at break of day was announced,[1] when Carathis
and Vathek ascended the steps, which led to the summit of
the tower; where they remained for some time though the
weather was lowering and wet. This impending gloom
corresponded with their malignant dispositions; but when
the sun began to break through the clouds, they ordered a
pavilion to be raised, as a screen against the intrusion of
his beams. The Caliph, overcome with fatigue, sought
refreshment from repose; at the same time, hoping that
significant dreams might attend on his slumbers; whilst
the indefatigable Carathis, followed by a party of her mutes,
descended to prepare whatever she judged proper, for the
oblation of the approaching night.

By secret stairs, contrived within the thickness of the
wall, and known only to herself and her son, she first

repaired to the mysterious recesses in which were deposited
the mummies[1] that had been wrested from the catacombs
of the ancient Pharaohs. Of these she ordered several to be
taken. From thence, she resorted to a gallery; where, under
the guard of fifty female negroes mute and blind of the
right eye, were preserved the oil of the most venomous
serpents; rhinoceros' horns; and woods of a subtile and
penetrating odour, procured from the interior of the Indies,
together with a thousand other horrible rarities. This collection had been formed for a purpose like the present, by
Carathis herself; from a presentiment, that she might one
day, enjoy some intercourse with the infernal powers: to
whom she had ever been passionately attached, and to
whose taste she was no stranger.

To familiarize herself the better with the horrors in view,
the Princess remained in the company of her negresses,
who squinted in the most amiable manner from the only
eye they had; and leered with exquisite delight, at the
sculls and skeletons which Carathis had drawn forth from
her cabinets; all of them making the most frightful contortions and uttering such shrill chatterings, that the Princess
stunned by them and suffocated by the potency of the
exhalations, was forced to quit the gallery, after stripping
it of a part of its abominable treasures.

Whilst she was thus occupied, the Caliph, who instead
of the visions he expected, had acquired in these un-
substantial regions a voracious appetite, was greatly provoked at the mutes. For having totally forgotten their
deafness, he had impatiently asked them for food; and
seeing them regardless of his demand, he began to cuff,
pinch, and bite them, till Carathis arrived to terminate a
scene so indecent, to the great content of these miserable

creatures: 'Son! what means all this?' said she, panting for breath. 'I thought I heard as I came up, the shrieks of a thousand bats, torn from their crannies in the recesses of a cavern; and it was the outcry only of these poor mutes, whom you were so unmercifully abusing. In truth, you but ill deserve the admirable provision I have brought you.'—'Give it me instantly,' exclaimed the Caliph; 'I am perishing for hunger!'—'As to that,' answered she, 'you must have an excellent stomach if it can digest what I have brought.'—'Be quick,' replied the Caliph;—'but, oh heavens! what horrors! what do you intend?' 'Come; come;' returned Carathis, 'be not so squeamish; but help me to arrange every thing properly; and you shall see that, what you reject with such symptoms of disgust, will soon complete your felicity. Let us get ready the pile, for the sacrifice of to-night; and think not of eating, till that is performed: know you not, that all solemn rites ought to be preceded by a rigorous abstinence?'

The Caliph, not daring to object, abandoned himself to grief and the wind that ravaged his entrails, whilst his mother went forward with the requisite operations. Phials of serpents' oil, mummies, and bones, were soon set in order on the balustrade of the tower. The pile began to rise; and in three hours was twenty cubits high. At length darkness approached, and Carathis, having stripped herself to her inmost garment, clapped her hands in an impulse of ecstacy; the mutes followed her example; but Vathek, extenuated[1] with hunger and impatience, was unable to support himself, and fell down in a swoon. The sparks had already kindled the dry wood; the venomous oil burst into a thousand blue flames; the mummies, dissolving, emitted a thick dun vapour; and the rhinoceros' horns, beginning to consume; all together diffused such a stench, that the Caliph, recovering, started from his trance, and gazed wildly on the scene in full blaze around him. The oil gushed forth in a plenitude of streams; and the negresses, who supplied it without intermission, united their cries to those of the Princess. At last, the fire became so violent, and the flames reflected from the polished marble so dazzling, that the Caliph, unable to withstand the heat and the blaze, effected his escape; and took shelter under the imperial standard.

In the mean time, the inhabitants of Samarah, scared at the light which shone over the city, arose in haste; ascended their roofs; beheld the tower on fire, and hurried, half naked to the square. Their love for their sovereign immediately awoke; and, apprehending him in danger of perishing in his tower, their whole thoughts were occupied with the means of his safety. Morakanabad flew from his retirement, wiped away his tears, and cried out for water like the rest. Bababalouk, whose olfactory nerves were more familiarized to magical odours, readily conjecturing, that Carathis was engaged in her favourite amusements, strenuously exhorted them not to be alarmed. Him, however, they treated as an old poltroon, and styled him a rascally traitor. The camels and dromedaries were advancing with water; but, no one knew by which way to enter the tower. Whilst the populace was obstinate in forcing the doors, a violent north-east wind drove an immense volume of flame against them. At first, they recoiled, but soon came back with redoubled zeal. At the same time, the stench of the horns and mummies increasing, most of the crowd fell backward in a state of suffocation. Those that kept their feet, mutually wondered at the cause of the smell; and admonished each other to retire. Morakanabad, more sick than the rest, remained in a piteous condition. Holding his nose with one hand, every one persisted in his efforts with the other to burst open the doors and obtain admission. A hundred and forty of the strongest and most resolute, at length accomplished their purpose. Having gained the stair-case, by their violent exertions, they attained a great height in a quarter of an hour.

Carathis, alarmed at the signs of her mutes, advanced to the stair-case; went down a few steps, and heard several voices calling out from below: 'You shall, in a moment have water!' Being rather alert, considering her age, she presently regained the top of the tower; and bade her son suspend the sacrifice for some minutes; adding,—'We shall soon be enabled to render it more grateful. Certain dolts of your subjects, imagining no doubt that we were on fire, have been rash enough to break through those doors, which had hitherto remained inviolate; for the sake of bringing up water. They are very kind, you must allow, so soon to forget the wrongs you have done them; but that is of little moment. Let us offer them to the Giaour,—let them come up; our mutes, who neither want strength nor experience, will soon dispatch them; exhausted as they are, with fatigue.'—'Be it so,' answered the Caliph, 'provided we finish, and I dine.' In fact, these good people, out of breath from ascending fifteen hundred stairs in such haste; and chagrined, at having spilt by the way, the water they had taken, were no sooner arrived at the top, than the blaze of the flames, and the fumes of the mummies, at once over-powered their senses. It was a pity! for they beheld not the agreeable smile, with which the mutes and negresses adjusted the cord to their necks: these amiable personages rejoiced, however, no less at the scene. Never before had the ceremony of strangling been performed with so much facility. They all fell, without the least resistance or struggle: so that Vathek, in the space of a few moments, found himself surrounded by the dead bodies of the most faithful of his subjects; all which were thrown on the top of the pile. Carathis, whose presence of mind never forsook her, perceiving that she had carcasses sufficient to complete her oblation, commanded the chains to be stretched across the stair-case, and the iron doors barricadoed, that no more might come up.

No sooner were these orders obeyed, than the tower shook; the dead bodies vanished in the flames; which, at once, changed from a swarthy crimson, to a bright rose colour: an ambient vapour emitted the most exquisite fragrance; the marble columns rang with harmonious sounds, and the liquified horns diffused a delicious perfume. Carathis, in transports, anticipated the success of her enter-prize; whilst her mutes and negresses, to whom these sweets had given the cholic, retired grumbling to their cells.

Scarcely were they gone, when, instead of the pile, horns, mummies and ashes, the Caliph both saw and felt, with a degree of pleasure which he could not express, a table, covered with the most magnificent repast: flaggons of wine, and vases of exquisite sherbet reposing on snow.[1] He availed himself, without scruple, of such an entertainment; and had already laid hands on a lamb stuffed with pis-tachios,[2] whilst Carathis was privately drawing from a filla-green urn, a parchment[3] that seemed to be endless; and which had escaped the notice of her son. Totally occupied in gratifying an importunate appetite, he left her to peruse it without interruption; which having finished, she said to him, in an authoritative tone, 'Put an end to your gluttony, and hear the splendid promises with which you are favoured!' She then read, as follows: 'Vathek, my well-beloved, thou hast surpassed my hopes: my nostrils have been regaled by the savour of thy mummies, thy horns; and, still more by the lives, devoted on the pile. At the full of the moon, cause the bands of thy musicians, and thy tymbals, to be heard; depart from thy palace, surrounded by all the pageants of majesty; thy most faithful slaves, thy best beloved wives; thy most magnificent litters; thy richest loaden camels; and set forward on thy way to Istakhar.[1] There, I await thy coming: that is the region of wonders: there shalt thou receive the diadem of Gian Ben Gian; the talismans of Soliman;[2] and the treasures of the pre-adamite sultans:[3] there shalt thou be solaced with all kinds of delight.—But, beware how thou enterest any dwelling[4] on thy route; or thou shalt feel the effects of my anger.'

The Caliph, notwithstanding his habitual luxury, had never before dined with so much satisfaction. He gave full scope to the joy of these golden tidings; and betook himself to drinking anew. Carathis, whose antipathy to wine was by no means insuperable, failed not to pledge him at every bumper he ironically quaffed to the health of Mahomet.[5] This infernal liquor completed their impious temerity, and prompted them to utter a profusion of blasphemies. They gave a loose to their wit, at the expense of the ass of Balaam, the dog of the seven sleepers, and the other animals admitted into the paradise of Mahomet.[6] In this sprightly humour, they descended the fifteen hundred stairs, diverting themselves as they went, at the anxious faces they saw on the square, through the barbacans and loop-holes of the

tower; and, at length, arrived at the royal apartments, by
the subterranean passage. Bababalouk was parading to and
fro, and issuing his mandates, with great pomp to the
eunuchs; who were snuffing the lights and painting the
eyes of the Circassians.[1] No sooner did he catch sight of
the Caliph and his mother, than he exclaimed, 'Hah! you
have, than, I perceive, escaped from the flames: I was not,
however, altogether out of doubt.'—'Of what moment is it
to us what you thought, or think?' cried Carathis: 'go;
speed; tell Morakanabad that we immediately want him:
and take care, not to stop by the way, to make your insipid
reflections.'

Morakanabad delayed not to obey the summons; and
was received by Vathek and his mother, with great solemnity. They told him, with an air of composure and
commiseration, that the fire at the top of the tower was
extinguished; but that it had cost the lives of the brave
people who sought to assist them.

'Still more misfortunes!' cried Morakanabad, with a
sigh. 'Ah, commander of the faithful, our holy prophet is
certainly irritated against us! it behoves you to appease
him.'—'We will appease him, hereafter!' replied the Caliph,
with a smile, that augured nothing of good. 'You will have
leisure sufficient for your supplications, during my absence:
for this country is the bane of my health. I am disgusted
with the mountain of the four fountains, and am resolved
to go and drink of the stream of Rocnabad.[2] I long to refresh myself, in the delightful vallies which it waters. Do
you, with the advice of my mother, govern my dominions,
and take care to supply whatever her experiments may
demand: for, you well know, that our tower abounds in
materials for the advancement of science.'

The tower but ill suited Morakanabad's taste. Immense treasures had been lavished upon it; and nothing had he ever seen carried thither but female negroes, mutes and abominable drugs. Nor did he know well what to think of Carathis, who, like a cameleon, could assume all possible colours. Her cursed eloquence had often driven the poor mussulman to his last shifts. He considered, however, that if she possessed but few good qualities, her son had still fewer; and that the alternative, on the whole, would be in her favour. Consoled, therefore, with this reflection; he went, in good spirits, to soothe the populace, and make the proper arrangements for his master's journey.

Vathek, to conciliate the Spirits of the subterranean palace, resolved that his expedition should be uncommonly splendid. With this view he confiscated, on all sides, the property of his subjects; whilst his worthy mother stripped the seraglios she visited, of the gems they contained. She collected all the sempstresses and embroiderers of Samarah and other cities, to the distance of sixty leagues; to prepare pavilions, palanquins; sofas, canopies, and litters for the train of the monarch. There was not left, in Masulipatan, a single piece of chintz; and so much muslin had been brought up to dress out Bababalouk and the other black eunuchs, that there remained not an ell of it in the whole Irak of Babylon.

During these preparations, Carathis, who never lost sight of her great object, which was to obtain favour with the powers of darkness, made select parties of the fairest and most delicate ladies of the city: but in the midst of their gaiety, she contrived to introduce vipers amongst them, and to break pots of scorpions under the table. They all bit to a wonder, and Carathis would have left her friends

to die, were it not that, to fill up the time, she now and then
amused herself in curing their wounds, with an excellent
anodyne of her own invention:[1] for this good Princess
abhorred being indolent.

Vathek, who was not altogether so active as his mother,
devoted his time to the sole gratification of his senses, in
the palaces which were severally dedicated to them. He
disgusted himself no more with the divan, or the mosque.
One half of Samarah followed his example, whilst the other
lamented the progress of corruption.

In the midst of these transactions, the embassy returned,
which had been sent, in pious times, to Mecca. It consisted
of the most reverend Moullahs[2] who had fulfilled their
commission, and brought back one of those precious be-
soms which are used to sweep the sacred Cahaba:[3] a present
truly worthy of the greatest potentate on earth!

The Caliph happened at this instant to be engaged in
an apartment[4] by no means adapted to the reception of
embassies. He heard the voice of Bababalouk, calling out
from between the door and the tapestry that hung before
it: 'Here are the excellent Edris al Shafei,[5] and the sera-
phic Al Mouhateddin, who have brought the besom from
Mecca, and, with tears of joy, entreat they may present it
to your majesty in person.'—'Let them bring the besom
hither, it may be of use,' said Vathek. 'How!' answered
Bababalouk, half aloud and amazed. 'Obey,' replied the
Caliph, 'for it is my sovereign will; go instantly, vanish!
for here will I receive the good folk who have thus filled
thee with joy.'

The eunuch departed muttering, and bade the venerable
train attend him. A sacred rapture was diffused amongst
these reverend old men. Though fatigued with the length

of their expedition, they followed Bababalouk with an alertness almost miraculous, and felt themselves highly flattered, as they swept along the stately porticos, that the Caliph would not receive them like ambassadors in ordinary in his hall of audience. Soon reaching the interior of the harem (where, through blinds of Persian, they perceived large soft eyes, dark and blue, that came and went like lightning) penetrated with respect and wonder, and full of their celestial mission, they advanced in procession towards the small corridors that appeared to terminate in nothing, but, nevertheless, led to the cell where the Caliph expected their coming.

'What! is the commander of the faithful sick?' said Edris al Shafei, in a low voice to his companion—'I rather think he is in his oratory,' answered Al Mouhateddin. Vathek, who heard the dialogue, cried out:—'What imports it you, how I am employed? approach without delay.' They advanced, whilst the Caliph, without shewing himself, put forth his hand from behind the tapestry that hung before the door, and demanded of them the besom. Having prostrated themselves as well as the corridor would permit, and, even in a tolerable semicircle, the venerable Al Shafei, drawing forth the besom from the embroidered and perfumed scarves, in which it had been enveloped, and secured from the profane gaze of vulgar eyes, arose from his associates, and advanced, with an air of the most awful solemnity towards the supposed oratory; but, with what astonishment! with what horror was he seized!——Vathek, bursting out into a villainous laugh, snatched the besom from his trembling hand, and, fixing upon some cobwebs, that hung from the ceiling, gravely brushed them away till not a single one remained. The old men, overpowered with amazement, were unable to lift their beards from the ground: for, as Vathek had carelessly left the tapestry between them half drawn, they were witnesses of the whole transaction. Their tears bedewed the marble. Al Mouhated-din swooned through mortification and fatigue, whilst the Caliph, throwing himself backward on his seat, shouted, and clapped his hands without mercy. At last, addressing himself to Bababalouk!—'My dear black,' said he, 'go, regale these pious poor souls, with my good wine from Shiraz,[1] since they can boast of having seen more of my palace than any one besides.' Having said this, he threw the besom in their face, and went to enjoy the laugh with Carathis. Bababalouk did all in his power to console the ambassadors; but the two most infirm expired on the spot: the rest were carried to their beds, from whence, being heart-broken with sorrow and shame, they never arose.

The succeeding night, Vathek, attended by his mother, ascended the tower to see if every thing were ready for his journey: for, he had great faith in the influence of the stars. The planets appeared in their most favourable aspects. The Caliph, to enjoy so flattering a sight, supped gaily on the roof; and fancied that he heard, during his repast, loud shouts of laughter resound through the sky, in a manner, that inspired the fullest assurance.

All was in motion at the palace; lights were kept burning through the whole of the night: the sound of implements, and of artizans finishing their work; the voices of women, and their guardians, who sung at their embroidery: all conspired to interrupt the stillness of nature, and infinitely delighted the heart of Vathek who imagined himself going in triumph to sit upon the throne of Soliman. The people were not less satisfied than himself: all assisted to accelerate the moment, which should rescue them from the wayward caprices of so extravagant a master.

The day preceding the departure of this infatuated Prince, was employed by Carathis, in repeating to him the decrees of the mysterious parchment; which she had thoroughly gotten by heart; and, in recommending him, not to enter the habitation of any one by the way: 'for, well thou knowest,' added she, 'how liquorish thy taste is after good dishes and young damsels; let me, therefore, enjoin thee, to be content with thy old cooks, who are the best in the world: and not to forget that, in thy ambulatory seraglio, there are at least three dozen of pretty faces which Bababalouk hath not yet unveiled. I myself have a great desire to watch over thy conduct, and visit the subterranean palace, which, no doubt, contains whatever can interest persons, like us. There is nothing so pleasing as retiring to caverns: my taste for dead bodies, and every thing like mummy is decided: and, I am confident, thou wilt see the most exquisite of their kind. Forget me not then, but the moment thou art in possession of the talismans which are to open the way to the mineral kingdoms and the centre of the earth itself, fail not to dispatch some trusty genius to take me and my cabinet: for the oil of the serpents I have pinched to death will be a pretty present to the Giaour who cannot but be charmed with such dainties.'

Scarcely had Carathis ended this edifying discourse, when the sun, setting behind the mountain of the four fountains, gave place to the rising moon. This planet, being that evening at full, appeared of unusual beauty and magnitude, in the eyes of the women, the eunuchs and the pages who were all impatient to set forward. The city re-echoed with shouts of joy, and flourishing of trumpets. Nothing was visible, but plumes, nodding on pavilions, and aigrets shining in the mild lustre of the moon. The spacious square resembled an immense parterre variegated with the most stately tulips of the east.[1]

Arrayed in the robes which were only worn at the most distinguished ceremonials, and supported by his vizir and Bababalouk, the Caliph descended the great staircase of the tower in the sight of all his people. He could not forbear pausing, at intervals, to admire the superb appearance which every where courted his view: whilst the whole multitude, even to the camels with their sumptuous burthens, knelt down before him. For some time a general stillness prevailed, which nothing happened to disturb, but the shrill screams of some eunuchs in the rear. These vigilant guards, having remarked certain cages of the ladies[2] swagging somewhat awry, and discovered that a few adventurous gallants had contrived to get in, soon dislodged[3] the enraptured culprits and consigned them, with good commendations, to the surgeons of the serail. The majesty of so magnificent a spectacle, was not, however, violated by incidents like these. Vathek, meanwhile, saluted the moon with an idolatrous air, that neither pleased Morakanabad, nor the doctors of the law, any more than the vizirs and grandees of his court, who were all assembled to enjoy the last view of their sovereign.

At length, the clarions and trumpets from the top of the tower, announced the prelude of departure. Though the instruments were in unison with each other, yet a singular dissonance was blended with their sounds. This proceeded from Carathis who was singing her direful orisons to the Giaour, whilst the negresses and mutes supplied thorough base, without articulating a word. The good Mussulmans fancied that they heard the sullen hum of those nocturnal insects, which presage evil; and importuned Vathek to beware how he ventured his sacred person.

On a given signal, the great standard of the Califat was displayed; twenty thousand lances shone around it; and the Caliph, treading royally on the cloth of gold, which had been spread for his feet, ascended his litter, amidst the general acclamations of his subjects.

The expedition commenced with the utmost order and so entire a silence, that, even the locusts were heard from the thickets on the plain of Catoul.[1] Gaiety and good humour prevailing, they made full six leagues before the dawn; and the morning star was still glittering in the firmament, when the whole of this numerous train had halted on the banks of the Tigris, where they encamped to repose for the rest of the day.

The three days that followed were spent in the same manner; but, on the fourth, the heavens looked angry; lightnings broke forth, in frequent flashes; re-echoing peals of thunder succeeded; and the trembling Circassians clung with all their might, to their ugly guardians. The Caliph himself, was greatly inclined to take shelter in the large town of Ghulchissar, the governor of which, came forth to meet him, and tendered every kind of refreshment the place could supply. But, having examined his tablets, he suffered the rain to soak him, almost to the bone, notwithstanding the importunity of his first favourites. Though he began to regret the palace of the senses; yet, he lost not sight of his enterprize, and his sanguine expectation confirmed his resolution. His geographers were ordered to attend him; but, the weather proved so terrible that these poor people exhibited a lamentable appearance: and their maps of the different countries spoiled by the rain, were in a still worse plight than themselves. As no long journey had been undertaken since the time of Haroun al Raschid, every one was ignorant which way to turn; and Vathek, though well versed in the course of the heavens, no longer knew his situation on earth. He thundered even louder than the elements; and muttered forth certain hints of the bow-string which were not very soothing to literary ears. Disgusted at the toilsome weariness of the way, he determined to cross over the craggy heights and follow the guidance of a peasant, who undertook to bring him, in four days, to Rocnabad. Remonstrances were all to no purpose; his resolution was fixed.

The females and eunuchs uttered shrill wailings at the sight of the precipices below them, and the dreary prospects that opened, in the vast gorges of the mountains. Before they could reach the ascent of the steepest rock, night over-took them, and a boisterous tempest arose, which, having rent the awnings of the palanquins and cages, exposed to the raw gusts the poor ladies within, who had never before felt so piercing a cold. The dark clouds that overcast the face of the sky deepened the horrors of this disastrous night, insomuch that nothing could be heard distinctly, but the mewling of pages and lamentations of sultanas.

To increase the general misfortune, the frightful up-roar of wild beasts resounded at a distance; and there were soon perceived in the forest they were skirting, the glaring of eyes, which could belong only to devils or tigers. The pioneers, who, as well as they could, had marked out a track; and a part of the advanced guard, were devoured, before they had been in the least apprized of their danger. The confusion that prevailed was extreme. Wolves, tigers,

and other carnivorous animals, invited by the howling of
their companions, flocked together from every quarter.
The crashing of bones was heard on all sides, and a fearful
rush of wings over head; for now vultures also began to be
of the party.

The terror at length reached the main body of the troops
which surrounded the monarch and his harem at the distance of two leagues from the scene. Vathek (voluptuously
reposed in his capacious litter upon cushions of silk, with
two little pages[1] beside him of complexions more fair than
the enamel of Franguistan, who were occupied in keeping
off flies) was soundly asleep, and contemplating in his
dreams the treasures of Soliman. The shrieks however of
his wives, awoke him with a start; and, instead of the Giaour
with his key of gold, he beheld Bababalouk full of consternation. 'Sire,' exclaimed this good servant of the most
potent of monarchs, 'misfortune is arrived at its height,
wild beasts, who entertain no more reverence for your
sacred person, than for a dead ass, have beset your camels
and their drivers; thirty of the most richly laden are already
become their prey, as well as your confectioners, your
cooks,[2] and purveyors: and, unless our holy Prophet
should protect us, we shall have all eaten our last meal.'
At the mention of eating, the Caliph lost all patience. He
began to bellow, and even beat himself (for there was no
seeing in the dark). The rumour every instant increased;
and Bababalouk, finding no good could be done with his
master, stopped both his ears against the hurlyburly of the
harem, and called out aloud: 'Come, ladies, and brothers!
all hands to work: strike light in a moment! never shall it
be said, that the commander of the faithful served to regale
these infidel brutes.' Though there wanted not in this bevy

of beauties, a sufficient number of capricious and wayward; yet, on the present occasion, they were all compliance. Fires were visible, in a twinkling, in all their cages. Ten thousand torches were lighted at once.[1] The Caliph, himself, seized a large one of wax: every person followed his example; and, by kindling ropes ends, dipped in oil and fastened on poles, an amazing blaze was spread. The rocks were covered with the splendour of sun-shine. The trails of sparks, wafted by the wind, communicated to the dry fern, of which there was plenty. Serpents were observed to crawl forth from their retreats, with amazement and hissings; whilst the horses snorted, stamped the ground, tossed their noses in the air, and plunged about, without mercy.

One of the forests of cedar that bordered their way, took fire;[2] and the branches that overhung the path, extending their flames to the muslins and chintzes, which covered the cages of the ladies obliged them to jump out, at the peril of their necks. Vathek, who vented on the occasion a thousand blasphemies, was himself compelled to touch, with his sacred feet, the naked earth.

Never had such an incident happened before. Full of mortification, shame, and despondence, and not knowing how to walk, the ladies fell into the dirt. 'Must I go on foot!' said one: 'Must I wet my feet!' cried another: 'Must I soil my dress!' asked a third: 'Execrable Bababalouk!' exclaimed all: 'Outcast of hell! what hast thou to do with torches! Better were it to be eaten by tigers, than to fall into our present condition! we are for ever undone! Not a porter is there in the army nor a currier of camels; but hath seen some part of our bodies; and, what is worse, our very faces!'[3] On saying this, the most bashful amongst

them hid their foreheads on the ground, whilst such as
had more boldness flew at Bababalouk; but he, well apprized
of their humour and not wanting in shrewdness, betook
himself to his heels along with his comrades, all dropping
their torches and striking their tymbals.

It was not less light than in the brightest of the dog-days,
and the weather was hot in proportion; but how degrading
was the spectacle, to behold the Caliph bespattered, like
an ordinary mortal! As the exercise of his faculties seemed
to be suspended, one of his Ethiopian wives (for he delighted
in variety) clasped him in her arms; threw him upon her
shoulder, like a sack of dates, and, finding that the fire was
hemming them in, set off, with no small expedition, considering the weight of her burden. The other ladies, who
had just learnt the use of their feet, followed her; their
guards galloped after; and the camel-drivers brought up
the rear, as fast as their charge would permit.

They soon reached the spot, where the wild beasts had
commenced the carnage, but which they had too much
good sense not to leave at the approaching of the tumult,
having made besides a most luxurious supper. Bababalouk,
nevertheless, seized on a few of the plumpest, which were
unable to budge from the place, and began to flea them
with admirable adroitness. The cavalcade having proceeded so far from the conflagration, that the heat felt
rather grateful than violent, it was, immediately, resolved
on to halt. The tattered chintzes were picked up; the
scraps, left by the wolves and tigers, interred; and vengeance was taken on some dozens of vultures, that were too
much glutted to rise on the wing. The camels, which had
been left unmolested to make sal ammoniac, being numbered; and the ladies once more inclosed in their cages;

the imperial tent was pitched on the levellest ground they could find.

Vathek, reposing upon a mattress of down, and tolerably recovered from the jolting of the Ethiopian, who, to his feelings, seemed the roughest trotting jade he had hitherto mounted, called out for something to eat. But, alas! those delicate cakes, which had been baked in silver ovens, for his royal mouth;[1] those rich manchets;[2] amber comfits; flaggons of Schiraz wine; porcelain vases of snow;[3] and grapes from the banks of the Tigris; were all irremediably lost!—And nothing had Bababalouk to present in their stead, but a roasted wolf; vultures à la daube; aromatic herbs of the most acrid poignancy; rotten truffles; boiled thistles: and such other wild plants, as must ulcerate the throat and parch up the tongue. Nor was he better provided, in the article of drink: for he could procure nothing to accompany these irritating viands, but a few phials of abominable brandy which had been secreted by the scullions in their slippers. Vathek made wry faces at so savage a repast; and Bababalouk answered them, with shrugs and contortions. The Caliph, however, eat with tolerable appetite; and fell into a nap, that lasted six hours.

The splendour of the sun, reflected from the white cliffs of the mountains, in spite of the curtains that inclosed Vathek, at length disturbed his repose. He awoke, terrified; and stung to the quick by wormwood-colour flies, which emitted from their wings a suffocating stench. The miserable monarch was perplexed how to act; though his wits were not idle, in seeking expedients, whilst Bababalouk lay snoring, amidst a swarm of those insects that busily thronged, to pay court to his nose. The little pages, famished with hunger, had dropped their fans on the ground;

and exerted their dying voices, in bitter reproaches on the Caliph; who now, for the first time, heard the language of truth.

Thus stimulated, he renewed his imprecations against the Giaour; and bestowed upon Mahomet some soothing expressions. 'Where am I?' cried he: 'What are these dreadful rocks? these valleys of darkness! are we arrived at the horrible Kaf![1] is the Simurgh[2] coming to pluck out my eyes, as a punishment for undertaking this impious enterprize!' Having said this he turned himself towards an outlet in the side of his pavilion, but, alas! what objects occurred to his view? on one side, a plain of black sand that appeared to be unbounded; and, on the other, perpendicular crags, bristled over with those abominable thistles, which had, so severely, lacerated his tongue. He fancied, however, that he perceived, amongst the brambles and briars, some gigantic flowers but was mistaken: for, these were only the dangling palampores[3] and variegated tatters of his gay retinue. As there were several clefts in the rock from whence water seemed to have flowed, Vathek applied his ear with the hope of catching the sound of some latent torrent; but could only distinguish the low murmurs of his people who were repining at their journey, and complaining for the want of water. 'To what purpose,' asked they, 'have we been brought hither? hath our Caliph another tower to build? or have the relentless afrits,[4] whom Carathis so much loves, fixed their abode in this place?'

At the name of Carathis, Vathek recollected the tablets he had received from his mother; who assured him, they were fraught with preternatural qualities,[5] and advised him to consult them, as emergencies might require. Whilst he was engaged in turning them over, he heard a shout of

joy, and a loud clapping of hands. The curtains of his
pavilion were soon drawn back and he beheld Bababalouk,
followed by a troop of his favourites, conducting two
dwarfs[1] each a cubit high; who brought between them a
large basket of melons, oranges, and pomegranates. They
were singing in the sweetest tones the words that follow:
'We dwell on the top of these rocks, in a cabin of rushes and
canes; the eagles envy us our nest: a small spring supplies
us with water for the Abdest, and we daily repeat prayers,[2]
which the Prophet approves. We love you, O commander
of the faithful! our master, the good Emir Fakreddin,[3]
loves you also: he reveres, in your person, the vicegerent
of Mahomet. Little as we are, in us he confides: he knows
our hearts to be as good, as our bodies are contemptible;
and hath placed us here to aid those who are bewildered on
these dreary mountains. Last night, whilst we were occupied within our cell in reading the holy Koran, a sudden
hurricane blew out our lights, and rocked our habitation.
For two whole hours, a palpable darkness prevailed; but
we heard sounds at a distance, which we conjectured to
proceed from the bells of a Cafila,[4] passing over the rocks.
Our ears were soon filled with deplorable shrieks, frightful
roarings, and the sound of tymbals. Chilled with terror,
we concluded that the Deggial,[5] with his exterminating
angels, had sent forth his plagues on the earth. In the midst
of these melancholy reflections, we perceived flames of
the deepest red, glow in the horizon; and found ourselves,
in a few moments, covered with flakes of fire. Amazed at
so strange an appearance, we took up the volume dictated
by the blessed intelligence, and, kneeling, by the light of
the fire that surrounded us, we recited the verse which
says: 'Put no trust in any thing but the mercy of Heaven:

there is no help, save in the holy Prophet: the mountain of Kaf, itself, may tremble; it is the power of Alla only, that cannot be moved.' After having pronounced these words, we felt consolation, and our minds were hushed into a sacred repose. Silence ensued, and our ears clearly distinguished a voice in the air, saying: 'Servants of my faithful servant! go down to the happy valley of Fakreddin: tell him that an illustrious opportunity now offers to satiate the thirst of his hospitable heart. The commander of true believers is, this day, bewildered amongst these mountains and stands in need of thy aid.'—We obeyed, with joy, the angelic mission; and our master, filled with pious zeal, hath culled, with his own hands, these melons, oranges, and pomegranates. He is following us, with a hundred dromedaries, laden with the purest waters of his fountains; and is coming to kiss the fringe of your consecrated robe, and implore you to enter his humble habitation which, placed amidst these barren wilds, resembles an emerald set in lead.' The dwarfs, having ended their address, remained still standing, and, with hands crossed upon their bosoms, preserved a respectful silence.

Vathek, in the midst of this curious harangue, seized the basket; and, long before it was finished, the fruits had dissolved in his mouth. As he continued to eat, his piety increased; and, in the same breath, he recited his prayers and called for the Koran and sugar.[1]

Such was the state of his mind, when the tablets, which were thrown by, at the approach of the dwarfs, again attracted his eye. He took them up; but was ready to drop on the ground, when he beheld in large red characters[2] inscribed by Carathis, these words; which were, indeed, enough to make him tremble; 'Beware of old doctors and

their puny messengers of but one cubit high: distrust their
pious frauds; and, instead of eating their melons, empale
on a spit the bearers of them. Shouldest thou be such a
fool as to visit them, the portal of the subterranean palace
will shut in thy face with such force, as shall shake thee
asunder: thy body shall be spit upon,[1] and bats will nestle
in thy belly.'[2]

'To what tends this ominous rhapsody?' cries the Caliph:
'and must I then perish in these deserts, with thirst; whilst
I may refresh myself in the delicious valley of melons and
cucumbers?—Accursed be the Giaour with his portal of
ebony! he hath made me dance attendance, too long
already. Besides, who shall prescribe laws to me?—I,
forsooth, must not enter any one's habitation! Be it so:
but, what one can I enter, that is not my own!' Bababalouk,
who lost not a syllable of this soliloquy, applauded it with
all his heart; and the ladies, for the first time, agreed with
him in opinion.

The dwarfs were entertained, caressed, and seated, with
great ceremony, on little cushions of satin. The symmetry
of their persons was a subject of admiration; not an inch
of them was suffered to pass unexamined. Knick-nacks
and dainties were offered in profusion; but all were declined, with respectful gravity. They climbed up the sides
of the Caliph's seat; and, placing themselves each on one
of his shoulders, began to whisper prayers in his ears. Their
tongues quivered, like aspen leaves; and the patience of
Vathek was almost exhausted, when the acclamations of
the troops announced the approach of Fakreddin, who was
come with a hundred old grey-beards, and as many Korans
and dromedaries. They instantly set about their ablutions, and began to repeat the Bismillah.[3] Vathek, to get

rid of these officious monitors, followed their example; for his hands were burning.

The good emir, who was punctiliously religious, and likewise a great dealer in compliments, made an harangue five times more prolix and insipid than his little harbingers had already delivered. The Caliph, unable any longer to refrain, exclaimed: 'For the love of Mahomet, my dear Fakreddin, have done! let us proceed to your valley, and enjoy the fruits that Heaven hath vouchsafed you.' The hint of proceeding, put all into motion. The venerable attendants of the emir set forward, somewhat slowly; but Vathek, having ordered his little pages, in private, to goad on the dromedaries, loud fits of laughter broke forth from the cages; for, the unwieldy curvetting of these poor beasts, and the ridiculous distress of their superannuated riders, afforded the ladies no small entertainment.

They descended, however, unhurt into the valley, by the easy slopes which the emir had ordered to be cut in the rock; and already, the murmuring of streams and the rustling of leaves began to catch their attention. The cavalcade soon entered a path, which was skirted by flowering shrubs, and extended to a vast wood of palm trees, whose branches overspread a vast building of free stone. This edifice was crowned with nine domes, and adorned with as many portals of bronze, on which was engraven the following inscription: 'This is the asylum of pilgrims, the refuge of travellers, and the depositary of secrets from all parts of the world.'

Nine pages, beautiful as the day, and decently clothed in robes of Egyptian linen, were standing at each door. They received the whole retinue with an easy and inviting air. Four of the most amiable placed the Caliph on a

magnificent tecthtrevan:[1] four others, somewhat less graceful, took charge of Bababalouk, who capered for joy at the
snug little cabin that fell to his share; the pages that remained waited on the rest of the train.

Every man being gone out of sight, the gate of a large
inclosure, on the right, turned on its harmonious hinges;
and a young female, of a slender form, came forth. Her
light brown hair floated in the hazy breeze of the twilight.
A troop of young maidens, like the Pleiades, attended her
on tip-toe. They hastened to the pavilions that contained
the sultanas: and the young lady, gracefully bending, said
to them: 'Charming princesses, every thing is ready: we
have prepared beds for your repose, and strewed your
apartments with jasmine: no insects will keep off slumber
from visiting your eye-lids; we will dispel them with a
thousand plumes. Come then, amiable ladies, refresh your
delicate feet, and your ivory limbs, in baths of rose water;[2]
and, by the light of perfumed lamps, your servants will
amuse you with tales.' The sultanas accepted, with pleasure, these obliging offers; and followed the young lady
to the emir's harem; where we must, for a moment, leave
them, and return to the Caliph.

Vathek found himself beneath a vast dome, illuminated
by a thousand lamps of rock crystal: as many vases of the
same material, filled with excellent sherbet, sparkled on a
large table, where a profusion of viands were spread.
Amongst others, were rice boiled in milk of almonds,
saffron soups, and lamb à la crême;[3] of all which the
Caliph was amazingly fond. He took of each, as much as
he was able, testified his sense of the emir's friendship, by
the gaiety of his heart; and made the dwarfs dance, against
their will:[4] for these little devotees durst not refuse the

commander of the faithful.[1] At last, he spread himself on the sopha, and slept sounder than he ever had before.

Beneath this dome, a general silence prevailed; for there was nothing to disturb it but the jaws of Bababalouk, who had untrussed himself to eat with greater advantage; being anxious to make amends for his fast, in the mountains. As his spirits were too high to admit of his sleeping; and hating to be idle, he proposed with himself to visit the harem and repair to his charge of the ladies: to examine if they had been properly lubricated with the balm of Mecca;[2] if their eye-brows, and tresses, were in order; and, in a word, to perform all the little offices they might need. He sought for a long time together but without being able to find out the door. He durst not speak aloud for fear of disturbing the Caliph; and not a soul was stirring in the precincts of the palace. He almost despaired of effecting his purpose, when a low whispering just reached his ear. It came from the dwarfs, who were returned to their old occupation, and, for the nine hundred and ninety-ninth time in their lives, were reading over the Koran. They very politely invited Bababalouk to be of their party; but his head was full of other concerns. The dwarfs, though not a little scandalized at his dissolute morals, directed him to the apartments he wanted to find. His way thither lay through a hundred dark corridors, along which he groped as he went; and at last, began to catch, from the extremity of a passage, the charming gossiping of the women which not a little delighted his heart. 'Ah, ha! what not yet asleep?' cried he; and, taking long strides as he spoke, 'did you not suspect me of abjuring my charge?' Two of the black eunuchs, on hearing a voice so loud, left their party in haste, sabre in hand,[3] to discover the cause: but, presently, was repeated on all sides: ''Tis

only Bababalouk! no one but Bababalouk!' This circum-
spect guardian, having gone up to a thin veil of carnation-
colour silk that hung before the door-way, distinguished,
by means of the softened splendor that shone through it,
an oval bath of dark porphyry surrounded by curtains,
festooned in large folds. Through the apertures between
them, as they were not drawn close, groups of young slaves
were visible; amongst whom, Bababalouk perceived his
pupils, indulgingly expanding their arms, as if to embrace
the perfumed water, and refresh themselves after their
fatigues. The looks of tender languor; their confidential
whispers; and the enchanting smiles with which they were
imparted; the exquisite fragrance of the roses: all combined
to inspire a voluptuousness, which even Bababalouk himself was scarce able to withstand.

He summoned up, however, his usual solemnity, and in
the peremptory tone of authority, commanded the ladies,
instantly, to leave the bath. Whilst he was issuing these
mandates, the young Nouronihar,[1] daughter of the emir,
who was as sprightly as an antelope, and full of wanton
gaiety, beckoned one of her slaves to let down the great
swing[2] which was suspended to the ceiling by cords of silk;
and whilst this was doing, winked to her companions in
the bath: who, chagrined to be forced from so soothing a
state of indolence, began to twist and entangle their hair
to plague and detain Bababalouk; and teased him besides
with a thousand vagaries.

Nouronihar perceiving that he was nearly out of patience
accosted him, with an arch air of respectful concern, and
said: 'My lord! it is not, by any means decent, that the chief
eunuch of the Caliph our sovereign should thus continue
standing: deign but to recline your graceful person upon

this sofa which will burst with vexation, if it have not the honour to receive you.' Caught by these flattering accents, Bababalouk gallantly replied: 'Delight of the apple of my eye! I accept the invitation of your honied lips; and, to say truth, my senses are dazzled with the radiance that beams from your charms.'¹—'Repose, then, at your ease,' replied the beauty; as she placed him on the pretended sofa which, quicker than lightning, flew up all at once. The rest of the women, having aptly conceived her design, sprang naked from the bath, and plied the swing, with such unmerciful jerks, that it swept through the whole compass of a very lofty dome, and took from the poor victim all power of respiration. Sometimes, his feet rased the surface of the water; and, at others, the skylight almost flattened his nose. In vain did he fill the air with the cries of a voice that resembled the ringing of a cracked jar; their peals of laughter were still predominant.

Nouronihar, in the inebriety of youthful spirits, being used only to eunuchs of ordinary harems; and having never seen any thing so eminently disgusting, was far more diverted than all of the rest. She began to parody some Persian verses and sang with an accent most demurely piquant: 'Oh gentle white dove, as thou soar'st through the air, vouchsafe one kind glance on the mate of thy love: melodious Philomel, I am thy rose;² warble some couplet to ravish my heart!'

The sultanas and their slaves, stimulated by these pleasantries, persevered at the swing, with such unremitted assiduity, that at length, the cord which had secured it, snapt suddenly asunder; and Bababalouk fell, floundering like a turtle, to the bottom of the bath. This accident occasioned an universal shout. Twelve little doors, till now

unobserved, flew open at once; and the ladies, in an instant,
made their escape; but not before having heaped all the
towels on his head and put out the lights that remained.

The deplorable animal, in water to the chin, overwhelmed
with darkness, and unable to extricate himself from the
wrappers that embarrassed him, was still doomed to hear,
for his further consolation, the fresh bursts of merriment
his disaster occasioned. He bustled, but in vain, to get from
the bath; for, the margin was become so slippery, with the
oil spilt in breaking the lamps,[1] that, at every effort, he
slid back with a plunge which resounded aloud through
the hollow of the dome. These cursed peals of laughter,
were redoubled at every relapse, and he, who thought the
place infested rather by devils than women, resolved to
cease groping, and abide in the bath; where he amused
himself with soliloquies, interspersed with imprecations,
of which his malicious neighbours, reclining on down,
suffered not an accent to escape. In this delectable plight,
the morning surprised him. The Caliph, wondering at his
absence, had caused him to be sought for every where. At
last, he was drawn forth almost smothered from under the
wisp of linen, and wet even to the marrow. Limping, and
his teeth chattering with cold, he approached his master;
who inquired what was the matter, and how he came soused
in so strange a pickle?—'And why did you enter this
cursed lodge?' answered Bababalouk, gruffly.—'Ought a
monarch like you to visit with his harem, the abode of a
grey-bearded emir, who knows nothing of life?—And, with
what gracious damsels doth the place too abound! Fancy
to yourself how they have soaked me like a burnt crust;
and made me dance like a jack-pudding,[2] the live-long
night through, on their damnable swing. What an excellent

lesson for your sultanas, into whom I had instilled such
reserve and decorum!' Vathek, comprehending not a
syllable of all this invective, obliged him to relate minutely
the transaction: but, instead of sympathizing with the
miserable sufferer, he laughed immoderately at the device
of the swing and the figure of Bababalouk, mounted upon
it. The stung eunuch could scarcely preserve the semblance
of respect. 'Aye, laugh, my lord! laugh,' said he; 'but I
wish this Nouronihar would play some trick on you; she
is too wicked to spare even majesty itself.' These words
made, for the present, but a slight impression on the
Caliph; but they, not long after, recurred to his mind.

This conversation was cut short by Fakreddin, who
came to request that Vathek would join in the prayers and
ablutions, to be solemnized on a spacious meadow watered
by innumerable streams. The Caliph found the waters
refreshing, but the prayers abominably irksome. He
diverted himself, however, with the multitude of calenders,[1] santons,[2] and derviches,[3] who were continually coming and going; but especially with the bramins,[4] faquirs,[5]
and other enthusiasts, who had travelled from the heart of
India, and halted on their way with the emir. These latter
had each of them some mummery peculiar to himself. One
dragged a huge chain wherever he went; another an ouran-
outang; whilst a third, was furnished with scourges; and
all performed to a charm. Some would climb up trees,
holding one foot in the air; others poise themselves over
a fire, and, without mercy, fillip their noses. There were
some amongst them that cherished vermin,[6] which were
not ungrateful in requiting their caresses. These rambling
fanatics revolted the hearts of the derviches, the calenders,
and santons; however, the vehemence of their aversion soon

subsided, under the hope that the presence of the Caliph would cure their folly, and convert them to the mussulman faith. But, alas! how great was their disappointment! for Vathek, instead of preaching to them, treated them as buffoons, bade them present his compliments to Visnow and Ixhora,[1] and discovered a predilection for a squat old man from the Isle of Serendib, who was more ridiculous than any of the rest. 'Come!' said he, 'for the love of your gods, bestow a few slaps on your chops to amuse me.' The old fellow, offended at such an address, began loudly to weep; but, as he betrayed a villainous drivelling in shedding tears, the Caliph turned his back and listened to Bababa-louk, who whispered, whilst he held the umbrella over him: 'Your majesty should be cautious of this odd assembly; which hath been collected, I know not for what. Is it neces-sary to exhibit such spectacles to a mighty potentate, with interludes of talapoins[2] more mangy than dogs? Were I you, I would command a fire to be kindled, and at once rid the estates of the emir, of his harem, and all his menagerie.' —'Tush, dolt,' answered Vathek; 'and know, that all this infinitely charms me. Nor shall I leave the meadow, till I have visited every hive of these pious mendicants.'

Wherever the Caliph directed his course, objects of pity were sure to swarm round him;[3] the blind, the purblind, smarts without noses, damsels without ears, each to extol the munificence of Fakreddin, who, as well as his attendant grey-beards, dealt about, gratis, plasters and cataplasms to all that applied. At noon, a superb corps of cripples made its appearance; and soon after advanced, by platoons, on the plain, the completest association of invalids that had ever been embodied till then. The blind went groping with the blind, the lame limped on together, and the maimed made gestures to each other with the only arm that remained. The sides of a considerable water-fall were crowded by the deaf; amongst whom were some from Pegû, with ears uncommonly handsome and large, but who were still less able to hear than the rest. Nor were there wanting others in abundance with hump-backs; wenny necks; and even horns of an exquisite polish.

The emir, to aggrandize the solemnity of the festival, in honour of his illustrious visitant, ordered the turf to be spread, on all sides, with skins and table-cloths; upon which were served up for the good Mussulmans, pilaus of every hue, with other orthodox dishes; and, by the express order of Vathek, who was shamefully tolerant, small plates of abominations[1] were prepared, to the great scandal of the faithful. The holy assembly began to fall to. The Caliph, in spite of every remonstrance from the chief of his eunuchs, resolved to have a dinner dressed on the spot. The complaisant emir immediately gave orders for a table to be placed in the shade of the willows. The first service consisted of fish, which they drew from a river, flowing over sands of gold at the foot of a lofty hill. These were broiled as fast as taken, and served up with a sauce of vinegar, and small herbs that grew on mount Sinai:[2] for every thing with the emir was excellent and pious.

The desert was not quite set on, when the sound of lutes, from the hill, was repeated by the echoes of the neighbouring mountains. The Caliph, with an emotion of pleasure and surprize, had no sooner raised up his head, than a handful of jasmine dropped on his face. An abundance of tittering succeeded the frolic, and instantly appeared, through the bushes, the elegant forms of several young females, skipping and bounding like roes. The fragrance diffused from their hair, struck the sense of Vathek, who, in an ecstacy, suspending his repast, said to Bababalouk: 'Are the peries¹ come down from their spheres? Note her, in particular, whose form is so perfect; venturously running on the brink of the precipice, and turning back her head, as regardless of nothing but the graceful flow of her robe. With what captivating impatience doth she contend with the bushes for her veil? could it be her who threw the jasmine at me!'—'Aye! she it was; and you too would she throw, from the top of the rock,' answered Bababalouk; 'for that is my good friend Nouronihar, who so kindly lent me her swing. My dear lord and master,' added he, wresting a twig from a willow, 'let me correct her for her want of respect: the emir will have no reason to complain; since (bating what I owe to his piety) he is much to be blamed for keeping a troop of girls on the mountains, where the sharpness of the air gives their blood too brisk a circulation.'

'Peace! blasphemer,' said the Caliph; 'speak not thus of her, who, over these mountains, leads my heart a willing captive. Contrive, rather, that my eyes may be fixed upon hers: that I may respire her sweet breath as she bounds panting along these delightful wilds!' On saying these words, Vathek extended his arms towards the hill, and directing his eyes, with an anxiety unknown to him before, endeavoured to keep within view the object that enthralled his soul: but her course was as difficult to follow, as the flight of one of those beautiful blue butterflies of Cachemire,² which are, at once, so volatile and rare.

The Caliph, not satisfied with seeing, wished also to hear Nouronihar, and eagerly turned to catch the sound of her voice. At last, he distinguished her whispering to one of her companions behind the thicket from whence she had thrown the jasmine: 'A Caliph, it must be owned, is a fine thing to see; but my little Gulchenrouz[1] is much more amiable: one lock of his hair is of more value to me than the richest embroidery of the Indies. I had rather that his teeth should mischievously press my finger, than the richest ring of the imperial treasure. Where have you left him, Sutlememe?[2] and why is he not here?'

The agitated Caliph still wished to hear more; but she immediately retired with all her attendants. The fond monarch pursued her with his eyes till she was gone out of sight; and then continued like a bewildered and be-nighted traveller, from whom the clouds had obscured the constellation that guided his way. The curtain of night seemed dropped before him: every thing appeared dis-coloured. The falling waters filled his soul with dejection, and his tears trickled down the jasmines he had caught from Nouronihar, and placed in his inflamed bosom. He snatched up a few shining pebbles, to remind him of the scene where he felt the first tumults of love. Two hours were elapsed, and evening drew on, before he could resolve to depart from the place. He often, but in vain, attempted to go: a soft languor enervated the powers of his mind. Extending himself on the brink of the stream, he turned his eyes towards the blue summits of the mountain, and exclaimed, 'What concealest thou behind thee, pitiless rock? what is passing in thy solitudes? Whither is she gone? O heaven! perhaps she is now wandering in thy grottoes with her happy Gulchenrouz!'

In the mean time, the damps began to descend; and the emir, solicitous for the health of the Caliph, ordered the imperial litter to be brought. Vathek, absorbed in his reveries, was imperceptibly removed and conveyed back

to the saloon, that received him the evening before. But,
let us leave the Caliph immersed in his new passion: and
attend Nouronihar beyond the rocks where she had again
joined her beloved Gulchenrouz.

This Gulchenrouz was the son of Ali Hassan, brother
to the emir: and the most delicate and lovely creature in the
world. Ali Hassan, who had been absent ten years, on a
voyage to the unknown seas, committed, at his departure,
this child, the only survivor of many, to the care and protection of his brother. Gulchenrouz could write in various
characters with precision, and paint upon vellum the most
elegant arabesques that fancy could devise. His sweet voice
accompanied the lute in the most enchanting manner; and,
when he sang the loves of Megnoun and Leilah,[1] or some
unfortunate lovers of ancient days, tears insensibly over-
flowed the cheeks of his auditors. The verses he composed
(for, like Megnoun, he, too, was a poet) inspired that un-
resisting languor, so frequently fatal to the female heart.
The women all doated upon him; and, though he had
passed his thirteenth year, they still detained him in the
harem. His dancing was light as the gossamer waved by
the zephyrs of spring; but his arms, which twined so gracefully with those of the young girls in the dance, could
neither dart the lance in the chace,[2] nor curb the steeds
that pastured in his uncle's domains. The bow, however,
he drew with a certain aim, and would have excelled his
competitors in the race, could he have broken the ties that
bound him to Nouronihar.

The two brothers had mutually engaged their children
to each other;[3] and Nouronihar loved her cousin, more than
her own beautiful eyes.[4] Both had the same tastes and
amusements; the same long, languishing looks;[5] the same

tresses; the same fair complexions; and, when Gulchenrouz appeared in the dress of his cousin, he seemed to be
more feminine than even herself. If, at any time, he left
the harem, to visit Fakreddin; it was with all the bashful-
ness of a fawn, that consciously ventures from the lair of
its dam: he was, however, wanton enough to mock the
solemn old grey-beards, though sure to be rated without
mercy in return. Whenever this happened, he would hastily
plunge into the recesses of the harem; and, sobbing, take
refuge in the fond arms of Nouronihar who loved even his
faults beyond the virtues of others.

It fell out this evening, that, after leaving the Caliph in
the meadow, she ran with Gulchenrouz over the green
sward of the mountain, that sheltered the vale where
Fakreddin had chosen to reside. The sun was dilated on
the edge of the horizon; and the young people, whose
fancies were lively and inventive, imagined they beheld, in
the gorgeous clouds of the west, the domes of Shaddukian
and Ambreabad,[1] where the Peries have fixed their abode.
Nouronihar, sitting on the slope of the hill, supported on
her knees the perfumed head of Gulchenrouz. The unexpected arrival of the Caliph and the splendour that
marked his appearance, had already filled with emotion
the ardent soul of Nouronihar. Her vanity irresistibly
prompted her to pique the prince's attention; and this, she
before took good care to effect, whilst he picked up the
jasmine she had thrown upon him. But, when Gulchenrouz
asked after the flowers he had culled for her bosom,
Nouronihar was all in confusion. She hastily kissed his
forehead; arose in a flutter; and walked, with unequal steps,
on the border of the precipice. Night advanced, and the
pure gold of the setting sun had yielded to a sanguine red;

the glow of which, like the reflection of a burning furnace, flushed Nouronihar's animated countenance. Gulchenrouz, alarmed at the agitation of his cousin, said to her, with a supplicating accent—'Let us begone; the sky looks portentous; the tamarisks tremble more than common; and the raw wind chills my very heart. Come! let us begone; 'tis a melancholy night!' Then, taking hold of her hand, he drew it towards the path he besought her to go. Nouronihar, unconsciously followed the attraction; for, a thousand strange imaginations occupied her spirits. She passed the large round of honey-suckles, her favourite resort, without ever vouchsafing it a glance; yet Gulchenrouz could not help snatching off a few shoots in his way, though he ran as if a wild beast were behind.

The young females seeing them approach in such haste, and, according to custom, expecting a dance, instantly assembled in a circle and took each other by the hand: but, Gulchenrouz coming up out of breath, fell down at once on the grass. This accident struck with consternation the whole of this frolicsome party; whilst Nouronihar, half distracted and overcome, both by the violence of her exercise, and the tumult of her thoughts, sunk feebly down at his side; cherished his cold hands in her bosom, and chafed his temples with a fragrant perfume. At length, he came to himself; and, wrapping up his head in the robe of his cousin, intreated that she would not return to the harem. He was afraid of being snapped at by Shaban[1] his tutor; a wrinkled old eunuch of a surly disposition; for, having interrupted the wonted walk of Nouronihar, he dreaded lest the churl should take it amiss. The whole of this sprightly group, sitting round upon a mossy knoll, began to entertain themselves with various pastimes; whilst their superintendants, the eunuchs, were gravely conversing at a distance. The nurse of the emir's daughter, observing her pupil sit ruminating with her eyes on the ground, endeavoured to amuse her with diverting tales; to which Gulchenrouz, who had already forgotten his inquietudes, listened with a breathless attention. He laughed; he clapped his hands; and passed a hundred little tricks on the whole of the company, without omitting the eunuchs whom he provoked to run after him, in spite of their age and decrepitude.

During these occurrences, the moon arose, the wind subsided, and the evening became so serene and inviting, that a resolution was taken to sup on the spot. One of the eunuchs ran to fetch melons whilst others were employed in showering down almonds from the branches that overhung this amiable party. Sutlememe, who excelled in dressing a salad, having filled large bowls of porcelain with eggs of small birds, curds turned with citron juice, slices of cucumber, and the inmost leaves of delicate herbs, handed it round from one to another and gave each their shares with a large spoon of cocknos.[1] Gulchenrouz, nestling, as usual, in the bosom of Nouronihar, pouted out his vermillion little lips against the offer of Sutlememe; and would take it, only, from the hand of his cousin, on whose mouth he hung, like a bee inebriated with the nectar of flowers.

In the midst of this festive scene, there appeared a light on the top of the highest mountain, which attracted the notice of every eye. This light was not less bright than the moon when at full, and might have been taken for her, had not the moon already risen. The phenomenon occasioned a general surprize and no one could conjecture the cause.

It could not be a fire, for the light was clear and bluish: nor had meteors ever been seen of that magnitude or splendour. This strange light faded, for a moment; and immediately renewed its brightness. It first appeared motionless, at the foot of the rock; whence it darted in an instant, to sparkle in a thicket of palm-trees: from thence it glided along the torrent; and at last fixed in a glen that was narrow and dark. The moment it had taken its direction, Gulchenrouz, whose heart always trembled at any thing sudden or rare, drew Nouronihar by the robe and anxiously requested her to return to the harem. The women were importunate in seconding the intreaty; but the curiosity of the emir's daughter prevailed. She not only refused to go back, but resolved, at all hazards, to pursue the appearance.

Whilst they were debating what was best to be done, the light shot forth so dazzling a blaze that they all fled away shrieking. Nouronihar followed them a few steps; but, coming to the turn of a little bye path, stopped, and went back alone. As she ran with an alertness peculiar to herself, it was not long before she came to the place, where they had just been supping. The globe of fire now appeared stationary in the glen, and burned in majestic stillness. Nouronihar, pressing her hands upon her bosom, hesitated, for some moments, to advance. The solitude of her situation was new; the silence of the night, awful; and every object inspired sensations, which, till then, she never had felt. The affright of Gulchenrouz recurred to her mind, and she, a thousand times turned to go back; but this luminous appearance was always before her. Urged on by an irresistible impulse, she continued to approach it, in defiance of every obstacle that opposed her progress.

At length she arrived at the opening of the glen; but, instead of coming up to the light, she found herself surrounded by darkness; excepting that, at a considerable distance, a faint spark glimmered by fits. She stopped, a second time: the sound of water-falls mingling their murmurs; the hollow rustlings among the palm-branches; and the funereal screams of the birds from their rifted trunks: all conspired to fill her soul with terror. She imagined, every moment, that she trod on some venomous reptile. All the stories of malignant Dives[1] and dismal Goules[2] thronged into her memory: but, her curiosity was, notwithstanding, more predominant than her fears. She, therefore, firmly entered a winding track that led towards the spark; but, being a stranger to the path, she had not gone far, till she began to repent of her rashness. 'Alas!' said she, 'that I were but in those secure and illuminated apartments, where my evenings glided on with Gulchen-rouz! Dear child! how would thy heart flutter with terror, wert thou wandering in these wild solitudes, like me!' Thus speaking, she advanced, and, coming up to steps hewn in the rock, ascended them undismayed. The light, which was now gradually enlarging, appeared above her on the summit of the mountain, and as if proceeding from a cavern. At length, she distinguished a plaintive and melodious union of voices, that resembled the dirges which are sung over tombs. A sound, like that which arises from the filling of baths, struck her ear at the same time. She continued ascending, and discovered large wax torches in full blaze, planted here and there in the fissures of the rock. This appearance filled her with fear, whilst the subtle and potent odour, which the torches exhaled, caused her to sink, almost lifeless, at the entrance of the grot.

Casting her eyes within, in this kind of trance, she beheld a large cistern of gold, filled with a water, the vapour of which distilled on her face a dew of the essence of roses. A soft symphony resounded through the grot. On the sides of the cistern, she noticed appendages of royalty, diadems and feathers of the heron, all sparkling with carbuncles.[1] Whilst her attention was fixed on this display of magnificence, the music ceased, and a voice instantly demanded: 'For what monarch are these torches kindled, this bath prepared, and these habiliments which belong, not only to the sovereigns of the earth, but even to the talismanick powers!' To which a second voice answered: 'They are for the charming daughter of the emir Fakreddin.'— 'What,' replied the first, 'for that trifler, who consumes her time with a giddy child, immersed in softness, and who, at best, can make but a pitiful husband?'—'And can she,' rejoined the other voice, 'be amused with such empty toys, whilst the Caliph, the sovereign of the world, he who is destined to enjoy the treasures of the pre-adamite sultans; a prince six feet high; and whose eyes pervade the inmost soul of a female,[2] is inflamed with love for her. No! she will be wise enough to answer that passion alone, that can aggrandize her glory. No doubt she will; and despise the puppet of her fancy. Then all the riches this place contains, as well as the carbuncle of Giamschid,[3] shall be hers.'— 'You judge right,' returned the first voice; 'and I haste to Istakhar, to prepare the palace of subterranean fire for the reception of the bridal pair.'

The voices ceased; the torches were extinguished,[4] the most entire darkness succeeded; and Nouronihar recovering, with a start, found herself reclined on a sofa, in the harem of her father. She clapped her hands,[5] and immediately came together, Gulchenrouz and her women; who, in despair at having lost her, had dispatched eunuchs to seek her, in every direction. Shaban appeared with the rest, and began to reprimand her, with an air of consequence: 'Little impertinent,' said he, 'have you false keys, or are you beloved of some genius, that hath given you a picklock? I will try the extent of your power: come to the dark chamber, and expect not the company of Gulchenrouz:—be expeditious! I will shut you up, and turn the key twice upon you!' At these menaces, Nouronihar indignantly raised her head, opened on Shaban her black eyes, which, since the important dialogue of the enchanted grot, were considerably enlarged, and said: 'Go, speak thus to slaves; but learn to reverence her who is born to give laws and subject all to her power.'

Proceeding in the same style, she was interrupted by a sudden exclamation of, 'The Caliph! the Caliph!' All the curtains were thrown open, the slaves prostrated themselves in double rows, and poor little Gulchenrouz went to hide beneath the couch of a sofa. At first appeared a file of black eunuchs trailing after them long trains of muslin embroidered with gold, and holding in their hands censers, which dispensed, as they passed, the grateful perfume of the wood of aloes. Next marched Bababalouk with a solemn strut, and tossing his head, as not overpleased at the visit. Vathek came close after, superbly robed: his gait was unembarrassed and noble; and his presence would have engaged admiration, though he had not been the sovereign of the world. He approached Nouronihar with a throbbing heart, and seemed enraptured at the full effulgence of her radiant eyes, of which he had before caught but a few glimpses: but she instantly depressed them, and her confusion augmented her beauty.

Bababalouk, who was a thorough adept in coincidences of this nature, and knew that the worst game should be played with the best face, immediately made a signal for all to retire; and no sooner did he perceive beneath the sofa the little one's feet, than he drew him forth without ceremony, set him upon his shoulders, and lavished on him, as he went off, a thousand unwelcome caresses. Gulchenrouz cried out, and resisted till his cheeks became the colour of the blossom of pomegranates, and his tearful eyes sparkled with indignation. He cast a significant glance at Nouronihar, which the Caliph noticing, asked, 'Is that, then, your Gulchenrouż?'—'Sovereign of the world!' answered she, 'spare my cousin, whose innocence and gentleness deserve not your anger!'—'Take comfort,' said Vathek, with a smile; 'he is in good hands. Bababalouk is fond of children; and never goes without sweetmeats and comfits.' The daughter of Fakreddin was abashed, and suffered Gulchenrouz to be borne away without adding a word. The tumult of her bosom betrayed her confusion, and Vathek becoming still more impassioned, gave a loose to his frenzy; which had only not subdued the last faint strugglings of reluctance, when the emir suddenly bursting in, threw his face upon the ground, at the feet of the Caliph, and said: 'Commander of the faithful! abase not yourself to the meanness of your slave.'—'No, emir,' replied Vathek, 'I raise her to an equality with myself: I declare her my wife; and the glory of your race shall extend from one generation to another.'—'Alas! my lord,' said Fakreddin, as he plucked off a few grey hairs of his beard; 'cut short the days of your faithful servant, rather than force him to depart from his word. Nouronihar is solemnly promised to Gulchenrouz, the son of my brother Ali

Hassan: they are united, also, in heart; their faith is mutually plighted; and affiances, so sacred, cannot be broken.'
—'What then!' replied the Caliph, bluntly, 'would you
surrender this divine beauty to a husband more womanish
than herself; and can you imagine, that I will suffer her
charms to decay in hands so inefficient and nerveless? No!
she is destined to live out her life within my embraces: such
is my will: retire; and disturb not the night I devote to the
worship of her charms.'

The irritated emir drew forth his sabre, presented it to
Vathek, and, stretching out his neck, said, in a firm tone
of voice: 'Strike your unhappy host, my lord! he has lived
long enough, since he hath seen the prophet's vicegerent
violate the rights of hospitality.'[1] At his uttering these
words, Nouronihar, unable to support any longer the conflict of her passions, sunk down in a swoon. Vathek, both
terrified for her life, and furious at an opposition to his will,
bade Fakreddin assist his daughter, and withdrew; darting
his terrible look at the unfortunate emir, who suddenly fell
backward, bathed in a sweat as cold as the damp of death.

Gulchenrouz, who had escaped from the hands of
Bababalouk and was, that instant, returned, called out for
help, as loudly as he could, not having strength to afford
it himself. Pale and panting, the poor child attempted to
revive Nouronihar by caresses; and it happened, that the
thrilling warmth of his lips restored her to life. Fakreddin
beginning also to recover from the look of the Caliph, with
difficulty tottered to a seat; and, after warily casting round
his eye, to see if this dangerous Prince were gone, sent for
Shaban and Sutlememe; and said to them apart: 'My
friends! violent evils require violent remedies: the Caliph
has brought desolation and horror into my family; and,

how shall we resist his power? Another of his looks will
send me to the grave. Fetch, then, that narcotick powder[1]
which a dervish brought me from Aracan. A dose of it, the
effect of which will continue three days, must be administered to each of these children. The Caliph will believe
them to be dead; for, they will have all the appearance of
death. We shall go, as if to inter them in the cave of Mei-
moune, at the entrance of the great desert of sand and near
the bower of my dwarfs. When all the spectators shall be
withdrawn, you, Shaban, and four select eunuchs, shall
convey them to the lake; where provision shall be ready to
support them a month: for, one day allotted to the surprize
this event will occasion; five, to the tears; a fortnight to
reflection; and the rest, to prepare for renewing his progress; will, according to my calculation, fill up the whole
time that Vathek will tarry; and I shall, then, be freed from
his intrusion.'

'Your plan is good,' said Sutlememe, 'if it can but be
effected. I have remarked, that Nouronihar is well able to
support the glances of the Caliph: and, that he is far from
being sparing of them to her: be assured, therefore, that
notwithstanding her fondness for Gulchenrouz, she will
never remain quiet, while she knows him to be here. Let
us persuade her, that both herself and Gulchenrouz are
really dead; and, that they were conveyed to those rocks,
for a limited season, to expiate the little faults, of which
their love was the cause. We will add, that we killed ourselves in despair; and that your dwarfs, whom they never
yet saw, will preach to them delectable sermons. I will
engage that every thing shall succeed to the bent of your
wishes.'—'Be it so!' said Fakreddin, 'I approve your proposal: let us lose not a moment to give it effect.'

They hastened to seek for the powder which, being mixed in a sherbet, was immediately administered to Gulchenrouz and Nouronihar. Within the space of an hour, both were seized with violent palpitations; and a general numbness gradually ensued. They arose from the floor where they had remained ever since the Caliph's departure; and, ascending to the sofa, reclined themselves upon it, clasped in each other's embraces. 'Cherish me, my dear Nouronihar!' said Gulchenrouz: 'put thy hand upon my heart; it feels as if it were frozen. Alas! thou art as cold as myself! hath the Caliph murdered us both, with his terrible look?'—'I am dying!' cried she, in a faultering voice: 'Press me closer; I am ready to expire!'—'Let us die then, together,' answered the little Gulchenrouz; whilst his breast laboured with a convulsive sigh: 'let me, at least, breathe forth my soul on thy lips!' They spoke no more, and became as dead.

Immediately, the most piercing cries were heard through the harem; whilst Shaban and Sutlememe personated with great adroitness, the parts of persons in despair. The emir, who was sufficiently mortified, to be forced into such untoward expedients; and had now, for the first time, made a trial of his powder, was under no necessity of counterfeiting grief. The slaves, who had flocked together from all quarters, stood motionless, at the spectacle before them. All lights were extinguished, save two lamps; which shed a wan glimmering over the faces of these lovely flowers that seemed to be faded in the spring-time of life. Funeral vestments were prepared; their bodies were washed,[1] with rose-water; their beautiful tresses were braided and incensed; and they were wrapped in symars whiter than alabaster.

At the moment, that their attendants were placing two wreaths of their favourite jasmines, on their brows, the Caliph, who had just heard the tragical catastrophe, arrived. He looked not less pale and haggard than the goules that wander, at night, among the graves. Forgetful of himself and every one else, he broke through the midst of the slaves; fell prostrate at the foot of the sofa; beat his bosom; called himself 'atrocious murderer!' and invoked upon his head, a thousand imprecations. With a trembling hand he raised the veil that covered the countenance of Nouronihar, and uttering a loud shriek, fell lifeless on the floor. The chief of the eunuchs dragged him off, with horrible grimaces, and repeated as he went, 'Aye, I foresaw she would play you some ungracious turn!'

No sooner was the Caliph gone, than the emir commanded biers to be brought, and forbad that any one should enter the harem. Every window was fastened; all instruments of music were broken;[1] and the Imans began to recite their prayers.[2] Towards the close of this melancholy day, Vathek sobbed in silence; for they had been forced to compose, with anodynes, his convulsions of rage and desperation.

At the dawn of the succeeding morning, the wide folding doors of the palace were set open, and the funeral procession moved forward for the mountain. The wailful cries of 'La Ilah illa Alla!'[3] reached the Caliph, who was eager to cicatrize himself, and attend the ceremonial: nor could he have been dissuaded, had not his excessive weakness disabled him from walking. At the few first steps he fell on the ground, and his people were obliged to lay him on a bed, where he remained many days in such a state of insensibility as excited compassion in the emir himself.

When the procession was arrived at the grot of Mei-
moune, Shaban and Sutlememe dismissed the whole of
the train, excepting the four confidential eunuchs who were
appointed to remain. After resting some moments near the
biers, which had been left in the open air; they caused
them to be carried to the brink of a small lake, whose banks
were overgrown with a hoary moss. This was the great
resort of herons and storks which preyed continually on
little blue fishes. The dwarfs, instructed by the emir, soon
repaired thither; and, with the help of the eunuchs, began
to construct cabins of rushes and reeds, a work in which
they had admirable skill. A magazine also was contrived
for provisions, with a small oratory for themselves, and a
pyramid of wood, neatly piled to furnish the necessary fuel:
for the air was bleak in the hollows of the mountains.

At evening two fires were kindled on the brink of the
lake, and the two lovely bodies, taken from their biers,
were carefully deposited upon a bed of dried leaves, within
the same cabin. The dwarfs began to recite the Koran,
with their clear, shrill voices; and Shaban and Sutlememe
stood at some distance, anxiously waiting the effects of the
powder. At length Nouronihar and Gulchenrouz faintly
stretched out their arms; and, gradually opening their eyes,
began to survey, with looks of increasing amazement, every
object around them. They even attempted to rise; but, for
want of strength, fell back again. Sutlememe, on this,
administered a cordial, which the emir had taken care to
provide.

Gulchenrouz, thoroughly aroused, sneezed out aloud:
and, raising himself with an effort that expressed his surprize, left the cabin and inhaled the fresh air, with the
greatest avidity. 'Yes,' said he, 'I breathe again! again do

I exist! I hear sounds! I behold a firmament, spangled over
with stars!'—Nouronihar, catching these beloved accents,
extricated herself from the leaves and ran to clasp Gulchenrouz to her bosom. The first objects she remarked,
were their long simars, their garlands of flowers, and their
naked feet: she hid her face in her hands to reflect. The
vision of the enchanted bath, the despair of her father, and,
more vividly than both, the majestic figure of Vathek,
recurred to her memory. She recollected also, that herself
and Gulchenrouz had been sick and dying; but all these
images bewildered her mind. Not knowing where she was,
she turned her eyes on all sides, as if to recognize the surrounding scene. This singular lake, those flames reflected
from its glassy surface, the pale hues of its banks, the
romantic cabins, the bullrushes, that sadly waved their
drooping heads; the storks, whose melancholy cries
blended with the shrill voices of the dwarfs, every thing
conspired to persuade her, that the angel of death had
opened the portal of some other world.[1]

Gulchenrouz, on his part, lost in wonder, clung to the
neck of his cousin. He believed himself in the region of
phantoms; and was terrified at the silence she preserved.
At length addressing her; 'Speak,' said he, 'where are we?
do you not see those spectres that are stirring the burning
coals? Are they Monker and Nekir[2] who are come to throw
us into them? Does the fatal bridge[3] cross this lake, whose
solemn stillness, perhaps, conceals from us an abyss, in
which, for whole ages, we shall be doomed incessantly to
sink.'

'No, my children,' said Sutlememe, going towards them,
'take comfort! the exterminating angel, who conducted
our souls hither after yours, hath assured us, that the

chastisement of your indolent and voluptuous life, shall be
restricted to a certain series of years,[1] which you must pass
in this dreary abode; where the sun is scarcely visible, and
where the soil yields neither fruits nor flowers. These,'
continued she, pointing to the dwarfs, 'will provide for
our wants; for souls, so mundane as ours, retain too strong
a tincture of their earthly extraction. Instead of meats, your
food will be nothing but rice; and your bread shall be
moistened in the fogs that brood over the surface of the
lake.'

At this desolating prospect, the poor children burst into
tears, and prostrated themselves before the dwarfs; who
perfectly supported their characters, and delivered an
excellent discourse, of a customary length, upon the sacred
camel;[2] which, after a thousand years, was to convey them
to the paradise of the faithful.

The sermon being ended, and ablutions performed, they
praised Alla and the Prophet; supped very indifferently;
and retired to their withered leaves. Nouronihar and her
little cousin, consoled themselves on finding that the dead
might lay in one cabin. Having slept well before, the
remainder of the night was spent in conversation on what
had befallen them; and both, from a dread of apparitions,
betook themselves for protection to one another's arms.

In the morning, which was lowering and rainy, the
dwarfs mounted high poles, like minarets, and called them
to prayers. The whole congregation, which consisted of
Sutlememe, Shaban, the four eunuchs, and a few storks
that were tired of fishing, was already assembled. The two
children came forth from their cabin with a slow and
dejected pace. As their minds were in a tender and melancholy mood, their devotions were performed with fervour.

No sooner were they finished than Gulchenrouz demanded of Sutlememe, and the rest, 'how they happened to die so opportunely for his cousin and himself?'—'We killed ourselves,' returned Sutlememe, 'in despair at your death.' On this, Nouronihar who, notwithstanding what had past, had not yet forgotten her vision said—'And the Caliph! is he also dead of his grief? and will he likewise come hither?' The dwarfs, who were prepared with an answer, most demurely replied: 'Vathek is damned beyond all redemption!'—'I readily believe so,' said Gulchenrouz; 'and am glad, from my heart, to hear it; for I am convinced it was his horrible look that sent us hither, to listen to sermons, and mess upon rice.' One week passed away, on the side of the lake, unmarked by any variety: Nouronihar ruminating on the grandeur of which death had deprived her; and Gulchenrouz applying to prayers and basket-making with the dwarfs, who infinitely pleased him.

Whilst this scene of innocence was exhibiting in the mountains, the Caliph presented himself to the emir in a new light.[1] The instant he recovered the use of his senses, with a voice that made Bababalouk quake, he thundered out: 'Perfidious Giaour! I renounce thee for ever! it is thou who hast slain my beloved Nouronihar! and I supplicate the pardon of Mahomet; who would have preserved her to me, had I been more wise. Let water be brought, to perform my ablutions, and let the pious Fakreddin be called to offer up his prayers with mine, and reconcile me to him. Afterwards, we will go together and visit the sepulchre of the unfortunate Nouronihar. I am resolved to become a hermit, and consume the residue of my days on this mountain, in hope of expiating my crimes.'—'And what do you intend to live upon there?' inquired

Bababalouk: 'I hardly know,' replied Vathek, 'but I will tell you when I feel hungry—which, I believe, will not soon be the case.'

The arrival of Fakreddin put a stop to this conversation. As soon as Vathek saw him, he threw his arms around his neck, bedewed his face with a torrent of tears, and uttered things so affecting, so pious, that the emir, crying for joy, congratulated himself, in his heart upon having performed so admirable and unexpected a conversion. As for the pilgrimage to the mountain, Fakreddin had his reasons not to oppose it; therefore, each ascending his own litter, they started.

Notwithstanding the vigilance with which his attendants watched the Caliph, they could not prevent his harrowing his cheeks with a few scratches, when on the place where he was told Nouronihar had been buried; they were even obliged to drag him away, by force of hands, from the melancholy spot. However he swore, with a solemn oath, that he would return thither every day. This resolution did not exactly please the emir—yet he flattered himself that the Caliph might not proceed farther, and would merely perform his devotions in the cavern of Meimouné. Besides, the lake was so completely concealed within the solitary bosom of those tremendous rocks, that he thought it utterly impossible any one could ever find it. This security of Fakreddin was also considerably strengthened by the conduct of Vathek, who performed his vow most scrupulously, and returned daily from the hill so devout, and so contrite, that all the grey-beards were in a state of ecstasy on account of it.

Nouronihar was not altogether so content; for though she felt a fondness for Gulchenrouz, who, to augment the attachment, had been left at full liberty with her, yet she still regarded him as but a bauble that bore no competition with the carbuncle of Giamschid. At times, she indulged doubts on the mode of her being; and scarcely could believe that the dead had all the wants and the whims of the living. To gain satisfaction, however, on so perplexing a topic; one morning, whilst all were asleep, she arose with a breathless caution from the side of Gulchenrouz: and, after having given him a soft kiss, began to follow the windings of the lake, till it terminated with a rock, the top of which was accessible, though lofty. This she climbed with considerable toil; and, having reached the summit, set forward in a run, like a doe before the hunter. Though she skipped with the alertness of an antelope, yet, at intervals, she was forced to desist, and rest beneath the tamarisks to recover her breath. Whilst she, thus reclined, was occupied with her little reflections on the apprehension that she had some knowledge of the place; Vathek, who, finding himself that morning but ill at ease, had gone forth before the dawn, presented himself, on a sudden, to her view. Motionless with surprise, he durst not approach the figure before him trembling and pale, but yet lovely to behold. At length, Nouronihar, with a mixture of pleasure and affliction, raising her fine eyes to him, said: 'My lord! are you then come hither to eat rice and hear sermons with me?'— 'Beloved phantom!' cried Vathek, 'thou dost speak; thou hast the same graceful form; the same radiant features: art thou palpable likewise?' and, eagerly embracing her, added: 'Here are limbs and a bosom, animated with a gentle warmth!—What can such a prodigy mean?'

Nouronihar, with indifference answered: 'You know, my lord, that I died on the very night you honoured me with your visit. My cousin maintains it was from one of your glances; but I cannot believe him: for, to me, they seem not so dreadful. Gulchenrouz died with me, and we were both brought into a region of desolation, where we are fed with a wretched diet. If you be dead also, and are come hither to join us, I pity your lot: for, you will be stunned with the clang of the dwarfs and the storks. Besides, it is mortifying in the extreme, that you, as well as myself, should have lost the treasures of the subterranean palace.'

At the mention of the subterranean palace, the Caliph suspended his caresses, (which indeed had proceeded pretty far) to seek from Nouronihar an explanation of her meaning. She then recapitulated her vision; what immediately followed; and the history of her pretended death; adding, also, a description of the place of expiation, from whence she had fled; and all, in a manner, that would have extorted his laughter, had not the thoughts of Vathek been too deeply engaged. No sooner, however, had she ended, than he again clasped her to his bosom and said: 'Light of my eyes! the mystery is unravelled; we both are alive! Your father is a cheat, who, for the sake of dividing us, hath deluded us both: and the Giaour, whose design, as far as I can discover, is, that we shall proceed together, seems scarce a whit better. It shall be some time, at least, before he finds us in his palace of fire. Your lovely little person, in my estimation, is far more precious than all the treasures of the pre-adamite sultans; and I wish to possess it at pleasure, and, in open day, for many a moon, before I go to burrow under ground, like a mole. Forget this little trifler, Gulchenrouz; and'—'Ah! my lord!' interposed Nouronihar, 'let me intreat that you do him no evil.'—'No,

no!' replied Vathek, 'I have already bid you forbear to
alarm yourself for him. He has been brought up too much
on milk and sugar to stimulate my jealousy. We will leave
him with the dwarfs; who, by the bye, are my old acquain-
tances: their company will suit him far better than yours.
As to other matters; I will return no more to your father's.
I want not to have my ears dinned by him and his dotards
with the violation of the rights of hospitality: as if it were
less an honour for you to espouse the sovereign of the
world, than a girl dressed up like a boy!'

Nouronihar could find nothing to oppose, in a discourse
so eloquent. She only wished the amorous monarch had
discovered more ardour for the carbuncle of Giamschid:
but flattered herself it would gradually increase; and,
therefore, yielded to his will, with the most bewitching
submission.

When the Caliph judged it proper, he called for Bababalouk, who was asleep in the cave of Meimouné, and dream-
ing that the phantom of Nouronihar, having mounted him
once more on her swing, had just given him such a jerk, that
he, one moment, soared above the mountains, and the next,
sunk into the abyss. Starting from his sleep at the sound
of his master, he ran, gasping for breath, and had nearly
fallen backward at the sight, as he believed, of the spectre,
by whom he had, so lately, been haunted in his dream. 'Ah,
my lord!' cried he, recoiling ten steps, and covering his
eyes with both hands, 'do you then perform the office of a
goul! have you dug up the dead? yet hope not to make her
your prey: for, after all she hath caused me to suffer, she
is wicked enough to prey even upon you.'

'Cease to play the fool,' said Vathek, 'and thou shalt soon
be convinced that it is Nouronihar herself, alive and well,

whom I clasp to my breast. Go and pitch my tents in the
neighbouring valley. There will I fix my abode, with this
beautiful tulip, whose colours I soon shall restore. There
exert thy best endeavours to procure whatever can augment the enjoyments of life, till I shall disclose to thee more
of my will.'

The news of so unlucky an event soon reached the ears
of the emir, who abandoned himself to grief and despair,
and began, as did his old grey-beards, to begrime his visage
with ashes. A total supineness ensued; travellers were no
longer entertained; no more plasters were spread; and,
instead of the charitable activity that had distinguished this
asylum, the whole of its inhabitants exhibited only faces
of half a cubit long, and uttered groans that accorded with
their forlorn situation.

Though Fakreddin bewailed his daughter, as lost to him
for ever, yet Gulchenrouz was not forgotten. He dispatched
immediate instruction to Sutlememe, Shaban, and the
dwarfs, enjoining them not to undeceive the child, in
respect to his state; but, under some pretence, to convey
him far from the lofty rock, at the extremity of the lake, to
a place which he should appoint, as safer from danger, for
he suspected that Vathek intended him evil.

Gulchenrouz, in the meanwhile, was filled with amazement, at not finding his cousin; nor were the dwarfs less
surprised; but Sutlememe, who had more penetration, immediately guessed what had happened. Gulchenrouz was
amused with the delusive hope of once more embracing
Nouronihar, in the interior recesses of the mountains, where
the ground, strewed over with orange blossoms and jasmines, offered beds much more inviting than the withered
leaves in their cabin; where they might accompany,

with their voices, the sounds of their lutes, and chase
butterflies. Sutlememe was far gone in this sort of description, when one of the four eunuchs beckoned her aside,
to apprize her of the arrival of a messenger from their
fraternity, who had explained the secret of the flight of
Nouronihar, and brought the commands of the emir. A
council with Shaban and the dwarfs was immediately held.
Their baggage being stowed in consequence of it, they
embarked in a shallop, and quietly sailed with the little
one, who acquiesced in all their proposals. Their voyage
proceeded in the same manner, till they came to the place
where the lake sinks beneath the hollow of a rock; but, as
soon as the bark had entered it and Gulchenrouz found
himself surrounded with darkness, he was seized with a
dreadful consternation, and incessantly uttered the most
piercing outcries; for he now was persuaded he should
actually be damned for having taken too many little free-
doms, in his life-time, with his cousin.

But let us return to the Caliph, and her who ruled over
his heart. Bababalouk had pitched the tents, and closed up
the extremities of the valley, with magnificent screens of
India cloth, which were guarded by Ethiopian slaves with
their drawn sabres. To preserve the verdure of this beautiful inclosure in its natural freshness, white eunuchs went
continually round it with gilt water vessels. The waving of
fans was heard near the imperial pavilion; where, by the
voluptuous light that glowed through the muslins, the
Caliph enjoyed, at full view, all the attractions of Nouronihar. Inebriated with delight, he was all ear to her charming
voice, which accompanied the lute: while she was not less
captivated with his descriptions of Samarah, and the tower
full of wonders; but especially with his relation of the

adventure of the ball, and the chasm of the Giaour, with its ebony portal.

In this manner they conversed the whole day, and at night they bathed together, in a basin of black marble, which admirably set off the fairness of Nouronihar. Bababalouk, whose good graces this beauty had regained, spared no attention, that their repasts might be served up with the minutest exactness: some exquisite rarity was ever placed before them; and he sent even to Schiraz, for that fragrant and delicious wine, which had been hoarded up in bottles, prior to the birth of Mahomet.[1] He had excavated little ovens in the rock,[2] to bake the nice manchets which were prepared by the hands of Nouronihar, from whence they had derived a flavour so grateful to Vathek, that he regarded the ragouts of his other wives as entirely maukish: whilst they would have died of chagrin at the emir's, at finding themselves so neglected, if Fakreddin, notwithstanding his resentment, had not taken pity upon them.

The sultana Dilara,[3] who, till then, had been the favourite, took this dereliction of the Caliph to heart, with a vehemence natural to her character: for, during her continuance in favour, she had imbibed from Vathek many of his extravagant fancies, and was fired with impatience to behold the superb tombs of Istakar, and the palace of forty columns; besides, having been brought up amongst the magi, she had fondly cherished the idea of the Caliph's devoting himself to the worship of fire: thus, his voluptuous and desultory life with her rival, was to her a double source of affliction. The transient piety of Vathek had occasioned her some serious alarms; but the present was an evil of far greater magnitude. She resolved, therefore, without hesitation, to write to Carathis, and acquaint her that all things went ill; that they had eaten, slept, and revelled at an old emir's, whose sanctity was very formidable; and that, after all, the prospect of possessing the treasures of the pre-adamite sultans, was no less remote than before. This letter was entrusted to the care of two woodmen, who were at work in one of the great forests of the mountains; and who, being acquainted with the shortest cuts, arrived in ten days at Samarah.

The Princess Carathis was engaged at chess with Morakanabad, when the arrival of these wood-fellers was announced. She, after some weeks of Vathek's absence, had forsaken the upper regions of her tower, because every thing appeared in confusion among the stars, which she consulted, relative to the fate of her son. In vain did she renew her fumigations, and extend herself on the roof, to obtain mystic visions; nothing more could she see in her dreams, than pieces of brocade, nosegays of flowers, and other unmeaning gew-gaws. These disappointments had thrown her into a state of dejection, which no drug in her power was sufficient to remove. Her only resource was in Morakanabad, who was a good man, and endowed with a decent share of confidence; yet, whilst in her company, he never thought himself on roses.

No person knew aught of Vathek, and, of course, a thousand ridiculous stories were propagated at his expense. The eagerness of Carathis may be easily guessed at receiving the letter, as well as her rage at reading the dissolute conduct of her son. 'Is it so!' said she: 'either I will perish, or Vathek shall enter the palace of fire. Let me expire in flames, provided he may reign on the throne of Soliman!' Having said this, and whirled herself round in a magical manner, which struck Morakanabad with such terror as

caused him to recoil, she ordered her great camel Alboufaki
to be brought, and the hideous Nerkes, with the unrelenting
Cafour,[1] to attend. 'I require no other retinue,' said she to
Morakanabad: 'I am going on affairs of emergency; a truce,
therefore, to parade! Take you care of the people; fleece
them well in my absence, for we shall expend large sums,
and one knows not what may betide.'

The night was uncommonly dark, and a pestilential blast
blew from the plain of Catoul, that would have deterred
any other traveller however urgent the call: but Carathis
enjoyed most whatever filled others with dread. Nerkes
concurred in opinion with her; and Cafour had a particular
predilection for a pestilence. In the morning this accomplished caravan, with the woodfellers, who directed their
route, halted on the edge of an extensive marsh, from
whence so noxious a vapour arose, as would have destroyed
any animal but Alboufaki, who naturally inhaled these
malignant fogs with delight. The peasants entreated their
convoy not to sleep in this place. 'To sleep,' cried Carathis,
'what an excellent thought! I never sleep, but for visions;
and, as to my attendants, their occupations are too many,
to close the only eye they have.' The poor peasants, who
were not over-pleased with their party, remained open-
mouthed with surprise.

Carathis alighted, as well as her negresses; and, severally
stripping off their outer garments, they all ran to cull from
those spots, where the sun shone fiercest, the venomous
plants that grew on the marsh. This provision was made
for the family of the emir; and whoever might retard the
expedition to Istakar. The woodmen were overcome with
fear, when they beheld these three horrible phantoms run;
and, not much relishing the company of Alboufaki, stood

aghast at the command of Carathis to set forward; notwithstanding it was noon, and the heat fierce enough to
calcine even rocks. In spite however, of every remonstrance,
they were forced implicitly to submit.

Alboufaki, who delighted in solitude, constantly snorted
whenever he perceived himself near a habitation; and
Carathis, who was apt to spoil him with indulgence, as
constantly turned him aside: so that the peasants were
precluded from procuring subsistence; for, the milch
goats and ewes, which Providence had sent towards the
district they traversed to refresh travellers with their milk,
all fled at the sight of the hideous animal and his strange
riders. As to Carathis, she needed no common aliment; for,
her invention had previously furnished her with an opiate,
to stay her stomach; some of which she imparted to her
mutes.

At dusk, Alboufaki making a sudden stop, stampt with
his foot; which, to Carathis, who knew his ways, was a
certain indication that she was near the confines of some
cemetery.[1] The moon shed a bright light on the spot, which
served to discover a long wall with a large door in it, standing a-jar; and so high that Alboufaki might easily enter.
The miserable guides, who perceived their end approaching, humbly implored Carathis, as she had now so good an
opportunity, to inter them; and immediately gave up the
ghost. Nerkes and Cafour, whose wit was of a style peculiar
to themselves, were by no means parsimonious of it on the
folly of these poor people; nor could any thing have been
found more suited to their taste, than the site of the bury-
ing ground, and the sepulchres which its precincts contained. There were, at least, two thousand of them on the
declivity of a hill. Carathis was too eager to execute her

plan, to stop at the view, charming as it appeared in her eyes. Pondering the advantages that might accrue from her present situation, she said to herself, 'So beautiful a cemetery must be haunted by gouls! they never want for intelligence: having heedlessly suffered my stupid guides to expire, I will apply for directions to them; and, as an inducement, will invite them to regale on these fresh corpses.' After this wise soliloquy, she beckoned to Nerkes and Cafour, and made signs with her fingers, as much as to say: 'Go; knock against the sides of the tombs and strike up your delightful warblings.'

The negresses, full of joy at the behests of their mistress; and promising themselves much pleasure from the society of the gouls, went, with an air of conquest, and began their knockings at the tombs. As their strokes were repeated, a hollow noise was heard in the earth; the surface hove up into heaps; and the gouls, on all sides, protruded their noses to inhale the effluvia, which the carcases of the wood-men began to emit. They assembled before a sarcophagus of white marble, where Carathis was seated between the bodies of her miserable guides. The Princess received her visitants with distinguished politeness; and, supper being ended, they talked of business. Carathis soon learnt from them every thing she wanted to discover; and, without loss of time, prepared to set forward on her journey. Her negresses, who were forming tender connexions with the gouls, importuned her, with all their fingers, to wait at least till the dawn. But Carathis, being chastity in the abstract, and an implacable enemy to love intrigues and sloth, at once rejected their prayer; mounted Alboufaki, and com-manded them to take their seats instantly. Four days and four nights, she continued her route without interruption.

On the fifth, she traversed craggy mountains, and half-burnt forests; and arrived on the sixth, before the beautiful screens which concealed from all eyes the voluptuous wanderings of her son.

It was day-break, and the guards were snoring on their posts in careless security, when the rough trot of Alboufaki awoke them in consternation. Imagining that a group of spectres, ascended from the abyss, was approaching, they all, without ceremony, took to their heels. Vathek was, at that instant, with Nouronihar in the bath; hearing tales, and laughing at Bababalouk, who related them: but, no sooner did the outcry of his guards reach him, than he flounced from the water like a carp; and as soon threw himself back at the sight of Carathis; who, advancing with her negresses, upon Alboufaki, broke through the muslin awnings and veils of the pavilion. At this sudden apparition, Nouronihar (for she was not, at all times, free from remorse) fancied, that the moment of celestial vengeance was come; and clung about the Caliph, in amorous despondence.

Carathis, still seated on her camel, foamed with indignation, at the spectacle which obtruded itself on her chaste view. She thundered forth without check or mercy: 'Thou double-headed and four-legged monster! what means all this winding and writhing? art thou not ashamed to be seen grasping this limber sapling; in preference to the sceptre of the pre-adamite sultans? Is it then, for this paltry doxy, that thou hast violated the conditions in the parchment of our Giaour! Is it on her, thou hast lavished thy precious moments! Is this the fruit of the knowledge I have taught thee! Is this the end of thy journey? Tear thyself from the arms of this little simpleton; drown

her, in the water before me; and, instantly follow my
guidance.'

In the first ebullition of his fury, Vathek had resolved to
rip open the body of Alboufaki and to stuff it with those of
the negresses and of Carathis herself, but the remembrance
of the Giaour, the palace of Istakar, the sabres, and the
talismans, flashing before his imagination, with the simul-
taneousness of lightning, he became more moderate, and
said to his mother, in a civil, but decisive tone; 'Dread
lady! you shall be obeyed; but I will not drown Nouronihar. She is sweeter to me than a Myrabolan comfit;[1] and
is enamoured of carbuncles; especially that, of Giamschid;
which hath also been promised to be conferred upon her:
she, therefore, shall go along with us; for, I intend to repose
with her upon the sofas of Soliman: I can sleep no more
without her.'—'Be it so!' replied Carathis, alighting; and,
at the same time, committing Alboufaki to the charge of
her black women.

Nouronihar, who had not yet quitted her hold, began
to take courage; and said, with an accent of fondness, to
the Caliph: 'Dear sovereign of my soul! I will follow thee,
if it be thy will, beyond the Kaf, in the land of the afrits.
I will not hesitate to climb, for thee, the nest of the Simurgh; who, this lady excepted, is the most awful of created
beings.'—'We have here then,' subjoined Carathis, 'a girl,
both of courage and science!' Nouronihar had certainly
both; but, notwithstanding all her firmness, she could not
help casting back a thought of regret upon the graces of
her little Gulchenrouz; and the days of tender endear-
ments she had participated with him. She, even, dropped
a few tears; which, the Caliph observed; and inadvertently
breathed out with a sigh: 'Alas! my gentle cousin! what

will become of thee!'—Vathek, at this apostrophe, knitted up his brows; and Carathis inquired what it could mean? 'She is preposterously sighing after a stripling with languishing eyes and soft hair, who loves her,' said the Caliph. 'Where is he?' asked Carathis. 'I must be acquainted with this pretty child: for,' added she, lowering her voice, 'I design, before I depart, to regain the favour of the Giaour. There is nothing so delicious, in his estimation, as the heart of a delicate boy palpitating with the first tumults of love.'

Vathek, as he came from the bath, commanded Bababalouk to collect the women, and other moveables of his harem; embody his troops; and hold himself in readiness to march within three days: whilst Carathis, retired alone to a tent, where the Giaour solaced her with encouraging visions: but, at length, waking, she found at her feet, Nerkes and Cafour, who informed her, by their signs, that having led Alboufaki to the borders of a lake; to browse on some grey moss, that looked tolerably venomous; they had discovered certain blue fishes,[1] of the same kind with those in the reservoir on the top of the tower. 'Ah! ha!' said she, 'I will go thither to them. These fish are past doubt of a species that, by a small operation, I can render oracular. They may tell me, where this little Gulchenrouz is; whom I am bent upon sacrificing.' Having thus spoken, she immediately set out, with her swarthy retinue.

It being but seldom that time is lost, in the accomplishment of a wicked enterprize, Carathis and her negresses soon arrived at the lake; where, after burning the magical drugs, with which they were always provided; they stripped themselves naked, and waded to their chins; Nerkes and Cafour waving torches around them, and Carathis

pronouncing her barbarous incantations. The fishes, with
one accord, thrust forth their heads from the water; which
was violently rippled by the flutter of their fins: and, at
length, finding themselves constrained, by the potency of
the charm, they opened their piteous mouths, and said:
'From gills to tail, we are yours; what seek ye to know?'
—'Fishes,' answered she, 'I conjure you, by your glittering
scales; tell me where now is Gulchenrouz?'—'Beyond the
rock,' replied the shoal, in full chorus: 'will this content
you? for we do not delight in expanding our mouths.'—'It
will,' returned the Princess: 'I am not to learn, that you
are not used to long conversations: I will leave you therefore to repose, though I had other questions to propound.'
The instant she had spoken, the water became smooth;
and the fishes, at once, disappeared.

Carathis, inflated with the venom of her projects, strode
hastily over the rock; and found the amiable Gulchenrouz,
asleep, in an arbour; whilst the two dwarfs were watching
at his side, and ruminating their accustomed prayers. These
diminutive personages possessed the gift of divining, whenever an enemy to good Mussulmans approached: thus, they
anticipated the arrival of Carathis; who, stopping short,
said to herself: 'How placidly doth he recline his lovely
little head! how pale, and languishing, are his looks! it is
just the very child of my wishes!' The dwarfs interrupted
this delectable soliloquy, by leaping, instantly, upon her;
and scratching her face, with their utmost zeal. But Nerkes
and Cafour, betaking themselves to the succour of their
mistress, pinched the dwarfs so severely, in return, that
they both gave up the ghost; imploring Mahomet to inflict
his sorest vengeance upon this wicked woman, and all her
household.

At the noise which this strange conflict occasioned in the valley, Gulchenrouz awoke; and, bewildered with terror, sprung impetuously and climbed an old fig-tree that rose against the acclivity of the rocks; from thence he gained their summits, and ran for two hours without once looking back. At last, exhausted with fatigue, he fell senseless into the arms of a good old genius, whose fondness for the company of children, had made it his sole occupation to protect them. Whilst performing his wonted rounds through the air, he had pounced on the cruel Giaour, at the instant of his growling in the horrible chasm, and had rescued the fifty little victims which the impiety of Vathek had devoted to his voracity. These the genius brought up in nests still higher than the clouds, and himself fixed his abode, in a nest more capacious than the rest, from which he had expelled the Rocs that had built it.

These inviolable asylums were defended against the dives and the afrits, by waving streamers; on which were inscribed in characters of gold, that flashed like lightning, the names of Alla and the Prophet. It was there that Gulchenrouz, who, as yet remained undeceived with respect to his pretended death, thought himself in the mansions of eternal peace. He admitted without fear the congratulations of his little friends, who were all assembled in the nest of the venerable genius, and vied with each other in kissing his serene forehead and beautiful eye-lids.—Remote from the inquietudes of the world; the impertinence of harems, the brutality of eunuchs, and the inconstancy of women; there he found a place truly congenial to the delights of his soul. In this peaceable society his days, months, and years glided on; nor was he less happy than the rest of his companions: for the genius, instead of burthening his pupils with perishable riches and vain sciences, conferred upon them the boon of perpetual childhood. .

Carathis, unaccustomed to the loss of her prey, vented a thousand execrations on her negresses, for not seizing the child, instead of amusing themselves with pinching to death two insignificant dwarfs from which they could gain no advantage. She returned into the valley murmuring; and, finding that her son was not risen from the arms of Nouronihar, discharged her ill-humour upon both. The idea, however, of departing next day for Istakar, and of cultivating, through the good offices of the Giaour, an intimacy with Eblis himself, at length consoled her chagrin. But fate had ordained it otherwise.

In the evening as Carathis was conversing with Dilara, who, through her contrivance had become of the party, and whose taste resembled her own, Bababalouk came to acquaint her that the sky towards Samarah looked of a fiery red, and seemed to portend some alarming disaster. Immediately recurring to her astrolabes[1] and instruments of magic, she took the altitude of the planets, and dis-covered, by her calculations, to her great mortification, that a formidable revolt had taken place at Samarah, that Motavakel, availing himself of the disgust, which was inveterate against his brother, had incited commotions amongst the populace, made himself master of the palace, and actually invested the great tower, to which Morakana-bad had retired, with a handful of the few that still remained faithful to Vathek.

'What!' exclaimed she; 'must I lose, then, my tower! my mutes! my negresses! my mummies! and, worse than all, the laboratory, the favourite resort of my nightly lucubrations, without knowing, at least, if my hair-brained

son will complete his adventure? No! I will not be the dupe!
immediately will I speed to support Morakanabad. By my
formidable art, the clouds shall pour grape-shot in the
faces of the assailants and shafts of red-hot iron on their
heads. I will let loose my stores of hungry serpents and
torpedos, from beneath them; and we shall soon see the
stand they will make against such an explosion!'

Having thus spoken, Carathis hasted to her son who was
tranquilly banqueting with Nouronihar, in his superb
carnation-coloured tent. 'Glutton, that thou art!' cried
she, 'were it not for me, thou wouldst soon find thyself the
mere commander of savoury pies. Thy faithful subjects
have abjured the faith they swore to thee. Motavakel,[1]
thy brother, now reigns on the hill of Pied Horses: and,
had I not some slight resources in the tower, would not be
easily persuaded to abdicate. But, that time may not be
lost, I shall only add a few words:—Strike tent to-night;
set forward; and beware how thou loiterest again by the
way. Though, thou hast forfeited the conditions of the
parchment, I am not yet without hope: for, it cannot be
denied, that thou hast violated, to admiration, the laws of
hospitality by seducing the daughter of the emir, after
having partaken of his bread and his salt. Such a conduct
cannot but be delightful to the Giaour; and if, on thy
march, thou canst signalize thyself, by an additional crime;
all will still go well, and thou shalt enter the palace of
Soliman, in triumph. Adieu! Alboufaki and my negresses
are waiting at the door.'

The Caliph had nothing to offer in reply: he wished his
mother a prosperous journey, and ate on till he had finished
his supper. At midnight, the camp broke up, amidst the
flourishing of trumpets and other martial instruments; but

loud indeed must have been the sound of the tymbals, to
overpower the blubbering of the emir, and his grey-beards;
who, by an excessive profusion of tears, had so far exhausted the radical moisture, that their eyes shrivelled up
in their sockets, and their hairs dropped off by the roots.
Nouronihar, to whom such a symphony was painful, did
not grieve to get out of hearing. She accompanied the
Caliph in the imperial litter; where they amused themselves, with imagining the splendour which was soon to
surround them. The other women, overcome with dejection were dolefully rocked in their cages; whilst Dilara
consoled herself, with anticipating the joy of celebrating
the rites of fire, on the stately terraces of Istakar.

In four days, they reached the spacious valley of Rocnabad. The season of spring was in all its vigour, and
the grotesque branches of the almond trees, in full blossom, fantastically chequered with hyacinths and jonquils,
breathed forth a delightful fragrance. Myriads of bees, and
scarce fewer of santons, had there taken up their abode. On
the banks of the stream, hives and oratories[1] were alter-
nately ranged; and their neatness and whiteness were set
off, by the deep green of the cypresses, that spired up
amongst them. These pious personages amused themselves,
with cultivating little gardens, that abounded with flowers
and fruits; especially, musk-melons, of the best flavour that
Persia could boast. Sometimes dispersed over the meadow,
they entertained themselves with feeding peacocks, whiter
than snow; and turtles, more blue than the sapphire. In this
manner were they occupied, when the harbingers of the
imperial procession began to proclaim: 'Inhabitants of
Rocnabad! prostrate yourselves on the brink of your pure
waters; and tender your thanksgivings to heaven, that

vouchsafeth to shew you a ray of its glory: for, lo! the
commander of the faithful draws near.'

The poor santons, filled with holy energy, having bustled
to light up wax torches in their oratories, and expand the
Koran on their ebony desks, went forth to meet the Caliph
with baskets of honeycomb, dates, and melons. But, whilst
they were advancing in solemn procession and with mea-
sured steps, the horses, camels, and guards, wantoned over
their tulips and other flowers, and made a terrible havoc
amongst them. The santons could not help casting from
one eye a look of pity on the ravages committing around
them; whilst, the other was fixed upon the Caliph and
heaven. Nouronihar, enraptured with the scenery of a
place which brought back to her remembrance the pleasing
solitudes where her infancy had passed, intreated Vathek
to stop: but he, suspecting that these oratories might be
deemed, by the Giaour, an habitation, commanded his
pioneers to level them all. The santons stood motionless
with horror, at the barbarous mandate; and, at last, broke
out into lamentations; but these were uttered with so ill a
grace, that Vathek bade his eunuchs to kick them from his
presence. He then descended from the litter, with Nouronihar. They sauntered together in the meadow; and amused
themselves with culling flowers, and passing a thousand
pleasantries on each other. But the bees, who were staunch
Mussulmans, thinking it their duty to revenge the insult
offered to their dear masters, the santons, assembled so
zealously to do it with good effect, that the Caliph and
Nouronihar were glad to find their tents prepared to
receive them.

Bababalouk, who, in capacity of purveyor, had acquitted
himself with applause, as to peacocks and turtles; lost no

time in consigning some dozens to the spit; and as many
more to be fricasseed. Whilst they were feasting, laughing,
carousing, and blaspheming at pleasure, on the banquet so
liberally furnished; the moullahs, the sheiks, the cadis,[1]
and imans of Schiraz (who seemed not to have met the
santons) arrived; leading by bridles of riband, inscribed
from the Koran,[2] a train of asses which were loaded with
the choicest fruits the country could boast. Having presented their offerings to the Caliph; they petitioned him,
to honour their city and mosques, with his presence.
'Fancy not,' said Vathek, 'that you can detain me. Your
presents I condescend to accept; but beg you will let me be
quiet; for, I am not over-fond of resisting temptation.
Retire then:—Yet, as it is not decent, for personages so
reverend, to return on foot; and, as you have not the
appearance of expert riders, my eunuchs shall tie you on
your asses with the precaution that your backs be not turned
towards me: for, they understand etiquette.'—In this depu-
tation, were some high-stomached sheiks who, taking
Vathek for a fool, scrupled not to speak their opinion.
These, Bababalouk girded with double cords; and having
well disciplined their asses with nettles behind, they all
started, with a preternatural alertness; plunging, kicking,
and running foul of one another, in the most ludicrous
manner imaginable.

Nouronihar and the Caliph mutually contended who
should most enjoy so degrading a sight. They burst out in
peals of laughter, to see the old men and their asses fall
into the stream. The leg of one was fractured; the shoulder
of another, dislocated; the teeth of a third, dashed out;
and the rest suffered still worse.

Two days more, undisturbed by fresh embassies, having

been devoted to the pleasures of Rocnabad, the expedition proceeded; leaving Schiraz on the right, and verging towards a large plain; from whence were discernible, on the edge of the horizon, the dark summits of the mountains of Istakar.

At this prospect, the Caliph and Nouronihar were unable to repress their transports. They bounded from their litter to the ground; and broke forth into such wild exclamations, as amazed all within hearing. Interrogating each other, they shouted, 'Are we not approaching the radiant palace of light? or gardens, more delightful than those of Sheddad?'[1]—Infatuated mortals! they thus indulged delusive conjecture, unable to fathom the decrees of the Most High!

The good Genii, who had not totally relinquished the superintendence of Vathek; repairing to Mahomet, in the seventh heaven; said: 'Merciful Prophet! stretch forth thy propitious arms, towards thy vicegerent; who is ready to fall, irretrievably, into the snare, which his enemies, the dives, have prepared to destroy him. The Giaour is awaiting his arrival, in the abominable palace of fire; where, if he once set his foot, his perdition will be inevitable.' Mahomet answered, with an air of indignation: 'He hath too well deserved to be resigned to himself; but I permit you to try if one effort more will be effectual to divert him from pursuing his ruin.'

One of these beneficent Genii,[2] assuming, without delay, the exterior of a shepherd, more renowned for his piety than all the derviches and santons of the region, took his station near a flock of white sheep, on the slope of a hill; and began to pour forth, from his flute, such airs of pathetic melody, as subdued the very soul; and, wakening remorse, drove, far from it, every frivolous fancy. At these energetic[1] sounds, the sun hid himself beneath a gloomy cloud; and the waters of two little lakes, that were naturally clearer than crystal, became of a colour like blood. The whole of this superb assembly was involuntarily drawn towards the declivity of the hill. With downcast eyes, they all stood abashed; each upbraiding himself with the evil he had done. The heart of Dilara palpitated; and the chief of the eunuchs, with a sigh of contrition, implored pardon of the women, whom, for his own satisfaction, he had so often tormented.

Vathek and Nouronihar turned pale in their litter; and, regarding each other with haggard looks, reproached themselves—the one with a thousand of the blackest crimes; a thousand projects of impious ambition;—the other, with the desolation of her family; and the perdition of the amiable Gulchenrouz. Nouronihar persuaded herself that she heard, in the fatal music, the groans of her dying father; and Vathek, the sobs of the fifty children he had sacrificed to the Giaour. Amidst these complicated pangs of anguish, they perceived themselves impelled towards the shepherd, whose countenance was so commanding that Vathek, for the first time, felt overawed; whilst Nouronihar concealed her face with her hands. The music paused; and the Genius, addressing the Caliph, said: 'Deluded prince! to whom Providence hath confided the care of innumerable subjects; is it thus that thou fulfillest thy mission? Thy crimes are already completed; and, art thou now hastening towards thy punishment? Thou knowest that, beyond these mountains, Eblis[2] and his accursed dives hold their infernal empire; and seduced by a malignant phantom, thou art proceeding to surrender thyself to them! This moment is

the last of grace allowed thee: abandon thy atrocious purpose: return: give back Nouronihar to her father, who still
retains a few sparks of life: destroy thy tower, with all its
abominations: drive Carathis from thy councils: be just
to thy subjects: respect the ministers of the Prophet; compensate for thy impieties, by an exemplary life:[1] and,
instead of squandering thy days in voluptuous indulgence,
lament thy crimes on the sepulchres of thy ancestors. Thou
beholdest the clouds that obscure the sun: at the instant
he recovers his splendour, if thy heart be not changed, the
time of mercy assigned thee will be past for ever.'

Vathek, depressed with fear, was on the point of prostrat-
ing himself at the feet of the shepherd; whom he perceived
to be of a nature superior to man: but, his pride prevailing,
he audaciously lifted his head, and, glancing at him one of
his terrible looks, said: 'Whoever thou art, withhold thy
useless admonitions: thou wouldst either delude me, or art
thyself deceive? If what I have done be so criminal, as
thou pretendest, there remains not for me a moment of
grace. I have traversed a sea of blood, to acquire a power,
which will make thy equals tremble: deem not that I shall
retire, when in view of the port; or, that I will relinquish
her, who is dearer to me than either my life, or thy mercy.
Let the sun appear! let him illume my career! it matters
not where it may end.' On uttering these words, which
made even the Genius shudder, Vathek threw himself into
the arms of Nouronihar; and commanded that his horses
should be forced back to the road.

There was no difficulty in obeying these orders: for, the
attraction had ceased: the sun shone forth in all his glory,
and the shepherd vanished with a lamentable scream.

The fatal impression of the music of the Genius,

remained, notwithstanding, in the heart of Vathek's attendants. They viewed each other with looks of consternation. At the approach of night, almost all of them escaped; and, of this numerous assemblage, there only remained the chief of the eunuchs, some idolatrous slaves, Dilara, and a few other women; who, like herself, were votaries of the religion of the Magi.

The Caliph, fired with the ambition of prescribing laws to the powers of darkness, was but little embarrassed at this dereliction. The impetuosity of his blood prevented him from sleeping; nor did he encamp any more, as before. Nouronihar, whose impatience, if possible exceeded his own, importuned him to hasten his march, and lavished on him a thousand caresses, to beguile all reflection. She fancied herself already more potent than Balkis,[1] and pictured to her imagination the Genii falling prostrate at the foot of her throne. In this manner they advanced by moon-light, till they came within view of the two towering rocks that form a kind of portal to the valley, at the extremity of which, rose the vast ruins of Istakar.[2] Aloft, on the mountain, glimmered the fronts of various royal mausoleums, the horror of which was deepened by the shadows of night. They passed through two villages, almost deserted; the only inhabitants remaining being a few feeble old men: who, at the sight of horses and litters, fell upon their knees, and cried out: 'O Heaven! is it then by these phantoms that we have been, for six months tormented! Alas! it was from the terror of these spectres and the noise beneath the mountains, that our people have fled, and left us at the mercy of the malificent spirits!' The Caliph, to whom these complaints were but unpromising auguries, drove over the bodies of these wretched old men; and, at length, arrived at the foot of the terrace of black marble. There he descended from his litter, handing down Nouronihar; both with beating hearts, stared wildly around them, and expected, with an apprehensive shudder, the approach of the Giaour. But nothing as yet announced his appearance.

A death-like stillness reigned over the mountain and through the air. The moon dilated on a vast platform, the shades of the lofty columns which reached from the terrace almost to the clouds. The gloomy watch-towers, whose number could not be counted, were covered by no roof; and their capitals, of an architecture unknown in the records of the earth, served as an asylum for the birds of night, which, alarmed at the approach of such visitants, fled away croaking.

The chief of the eunuchs, trembling with fear, besought Vathek that a fire might be kindled. 'No!' replied he, 'there is no time left to think of such trifles; abide where thou art, and expect my commands.' Having thus spoken, he presented his hand to Nouronihar; and, ascending the steps of a vast staircase, reached the terrace, which was flagged with squares of marble, and resembled a smooth expanse of water, upon whose surface not a blade of grass ever dared to vegetate. On the right rose the watch-towers, ranged before the ruins of an immense palace, whose walls were embossed with various figures. In front stood forth the colossal forms of four creatures, composed of the leopard and the griffin, and though but of stone, inspired emotions of terror. Near these were distinguished by the splendour of the moon, which streamed full on the place, characters like those on the sabres of the Giaour, and which possessed the same virtue of changing every moment. These, after vacillating for some time, fixed at last in Arabic letters, and prescribed to the Caliph the following words:—'Vathek! thou hast violated the conditions of my parchment, and deservest to be sent back, but in favour to thy companion, and, as the meed for what thou hast done to obtain it; Eblis permitteth that the portal of his palace shall be opened; and the subterranean fire will receive thee into the number of its adorers.'

He scarcely had read these words, before the mountain, against which the terrace was reared, trembled; and the watch-towers were ready to topple headlong upon them. The rock yawned,[1] and disclosed within it a staircase of polished marble, that seemed to approach the abyss. Upon each stair were planted two large torches, like those Nouronihar had seen in her vision; the camphorated vapour of which ascended and gathered itself into a cloud under the hollow of the vault.

This appearance, instead of terrifying, gave new courage to the daughter of Fakreddin. Scarcely deigning to bid adieu to the moon, and the firmament; she abandoned, without hesitation, the pure atmosphere, to plunge into these infernal exhalations. The gait of those impious personages was haughty, and determined. As they descended, by the effulgence of the torches, they gazed on each other with mutual admiration; and both appeared so resplendent, that they already esteemed themselves spiritual intelligences. The only circumstance that perplexed them, was their not arriving at the bottom of the stairs. On hastening their descent, with an ardent impetuosity, they felt their steps accelerated to such a degree, that they seemed not walking but falling from a precipice. Their progress, however, was at length impeded, by a vast portal of ebony which the Caliph, without difficulty, recognized. Here, the

Giaour awaited them, with the key in his hand. 'Ye are
welcome!' said he to them, with a ghastly smile, 'in spite
of Mahomet, and all his dependents. I will now usher you
into that palace, where you have so highly merited a place.'
Whilst he was uttering these words, he touched the
enameled lock with his key; and the doors, at once, flew
open with a noise still louder than the thunder of the dog
days, and as suddenly recoiled, the moment they had
entered.

The Caliph and Nouronihar beheld each other with
amazement, at finding themselves in a place, which,
though roofed with a vaulted ceiling, was so spacious and
lofty, that, at first, they took it for an immeasurable plain.
But their eyes, at length, growing familiar to the grandeur
of the surrounding objects, they extended their view to
those at a distance; and discovered rows of columns and
arcades, which gradually diminished, till they terminated
in a point radiant as the sun, when he darts his last beams
athwart the ocean. The pavement, strewed over with gold
dust and saffron, exhaled so subtile an odour, as almost
overpowered them. They, however, went on; and observed
an infinity of censers, in which, ambergrise and the wood
of aloes, were continually burning. Between the several
columns, were placed tables; each, spread with a profusion of viands; and wines, of every species, sparkling in
vases of crystal. A throng of Genii, and other fantastic
spirits, of either sex, danced lasciviously, at the sound of
music, which issued from beneath.

In the midst of this immense hall, a vast multitude was
incessantly passing; who severally kept their right hands
on their hearts; without once regarding any thing around
them. They had all, the livid paleness of death. Their eyes,

deep sunk in their sockets, resembled those phosphoric
meteors, that glimmer by night, in places of interment.
Some stalked slowly on; absorbed in profound reverie:
some shrieking with agony, ran furiously about like tigers,
wounded with poisoned arrows; whilst others, grinding
their teeth in rage, foamed along more frantic than the
wildest maniac. They all avoided each other; and, though
surrounded by a multitude that no one could number,
each wandered at random, unheedful of the rest, as if alone
on a desert where no foot had trodden.

Vathek and Nouronihar, frozen with terror, at a sight
so baleful, demanded of the Giaour what these appearances
might mean; and, why these ambulating spectres never
withdrew their hands from their hearts? 'Perplex not
yourselves, with so much at once,' replied he bluntly; 'you
will soon be acquainted with all: let us haste, and present
you to Eblis.' They continued their way, through the
multitude; but, notwithstanding their confidence at first,
they were not sufficiently composed to examine, with
attention, the various perspectives of halls and of galleries,
that opened on the right hand and left; which were all
illuminated by torches and braziers, whose flames rose in
pyramids to the centre of the vault. At length they came to
a place, where long curtains brocaded with crimson and
gold, fell from all parts in solemn confusion. Here, the
choirs and dances were heard no longer. The light which
glimmered, came from afar.

After some time, Vathek and Nouronihar perceived a
gleam brightening through the drapery, and entered a vast
tabernacle hung around with the skins of leopards. An
infinity of elders with streaming beards, and afrits in complete armour, had prostrated themselves before the ascent

of a lofty eminence; on the top of which, upon a globe of
fire, sat the formidable Eblis.[1] His person was that of a
young man, whose noble and regular features seemed to
have been tarnished by malignant vapours. In his large
eyes appeared both pride and despair: his flowing hair
retained some resemblance to that of an angel of light. In
his hand, which thunder had blasted, he swayed the iron
sceptre, that causes the monster Ouranbad,[2] the afrits, and
all the powers of the abyss to tremble. At his presence, the
heart of the Caliph sunk within him; and he fell prostrate
on his face. Nouronihar, however, though greatly dis-
mayed, could not help admiring the person of Eblis: for,
she expected to have seen some stupendous giant. Eblis,
with a voice more mild than might be imagined, but such
as penetrated the soul and filled it with the deepest melancholy, said: 'Creatures of clay,[3] I receive you into mine
empire: ye are numbered amongst my adorers: enjoy
whatever this palace affords: the treasures of the pre-
adamite sultans; their fulminating sabres; and those talismans, that compel the dives to open the subterranean
expanses of the mountain of Kaf, which communicate with
these. There, insatiable as your curiosity may be, shall you
find sufficient objects to gratify it. You shall possess the
exclusive privilege of entering the fortresses of Aherman,[4]
and the halls of Argenk,[5] where are pourtrayed all creatures
endowed with intelligence; and the various animals that
inhabited the earth prior to the creation of that contemptible being whom ye denominate the father of mankind.'

Vathek and Nouronihar feeling themselves revived and
encouraged by this harangue, eagerly said to the Giaour;
'Bring us instantly to the place which contains these precious talismans.'—'Come,' answered this wicked dive, with

his malignant grin, 'come and possess all that my sovereign
hath promised; and more.' He then conducted them into a
long aisle adjoining the tabernacle; preceding them with
hasty steps, and followed by his disciples with the utmost
alacrity. They reached, at length, a hall of great extent, and
covered with a lofty dome; around which appeared fifty
portals of bronze, secured with as many fastenings of iron.
A funereal gloom prevailed over the whole scene. Here,
upon two beds of incorruptible cedar, lay recumbent the
fleshless forms of the pre-adamite kings, who had been
monarchs of the whole earth. They still possessed enough
of life to be conscious of their deplorable condition. Their
eyes retained a melancholy motion: they regarded one
another with looks of the deepest dejection; each holding
his right hand, motionless, on his heart.[1] At their feet were
inscribed the events of their several reigns, their power,
their pride, and their crimes; Soliman Daki; and Soliman,
called Gian Ben Gian,[2] who, after having chained up the
dives in the dark caverns of Kaf, became so presumptuous
as to doubt of the Supreme Power. All these maintained
great state; though not to be compared with the eminence
of Soliman Ben Daoud.

This king, so renowned for his wisdom, was on the
loftiest elevation; and placed immediately under the dome.
He appeared to possess more animation than the rest.
Though, from time to time, he laboured with profound
sighs; and, like his companions, kept his right hand on his
heart; yet his countenance was more composed, and he
seemed to be listening to the sullen roar of a cataract visible
in part through one of the grated portals. This was the only
sound that intruded on the silence of these doleful mansions. A range of brazen vases surrounded the elevation.

'Remove the covers from these cabalistic depositaries,'
said the Giaour to Vathek; 'and avail thyself of the talismans
which will break asunder all these gates of bronze; and not
only render thee master of the treasures contained within
them, but also of the spirits by which they are guarded.'

The Caliph, whom this ominous preliminary had entirely
disconcerted, approached the vases with faltering foot-
steps; and was ready to sink with terror when he heard the
groans of Soliman. As he proceeded, a voice from the livid
lips of the prophet articulated these words:[1] 'In my life-
time, I filled a magnificent throne; having, on my right
hand, twelve thousand seats of gold, where the patriarchs
and the prophets heard my doctrines; on my left, the sages
and doctors, upon as many thrones of silver, were present
at all my decisions. Whilst I thus administered justice to
innumerable multitudes, the birds of the air, hovering
over me, served as a canopy against the rays of the sun. My
people flourished; and my palace rose to the clouds. I
erected a temple to the Most High, which was the wonder
of the universe: but, I basely suffered myself to be seduced
by the love of women, and a curiosity that could not be
restrained by sublunary things. I listened to the counsels
of Aherman, and the daughter of Pharaoh; and adored fire,
and the hosts of heaven. I forsook the holy city, and commanded the Genii to rear the stupendous palace of Istakar,
and the terrace of the watch towers; each of which was
consecrated to a star. There, for a while, I enjoyed myself
in the zenith of glory and pleasure. Not only men, but supernatural beings were subject also to my will. I began to think,
as these unhappy monarchs around had already thought,
that the vengeance of Heaven was asleep; when, at once,
the thunder burst my structures asunder, and precipitated

me hither: where, however, I do not remain, like the other
inhabitants, totally destitute of hope; for, an angel of light
hath revealed that in consideration of the piety of my early
youth, my woes shall come to an end, when this cataract
shall for ever cease to flow. Till then I am in torments,
ineffable torments! an unrelenting fire preys on my heart.'

Having uttered this exclamation, Soliman raised his
hands towards heaven, in token of supplication; and the
Caliph discerned through his bosom, which was trans-
parent as crystal, his heart enveloped in flames.[1] At a sight
so full of horror, Nouronihar fell back, like one petrified,
into the arms of Vathek, who cried out with a convulsive
sob; 'O Giaour! whither hast thou brought us! Allow us to
depart, and I will relinquish all thou hast promised. O
Mahomet! remains there no more mercy!'—'None! none!'
replied the malicious dive. 'Know, miserable prince! thou
art now in the abode of vengeance and despair. Thy heart,
also, will be kindled like those of the other votaries of Eblis.
A few days are allotted thee previous to this fatal period:
employ them as thou wilt; recline on these heaps of gold;
command the infernal potentates; range, at thy pleasure,
through these immense subterranean domains: no barrier
shall be shut against thee. As for me, I have fulfilled my
mission: I now leave thee to thyself.' At these words he
vanished.

The Caliph and Nouronihar remained in the most
abject affliction. Their tears were unable to flow, and
scarcely could they support themselves. At length, taking
each other, despondingly, by the hand, they went faltering
from this fatal hall; indifferent which way they turned their
steps. Every portal opened at their approach. The dives
fell prostrate before them. Every reservoir of riches was

disclosed to their view: but they no longer felt the incentives of curiosity, of pride, or avarice. With like apathy they heard the chorus of Genii, and saw the stately banquets prepared to regale them. They went wandering on, from chamber to chamber; hall to hall; and gallery to gallery; all without bounds or limit; all distinguishable by the same louring gloom; all adorned with the same awful grandeur; all traversed by persons in search of repose and consolation; but, who sought them in vain; for every one carried within him a heart tormented in flames. Shunned by these various sufferers, who seemed by their looks to be upbraiding the partners of their guilt, they withdrew from them to wait, in direful suspense, the moment which should render them to each other the like objects of terror.

'What!' exclaimed Nouronihar; 'will the time come when I shall snatch my hand from thine!'—'Ah!' said Vathek, 'and shall my eyes ever cease to drink from thine long draughts of enjoyment! Shall the moments of our reciprocal ecstasies be reflected on with horror! It was not thou that broughtest me hither; the principles by which Carathis perverted my youth, have been the sole cause of my perdition! it is but right she should have her share of it.' Having given vent to these painful expressions, he called to an afrit, who was stirring up one of the braziers, and bade him fetch the Princess Carathis from the palace of Samarah.

After issuing these orders, the Caliph and Nouronihar continued walking amidst the silent croud, till they heard voices at the end of the gallery. Presuming them to proceed from some unhappy beings, who, like themselves, were awaiting their final doom; they followed the sound, and found it to come from a small square chamber, where they discovered, sitting on sofas, four young men, of goodly figure, and a lovely female, who were holding a melancholy conversation by the glimmering of a lonely lamp. Each had a gloomy and forlorn air; and two of them were embracing each other with great tenderness. On seeing the Caliph and the daughter of Fakreddin enter, they arose, saluted, and made room for them. Then he who appeared the most considerable of the group, addressed himself thus to Vathek:—'Strangers! who doubtless are in the same state of suspense with ourselves, as you do not yet bear your hand on your heart, if you are come hither to pass the interval allotted, previous to the infliction of our common punishment, condescend to relate the adventures that have brought you to this fatal place; and we, in return, will acquaint you with ours, which deserve but too well to be heard. To trace back our crimes to their source, though we are not permitted to repent, is the only employment suited to wretches like us!'

The Caliph and Nouronihar assented to the proposal; and Vathek began, not without tears and lamentations, a sincere recital of every circumstance that had passed. When the afflicting narrative was closed, the young man entered on his own. Each person proceeded in order;[1] and, when the third prince had reached the midst of his adventures, a sudden noise interrupted him, which caused the vault to tremble and to open.

Immediately a cloud descended, which gradually dissipating, discovered Carathis on the back of an afrit,[2] who grievously complained of his burden. She, instantly springing to the ground, advanced towards her son, and said, 'What dost thou here, in this little square chamber? As the dives are become subject to thy beck, I expected to have found thee on the throne of the pre-adamite kings.'

'Execrable woman!' answered the Caliph; 'cursed be the day thou gavest me birth! Go, follow this afrit; let him conduct thee to the hall of the Prophet Soliman: there thou wilt learn to what these palaces are destined, and how much I ought to abhor the impious knowledge thou hast taught me.'

'Has the height of power, to which thou art arrived, turned thy brain?' answered Carathis: 'but I ask no more than permission to shew my respect for Soliman the prophet. It is, however, proper thou shouldest know that (as the afrit has informed me neither of us shall return to Samarah) I requested his permission to arrange my affairs; and he politely consented. Availing myself, therefore, of the few moments allowed me, I set fire to the tower, and consumed in it the mutes, negresses, and serpents, which have rendered me so much good service: nor should I have been less kind to Morakanabad, had he not prevented me, by deserting at last to thy brother. As for Bababalouk, who had the folly to return to Samarah, to provide husbands for thy wives, I undoubtedly would have put him to the torture; but being in a hurry, I only hung him, after having decoyed him in a snare, with thy wives: whom I buried alive by the help of my negresses; who thus spent their last moments greatly to their satisfaction. With respect to Dilara, who ever stood high in my favour, she hath evinced the greatness of her mind, by fixing herself near, in the service of one of the magi; and, I think, will soon be one of our society.'

Vathek, too much cast down to express the indignation excited by such a discourse, ordered the afrit to remove

Carathis from his presence, and continued immersed in thoughts which his companions durst not disturb.

Carathis, however, eagerly entered the dome of Soliman, and, without regarding in the least the groans of the prophet, undauntedly removed the covers of the vases, and violently seized on the talismans. Then, with a voice more loud than had hitherto been heard within these mansions, she compelled the dives to disclose to her the most secret treasures, the most profound stores, which the afrit himself had not seen. She passed, by rapid descents, known only to Eblis and his most favoured potentates; and thus penetrated the very entrails of the earth, where breathes the sansar, or the icy wind of death. Nothing appalled her dauntless soul. She perceived, however, in all the inmates who bore their hands on their heart, a little singularity, not much to her taste.

As she was emerging from one of the abysses, Eblis stood forth to her view; but, notwithstanding he displayed the full effulgence of his infernal majesty, she preserved her countenance unaltered; and even paid her compliments with considerable firmness.

This superb monarch thus answered: 'Princess, whose knowledge, and whose crimes, have merited a conspicuous rank in my empire; thou dost well to avail thyself of the leisure that remains: for, the flames and torments, which are ready to seize on thy heart, will not fail to provide thee soon with full employment.' He said, and was lost in the curtains of his tabernacle.

Carathis paused for a moment with surprise; but resolved to follow the advice of Eblis, she assembled all the choirs of genii, and all the dives, to pay her homage. Thus marched she, in triumph, through a vapour of perfumes, amidst the acclamations of all the malignant spirits; with most of whom she had formed a previous acquaintance. She even attempted to dethrone one of the Solimans, for the purpose of usurping his place; when a voice, proceeding from the abyss of death, proclaimed: 'All is accomplished!' Instantaneously, the haughty forehead of the intrepid princess became corrugated with agony: she uttered a tremendous yell; and fixed, no more to be withdrawn, her right hand upon her heart, which was become a receptacle of eternal fire.

In this delirium, forgetting all ambitious projects, and her thirst for that knowledge which should ever be hidden from mortals, she overturned the offerings of the genii; and, having execrated the hour she was begotten and the womb that had borne her, glanced off in a rapid whirl that rendered her invisible,[1] and continued to revolve without intermission.

Almost at the same instant, the same voice announced to the Caliph, Nouronihar, the four princes, and the princess, the awful, and irrevocable decree. Their hearts immediately took fire, and they, at once, lost the most precious gift of heaven:—HOPE.[2] These unhappy beings recoiled, with looks of the most furious distraction. Vathek beheld in the eyes of Nouronihar nothing but rage and vengeance; nor could she discern aught in his, but aversion and despair. The two princes who were friends, and, till that moment, had preserved their attachment, shrunk back, gnashing their teeth with mutual and unchangeable hatred. Kalilah and his sister made reciprocal gestures of imprecation; all testified their horror for each other by the most ghastly convulsions, and screams that could not be smothered. All severally plunged themselves into the accursed multitude, there to wander in an eternity of un-abating anguish.

Such was, and such should be, the punishment of unrestrained passions and atrocious deeds! Such shall be, the chastisement of that blind curiosity, which would transgress those bounds the wisdom of the Creator has prescribed to human knowledge; and such the dreadful disappointment of that restless ambition, which, aiming at discoveries reserved for beings of a supernatural order, perceives not, through its infatuated pride, that the condition of man upon earth is to be—humble and ignorant.

Thus the Caliph Vathek, who, for the sake of empty pomp and forbidden power, had sullied himself with a thousand crimes, became a prey to grief without end, and remorse without mitigation: whilst the humble, the despised Gulchenrouz passed whole ages in undisturbed tranquillity, and in the pure happiness of childhood.

EXPLANATORY NOTES

THE notes to the English translation of *Vathek* published in London in 1786 were compiled by the translator, Samuel Henley. The proportion of annotation to text in this edition is indicated by the fact that the story itself occupied 211 pages and the notes another 122 pages of smaller print. The later French editions have lighter annotation, most of it deriving from Henley's notes. In 1816, for the third edition of *Vathek* in English, Beckford severely pruned Henley's elaborate, learned but often irrelevant commentary, omitting many notes completely, shortening others, at times rephrasing them, and occasionally making additions of his own. (*1816* has 227 pages of text, 56 pages of notes.) In spite of Henley's excesses, Beckford had always considered an erudite apparatus as an integral part of his book and much of the original annotation was supplied with his approval and at times under his direction. Those notes which he selected for *1816* have been retained here. While no indication has normally been given here of notes omitted from *1816*, the relationship of the *1816* notes to those in *1786* has been concisely indicated in square brackets after each note. [*1786*] indicates, for example, that Beckford retained Henley's original note; any changes made by Beckford are then described. The titles of works cited in Henley's often cryptic references are given in full; a small amount of additional information from the notes to the French editions has been recorded; and any information from the Beckford-Henley correspondence as to Beckford's contribution to or interest in the original notes has been added. In this way, as clear a picture as possible is given of the extent of Beckford's own responsibility for the notes in *1816*, whether it took the form of passive retention, direct assistance, or alteration. Other complete notes within square brackets, concerned with source material and other explanatory matter, have been supplied for the present edition. It should be added that the phrases from the text used in *1816* to introduce the notes were not always accurately quoted but have been allowed to stand. Similarly, the French of Beckford, d'Herbelot and other writers has not been modernised.

(It seems not to have been noticed that Henley's original notes were restored in two editions in Beckford's lifetime, those published by Bentley in 1834 and 1836. The text follows *1816* but the notes are basically taken from *1786*. Any additions made in *1816* are conflated and, when Beckford had rewritten Henley's note, some kind of compromise is usually reached. A few notes no longer relevant to *1816* are omitted. Henley's learned notes, so highly praised by early reviewers, may have been reprinted by popular request. Beckford himself was almost certainly not consulted about the contents of these editions.)

ABBREVIATIONS

Arabian Nights	*Arabian Nights Entertainments . . . Translated . . . from the Arabian MSS. by M. Galland*, 4 vols., 1783. (First translated into English in 1708; but the edition cited was used by Henley for his notes.)
d'Herbelot	Barthélemy d'Herbelot de Molainville, *Bibliothèque Orientale, Ou Dictionaire Universel Contenant Généralement Tout ce qui regarde la connoissance des Peuples de l'Orient*, Paris, 1697.
d'Herbelot Suppl.	*Bibliothèque Orientale, Ou Dictionnaire Universel... Par Messieurs C. Visdelou et A. Galand. Pour Servir de Supplément à Celle de Monsieur D'Herbelot*, [Maestricht], 1780.
Habesci	Alexander Ghiga, *The Present State of the Ottoman Empire . . . Translated from the French Manuscript of Elias Habesci*, 1784.
Melville	Lewis Melville, *The Life and Letters of William Beckford of Fonthill*, 1910.
Parreaux	André Parreaux, *William Beckford, Auteur de Vathek (1760-1844): Étude de la Creation Littéraire*, Paris, 1960.
Religious Ceremonies	Jean Frédéric Bernard, *The Ceremonies and Religious Customs of the Various Nations of the Known World*, 7 vols., 1733-9 (numerous engravings by Bernard Picart); translated from *Cérémonies et Coutumes Religieuses de Tous les Peuples du Monde*, Amsterdam, 1723-43.

Richardson's
Dissertat.

John Richardson, *A Dissertation on the Languages, Literature, and Manners of the Eastern Nations,* Oxford, 1777; 2nd edn. expanded, 1778 (this is the edition cited by Henley).

Sale's *Koran*
and *Prelim.*
Disc.

George Sale, *The Koran, Commonly Called The Alcoran of Mohammed, Translated into English . . . To Which is Prefixed a Preliminary Discourse,* 1734; 2nd edn., 2 vols., 1764 (this edition is cited by Henley).

Tales from
Inatulla

Tales, Translated from the Persian of Inatulla of Delhi (by Alexander Dow), 2 vols., 1768.

Weber, *Tales*
of the East

Henry Weber, *Tales of the East: Comprising the Most Popular Romances of Oriental Origin; and the Best Imitations by European Authors,* 3 vols., Edinburgh, 1812.

Page 1. (1) *Caliph*: This title amongst the Mahometans implies the three characters of Prophet, Priest, and King: it signifies, in the Arabic, *Successor, or Vicar*; and, by appropriation, the *Vicar of God on Earth.* It is, at this day, one of the titles of the Grand Signior, as successor of Mahomet; and of the Sophi of Persia, as successor of Ali. *Habesci's State of the Ottoman Empire,* p. 9. *D'Herbelot,* p. 985. [*1786,* but *1816* rephrases slightly and adds second sentence.]

(2) *one of his eyes became so terrible*: The author of Nighiaristan hath preserved a fact that supports this account; and there is no history of Vathek, in which his *terrible eye* is not mentioned. [*1786.* Beckford's source was d'Herbelot's main account of Vathek, p. 912. (For the 'Nighiaristan', see d'Herbelot, p. 671.) But Beckford's use of the detail recalls Anthony Hamilton's *Fleur d'Epine,* where it is said of Radiant that 'Nobody had ever been able to look at them [her eyes] long enough to tell their colour, for if any one encountered her glance it was as though he had been struck by lightning.' Radiant's eyes do in fact start to decimate the court. (See Anthony Hamilton, *Fairy Tales and Romances,* trans. M. Lewis, H. T. Ryde, and C. Kenney, 1849, pp. 368 ff.) It is probably only coincidental that, as Boyd Alexander has pointed out (*England's Wealthiest Son,* 1962, p. 35), Beckford's father also had a 'ferocious eye'.]

(3) *Omar Ben Abdalaziz*: This Caliph was eminent above all others for temperance and self-denial; insomuch, that, according to the Mahometan faith, he was raised to Mahomet's bosom, as a reward for his abstinence in an age of corruption. *D'Herbelot*, p. 690. [*1786*, slightly revised in *1816*.]

(4) [*Alkoremi*: Parreaux, p. 159, suggests that Beckford was struck by the name of Babek Alkhorremi, who revolted against Vathek's father (d'Herbelot, p. 159). But Beckford probably had in mind the tradition that Adam, after his fall, entered an earthly paradise on the island of Serendib, where Caherman Catel built 'une Ville dans la grande Plaine qui est au pied de la Montagne, où Adam étoit enterré, & qu'il la nomma, Khorrem, Lieu de joye & de plaisirs, tels que les Grecs & les Latins ont crû qu'étoient les Champs Elysiens' (d'Herbelot, pp. 806, 995).]

(5) *Samarah*: A city of the Babylonian Irak; supposed to have stood on the site where Nimrod erected his tower. Khondemir relates, in his life of Motassem, that this prince, to terminate the disputes which were perpetually happening between the inhabitants of Bagda and his Turkish slaves, withdrew from thence, and, having fixed on a situation in the plain of Catoul, there founded Samarah. He is said to have had in the stables of this city, a hundred and thirty thousand *pied horses*; each of which carried, by his order, a sack of earth to a place he had chosen. By this accumulation, an elevation was formed that commanded a view of all Samarah, and served for the foundation of his magnificent palace. *D'Herbelot*, p. 752. 808. 985. *Anecdotes Arabes*, p. 413. [*1786*. For an account of Motassem and the building of Samarah, see also d'Herbelot, pp. 639-40. The second reference is to J. F. de la Croix, *Anecdotes Arabes et Musulmanes* (Paris, 1772).]

Page 2. (1) *in the most delightful succession*: The great men of the East have been always fond of music. Though forbidden by the Mahometan religion, it commonly makes a part of every entertainment. *Nitimur in vetitum semper.* Female slaves are generally kept to amuse them, and the ladies of their harems. [*1786*, but *1816* has omitted four-fifths of the original and added the phrase from Ovid, *Amores*, III. iv. 17.]

(2) *Mani*: This artist, whom Inatulla of Delhi styles *the far-famed*, lived in the reign of Schabur, or Sapor, the son of Ardschir Babegan; and was, by profession, a painter and sculptor. It appears, from the Arabian Nights, that Haroun al Raschid, Vathek's grandfather, had adorned his palace and furnished his magnificent pavilion, with the most capital performances of the Persian artists. [*1786*, but reduced to

one-half in *1816*. See *Tales from Inatulla*, i. 81, where 'the far-famed Mani of Chin' is described in a note as 'A famous painter of China'.]

Page 3. (1) *Houris*: The virgins of Paradise, called, from their large black eyes, *Hur al oyun*. An intercourse with these, according to the institution of Mahomet, is to constitute the principal felicity of the faithful. Not formed of clay, like mortal women, they are adorned with unfading charms, and deemed to possess the celestial privilege of an eternal youth. *Al Koran; passim*. [*1786*, but *1816* omits a long footnote.]

(2) [*theological controversy*: Beckford probably had in mind Vathek's persecution of those who believed in the divine origin of the Koran, mentioned in a note in *1786*, omitted in *1816*. See d'Herbelot, pp. 85–6, 911.]

Page 4. (1) *Mahomet in the seventh heaven*: In this heaven, the paradise of Mahomet is supposed to be placed contiguous to the throne of Alla. Hagi Khalfah relates, that Ben Iatmaiah, a celebrated doctor of Damascus, had the temerity to assert, that, when the Most High erected his throne, he reserved a vacant place for Mahomet upon it. [*1786*.]

(2) *Genii*: It is asserted, and not without plausible reasons, that the words *Genn, Ginn—Genius, Genie, Gian, Gigas, Giant, Geant* proceed from the same themes, viz. $Γή$, *the earth*, and $Γάω$ *to produce*; as if these supernatural agents had been an early production of the earth, long before Adam was modelled out from a lump of it. The $Ωντες$ and $Εωντες$ of Plato, bear a close analogy to these supposed intermediate creatures between God and man. From these premises arose the consequence that, boasting a higher order, formed of more subtile matter and possessed of much greater knowledge than man, they lorded over this planet and invisibly governed it with superior intellect. From this last circumstance, they obtained in Greece, the title of $Δαίμονες$, Demons, from $Δάημων$, *Sciens*, knowing. The Hebrew word נפלים Nephilim. (Gen. Cap. vi. 4.) translated by *Gigantes*, giants, claiming the same etymon with $Νεφέλη$ a cloud, seems also to indicate that these intellectual beings inhabited the void expanse of the terrestrial atmosphere. Hence the very ancient fable of men of enormous strength and size revolting against the Gods, and all the mythological lore relating to that mighty conflict; unless we trace the origin of this important event to the ambition of Satan, his revolt against the Almighty and his fall with the angels. [*1786*, but extensively revised and expanded in *1816*.]

(3) *Assist him to complete the tower*: The genii were famous for their

architectural skill. The pyramids of Egypt have been ascribed to Gian
Ben Gian their chief, most likely, because they could not, from records,
be attributed to any one else. According to the Koran, ch. 34, the genii
were employed by Solomon in the erection of his temple.

The reign of Gian Ben Gian, over the Peris, is said to have continued
for two thousand years; after which, EBLIS was sent by the Deity to
exile them, on account of their disorders, and confine them in the
remotest region of the earth. *D'Herbelot*, p. 396. *Bailly sur l'Atlantide*,
p. 147. [*1786*, but compressed in *1816*, which adds para. 2 and corrects
the references. See J. S. Bailly, *Lettres sur L'Atlantide de Platon et sur
l'Ancienne Histoire d'Asie* (1779).]

(4) [Parreaux, p. 339, suggests that Beckford may have had in mind
N. A. Boulanger, *Recherches sur l'Origine du Despotisme Oriental*
(Geneva, 1761), section xvi ('Tous les Despotes veulent commander
à la Nature même'), which states: 'L'Histoire ancienne nous offre
plusieurs exemples de Princes, qui se croyant une ame plus qu'humaine,
se sont portés à cet excès d'extravagance, de penser qu'ils pouvoient se
faire obéir des élémens.']

(5) [Beckford seems to echo the account of Nimrod's attempt to
reach heaven by building a tower, in d'Herbelot, p. 668: 'On travailla
trois ans entiers à ce bâtiment, & Nembrod étant monté jusqu'au plus
haut, fut bien étonné en regardant le Ciel, de le voir encore aussi
éloigné de luy, que s'il ne s'en fust pas approché.' For the connection
of Nimrod with Samarah see page 1, note 5 above.]

Page 5. (1) [M. P. Conant, *The Oriental Tale in England in the Eighteenth
Century* (New York, 1908), p. 16, drew attention to a not dissimilar
ironic episode, concerning a horrible and voracious Afrite, in Pétis de
la Croix, *Les Mille et un jours, Contes Persans* (see 'The Adventures
of Aboulfouaris, surnamed the Great Voyager. First Voyage', Weber,
Tales of the East, ii. 475-6).]

(2) *the stranger displayed such rarities as he had never before seen*: That
such curiosities were much sought after in the days of Vathek, may be
concluded from the encouragement which Haroun al Raschid gave to
the mechanic arts, and the present he sent, by his ambassadors, to
Charlemagne. This consisted of a clock, which, when put into motion,
by means of a clepsydra, not only pointed out the hours, but also, by
dropping small balls on a bell, struck them; and, at the same instant,
threw open as many little doors, to let out an equal number of horsemen.
Ann. Reg. Franc. Pip. Caroli, &c. ad ann. 807. *Weidler*, p. 205. [*1786,*

with omission of two sentences in *1816*. Henley cites J. F. Weidler, *Historia Astronomiae* (Wittemberg, 1741), pp. 204-5, where this incident is described from *Annalium Regum Francorum Pipini, Caroli M. & Ludouici Pii . . . ad ann 807*. See *Recueil Des Historiens Des Gaules et La France. Tome Cinquième* (Paris, 1744), p. 56.]

(3) [In describing such weapons, Beckford may have recalled 'The javelin which went of itself wherever one wanted it to go' in Voltaire's *The Black and the White* (1764); see *Zadig and Other Tales*, trans. R. B. Boswell, 1891, p. 351.]

Page 7. [This prison seems to derive from a passage in the account of Vathek's brother and successor Motavakel in d'Herbelot, p. 642: 'il avoit fait faire un fourneau de fer armé au dedans de pointes de clouds, qu'il faisoit échaufer plus ou moins pour punir ceux qu'il y faisoit enfermer.']

Page 8. [*Judiciary astrology*: the eventual doom of Carathis and Vathek may be hinted at. In his account of the subterranean temple at Persepolis or Istakhar, where they were eventually to be punished, Jean Chardin (Beckford's main source in this part of the story) describes the origins of 'cette vaine & superstitieuse Science qu'on appelle *Astrologie Judiciaire*', *Voyages... en Perse, et autres Lieux de l'Orient* (Amsterdam, 1711), iii. 131.]

Page 9. (1) [*coloured glass*: This detail recalls the coloured spectacles which Pooh-Pooh devises for looking at Radiant's dazzling eyes in Anthony Hamilton's *Fleur d'Epine* (*Fairy Tales and Romances*, trans. M. Lewis, H. T. Ryde, and C. Kenney, 1849, p. 373).]

(2) *their beards to be burnt*: The loss of the beard, from the earliest ages, was accounted highly disgraceful. An instance occurs, in the Tales of Inatulla, of one being *singed off*, as a mulct on the owner, for having failed to explain a question propounded; and, in the Arabian Nights, a proclamation may be seen similar to this of Vathek. Vol. I. p. 268. Vol. II. p. 228. [*1786*. The first reference is to Dow's *Tales from Inatulla*, the second to the *Arabian Nights*. Beckford's repeated jokes about the beards of the aged, pious, and sensible, perhaps imitate Anthony Hamilton's amusement at them, especially in *The Four Facardins* (see *Fairy Tales and Romances*, 1849, pp. 40, 45, 52, 53, 83, etc.).]

Page 13. [*nightingale . . . rose*: see page 58, note 2.]

Page 14. Giaour means *infidel.* [In replacing the two sentences in *1786* with this simple definition, *1816* follows the French editions.]

Page 16. (1) [*Bababalouk*: Beckford may have imitated the name from Voltaire, who was fond of such variants as Babouc, Bababec, and Bababou in his oriental tales.]

(2) *the Divan*: This was both the supreme council and court of justice, at which the caliphs of the race of the Abassides assisted in person, to redress the injuries of every appellant. *D'Herbelot*, p. 298. [*1786*.]

Page 17. the prime vizir: Vazir, vezir, or as we express it, vizir, literally signifies a *porter*; and, by metaphor, the minister who bears the principal burthen of the state, generally called the sublime Porte. [*1786*, but *1816* adds the last five words.]

Page 19. The Meuzins and their minarets: Valid, the son of Abdalmalek, was the first who erected a *minaret*, or turret; and this he placed on the grand mosque at Damascus; for the *meuzin*, or crier, to announce from it, the hour of prayer. This practice has constantly been kept to this day. *D'Herbelot*, p. 576. [*1786*.]

Page 22. Soliman Ben Daoud: The name of *David* in Hebrew is composed of the letter ו *Vau* between two ד *Daleths* דוד; and according to the Massoretic points ought to be pronounced *David*. Having no u consonant in their tongue, the Septuagint substituted the letter β for v, and wrote Δαβιδ, *Dabid*. The Syriac reads *Dad* or *Dod*; and the Arabs articulate *Daoud*. [Added in *1816*.]

Page 23. [*on the tapis*: under discussion or consideration.]

Page 25. [*The evening . . . eminences*: The development of this description is revealing. There is no equivalent in Lettice's early translation to the passage from 'shed a glow of ruddy light' to the end of the paragraph (see Parreaux, pp. 215, 513-14). Beckford later expanded the description but on 15 June 1785 Henley wrote that he had tried 'to throw a little more color' into the scene and gave his suggested revision, an indication of the freedom he felt he enjoyed to 'improve' the tale (Melville, p. 133):

> The sultry heat had subsided, the sky became serene, the air refreshing, and the flowers began to breathe their evening odours. The beams of the setting sun just breaking from the last cloud of the west lighted up the green bulges of the mountain with a golden verdure, and cast a ruddy glow over the sheep that grotesquely varied

their sidelong shadows as they gambolled down its steeps. No sounds were audible &c.

Beckford replied on 22 June (Melville, p. 134): 'Leave the description of the Eve: scene as it was originally—we have already more description than we know what to do with.' The Lausanne text, retained with some rephrasing and contraction in *1787* and *1815*, is clearly intermediary between those translated by Lettice and Henley (whereas *1816* follows *1786* without alteration):

> La soirée étoit belle, l'air frais, le ciel serein; les fleurs exhaloient leurs parfums. La nature en repos sembloit se réjouir aux rayons du soleil couchant, dont la douce clarté se reposoit sur la cime de la montagne aux quatre sources, & repandoit de-là une lueur favorable qui en embellissoit la descente, & animoit les troupeaux bondissans *etc.*]

Page 26. with the grin of an ogre: Thus, in the history of the punished vizir:—'The prince heard enough to convince him of his danger, and then perceived that the lady, who called herself the daughter of an *Indian* king, was an *ogress*; wife to one of those *savage demons*, called ogre, who stay in remote places, and make use of a thousand wiles to surprize and devour passengers.' *Arab. Nights*, vol. I. p. 56. [*1786*.]

Page 29. mutes: It has been usual, in eastern courts, from time immemorial, to retain a number of mutes. These are not only employed to amuse the monarch, but also to instruct his pages, in an art to us little known, that of communicating their thoughts by signs, lest the sounds of their voices should disturb the sovereign.—*Habesci's State of the Ottoman Empire*, p. 164.—The mutes are also the secret instruments of his private vengeance, in carrying the fatal string. [*1786*, slightly rephrased in *1816*, which adds last five words.]

Page 30. Prayer announced at break of day: The stated seasons of public prayer, in the twenty-four hours, were five: day-break, noon, midtime between noon and sun-set, immediately as the sun leaves the horizon, and an hour and half after it is down. [*1786*.]

Page 31. mummies: *Moumia* (from *moum*, wax and tallow) signifies the flesh of the human body preserved in the sand, after having been embalmed and wrapt in cerements. They are frequently found in the sepulchres of Egypt; but most of the Oriental mummies are brought from a cavern near Abin, in Persia. *D'Herbelot*, p. 647. [*1786*.]

Page 32. [*extenuated*: made thin or lean.]

Page 35. (1) [*1786* has a note on these delicacies, omitted in *1816*, but translated into French in *1787*, with an additional footnote, presumably by Beckford himself, on the phrase 'des vases de Fagfouri', which Henley had mistranslated or evaded. In *1815* only the additional footnote was retained: 'Les Orientaux donnent le nom de Fagfouri à la porcelaine de la Chine, dont l'usage est ancien chez eux. Ils appellent l'Empereur de la Chine, le Fagfour.' See d'Herbelot, p. 335. *sherbet reposing on snow*: cf. *Arabian Nights*, i. 307: 'he fill'd a large china cup with sherbet, and put snow into it'.]

(2) [*a lamb stuffed with pistachios*: Cf. *Arabian Nights*, ii. 117: 'what he boasted of more than all the rest, was a lamb fed with pistachio nuts.']

(3) *a parchment*: Parchments of the like mysterious import are frequently mentioned in the works of the Eastern writers. One in particular, amongst the Arabians, is held in high veneration. It was written by Ali, and Giafar Sadek, in mystic characters, and is said to contain the destiny of the Mahometan religion, and the great events which are to happen previous to the end of the world. This parchment is of *camel's skin*. [*1786*, but *1816* has omitted most of the last sentence and two source references, one to d'Herbelot, p. 366.]

Page 36. (1) *Istakhar*: This city was the ancient Persepolis and capital of Persia, under the kings of the three first races. The author of Lebtarikh writes, that Kischtab there established his abode, erected several temples to the element of fire, and hewed out, for himself and his successors, sepulchres in the rocks of the mountain contiguous to the city. The ruins of columns and broken figures which still remain, defaced as they were by Alexander, and mutilated by time, plainly evince that those ancient potentates had chosen it for the place of their interment. [*1786*, but *1816* has omitted the last two sentences and a reference to d'Herbelot, p. 327, which had been retained in *1815*.]

(2) *the talismans of Soliman*: The most famous *talisman* of the East, and which could control even the arms and magic of the dives, or giants, was *Mohur Solimani*, the seal or ring of Soliman Jared, fifth monarch of the world after Adam. By means of it, the possessor had the entire command, not only of the elements, but also of demons, and every created being. *Richardson's Dissertat.* p. 272. *D'Herbelot*, p. 820. [*1786*. References to the talismans are relatively common in English oriental tales: e.g. Steele, *The Guardian*, No. 167; John Hawkesworth, *Almoran and Hamet*, 1761, i. 12; James Ridley, *Tales of the Genii*, 1764, i. 129.]

(3) *pre-adamite sultans*: These monarchs, which were seventy-two in number, are said to have governed each a distinct species of rational beings, prior to the existence of Adam. [*1786*, but *1816* has omitted the last sentence and a reference to d'Herbelot, p. 820, which was probably Beckford's source for a later passage in the story: see p. 112 above.]

(4) *beware how thou enterest any dwelling*: Strange as this injunction may seem, it is by no means incongruous to the customs of the country. Dr. Pocock mentions his travelling with the train of the Governor of Faiume, who, instead of lodging in a village that was near, preferred to pass the night in a grove of palm-trees. *Travels*, vol. I. p. 56. [*1786*. See Richard Pococke, *A Description of the East, and Some Other Countries*, 2 vols., 1743-5.]

(5) *every bumper he ironically quaffed to the health of Mahomet*: There are innumerable proofs that the Grecian custom, συμπιειν κναθιζομενὸς, prevailed amongst the Arabs; but had these been wanted, Carathis could not be supposed a stranger to it. The practice was to hail the gods, in the first place; and then, those who were held in the highest veneration. [*1786*, but *1816* has omitted the last third, which concerns St. Ambrose.]

(6) *the ass of Balaam, the dog of the seven sleepers, and the other animals admitted into the paradise of Mahomet*: It was a tenet of the Mussulman creed, that all animals would be raised again, and many of them honoured with admission to paradise. The story of the seven sleepers, borrowed from Christian legends, was this:—In the days of the Emperor Decius, there were certain Ephesian youths of a good family, who, to avoid the flames of persecution, fled to a secret cavern, and there slept for a number of years. In their flight towards the cave, they were followed by a dog, which, when they attempted to drive him back, said: '*I love those who are dear unto God; go sleep, therefore, and I will guard you.*'—For this dog the Mahometans retain so profound a reverence, that their harshest sarcasm against a covetous person, is, 'He would not throw a bone to the dog of the seven sleepers.' It is even said, that their superstition induces them to write his name upon the letters they send to a distance, as a kind of talisman to secure them a safe conveyance. *Religious Ceremonies*, vol. VII. p. 74, n. *Sale's Koran*, ch. xviii. *and notes*. [*1786*.]

Page 37. (1) *painting the eyes of the Circassians*: It was an ancient custom in the East, which still continues, to tinge the eyes of women, particularly those of a fair complexion, with an impalpable powder,

prepared chiefly from crude antimony, and called *surmeh*. Ebni'l
Motezz, in a passage translated by Sir W. Jones, hath not only ascer-
tained its *purple* colour, but also likened the *violet* to it.

Viola collegit folia sua, similia
    Collyrionigro, quod bibit lachrymas die discessus,
Velut si esset super vasa in quibus fulgent
Primæ ignis flammulæ in sulphuris extremis partibus.

This pigment, when applied to the inner surface of the lids, com-
municates to the eye (especially if seen by the light of lamps) so tender
and fascinating a languor, as no language is competent to express.
Hence the epithet Ιοβλεφαρος, violet-colour eye-lids, attributed by the
Greeks to the goddess of beauty. [*1786*, but *1816* has omitted about a
third, containing classical and modern parallels, and several notes on
the note, giving further parallels. The verses quoted are from William
Jones, *Poeseos Asiaticae Commentariorum Libri Sex* (1774), p. 193.]

(2) *Rocnabad*: The stream thus denominated, flows near the city of
Schiraz. Its waters are uncommonly pure and limpid, and its banks
swarded with the finest verdure. Its praises are celebrated by Hafez,
in an animated song, which Sir W. Jones has admirably translated:—

> Boy, let yon liquid ruby flow,
> And bid thy pensive heart be glad,
> Whate'er the frowning zealots say:
> Tell them, their Eden cannot shew
> A stream so clear as Rocnabad,
> A bower so sweet as Mosella.

Mosella was an oratory on the banks of Rocnabad. [*1786*, but *1816* has
absorbed the last sentence from a footnote in *1786*. The verses quoted
are from 'A Persian Song of Hafiz' in William Jones, *Poems Consisting
Chiefly of Translations From The Asiatic Languages* (Oxford, 1772),
p. 72 (which reads 'Mosellay' for 'Mosella'). See d'Herbelot, p. 717.]

Page 39. (1) [*she contrived . . . invention*: Beckford has adapted to Carathis a passage concerning Vathek's brother Motavakel in d'Herbelot,
p. 641:

Il faisoit aussi quelquefois couler des serpens par dessous la Table,
& casser des pots pleins de scorpions au milieu de la Sale, où il
mangeoit sans qu'il fust permis à aucun de se lever de Table, ni de
changer de place; & lorsque quelqu'un de ses amis avoit été piqué

ou mordu par ces animaux, il le faisoit guerir avec une excellente Theriaque qu'il faisoit preparer.

A note on the phrase 'pots remplis de scorpions' in the French editions of *1787* and *1815* admitted to the adaptation: 'C'étoit un goût de famille. Motavekel, frère de Vathek, régaloit ses convives de la même manière, & s'amusoit aussi quelquefois à les guérir avec une thériaque admirable. *Herbelot*, p. 641.']

(2) *Moullahs*: Those amongst the Mahometans who were bred to the law, had this title; and the judges of cities and provinces were taken from their order. [*1786*, slightly rephrased in *1816*.]

(3) *the sacred Cahaba*: That part of the temple at Mecca which is chiefly revered, and, indeed, gives a sanctity to the rest, is a square stone building, the length of which, from north to south, is twenty-four cubits; and its breadth, from east to west, twenty-three. The door is on the east side, and stands about four cubits from the ground, the floor being level with the threshold. The Cahaba has a double roof, supported internally by three octangular pillars of aloes-wood; between which, on a bar of iron, hangs a row of silver lamps. The outside is covered with rich black damask, adorned with an embroidered band of gold. This hanging, which is changed every year, was formerly sent by the caliphs. *Sale's Preliminary Discourse*, p. 152. [*1786*, slightly shortened in *1816*. Beckford is probably indebted for the precious besom to an episode in Voltaire's *Travels of Scarmentado* (1756). At the court of Aurungzebe in Delhi, Scarmentado saw the monarch receive 'the celestial present which the Sherif of Mecca had sent him: it was the broom with which the Sacred House, the Kaaba, the Beit Allah had been swept. This broom is the symbol of the divine besom which sweeps away all defilement from the soul' (*Zadig and Other Tales*, trans. R. B. Boswell, 1891, p. 205).]

(4) [The textual notes to the following three paragraphs indicate more clearly the nature of Vathek's blasphemy, which was more explicitly gross in *1786*. When Beckford refined the passage for *1816*, he also omitted a note which had áppeared in *1786*:

The heinousness of Vathek's profanation can only be judged of by an orthodox Mussalman; or one who recollects the ablution and prayer indispensably required on the exoneration of nature. Sale's Prelim. Disc. p. 139. Al Koran, ch. 4. Habesci's State of the Ottoman Empire, p. 93.]

(5) [*Edris al Shafei*. Beckford probably derived this name from Sale's

Preliminary Discourse, sect. viii, p. 207, which discusses Mohammed Ebn Edris al Shâfeï, the 'author of the third orthodox sect' of the Mohammedans.]

Page 41. regale these pious poor souls with my good wine from Schiraz: The prohibition of wine in the Koran is so rigidly observed by the conscientious, especially if they have performed the pilgrimage to Mecca, that they deem it sinful to press grapes for the purpose of making it, and even to use the money arising from its sale. *Chardin, Voy. de Perse, tom.* II. p. 212.—*Schiraz* was famous in the East, for its wines of different sorts, but particularly for its *red*, which was esteemed more highly than even the white wine of *Kismische*. [*1786*. See Jean Chardin, *Voyages . . . en Perse, et autres Lieux de l'Orient* (3 vols., Amsterdam, 1711); and the *Koran*, chs. 1 and 5.]

Page 43. (1) *the most stately tulips of the East*: The tulip is a flower of eastern growth, and there held in great estimation. Thus, in an ode of Mesihi:—'The edge of the bower is filled with the light of Ahmed: among the plants, the fortunate *tulips* represent his companions.' [*1786*. The note quotes the prose translation accompanying William Jones's version of 'A Turkish Ode of Mesihi' in his *Poems* (Oxford, 1772), p. 105.]

(2) *certain cages of ladies*: There are many passages of the Moallakat in which these *cages* are fully described. Thus, in the poem of Lebeid:—

'How were thy tender affections raised, when the damsels of the tribe departed; when they hid themselves in carriages of cotton, like antelopes in their lair, and the tents as they were struck gave a piercing sound!

'They were concealed in vehicles, whose sides were well covered with awnings and carpets, with fine-spun curtains and pictured veils.'

Again, Zohair:—

'They are mounted in carriages covered with costly awnings, and with rose-coloured veils, the lining of which have the hue of crimson andemwood.' *Moallakat, by Sir W. Jones*, p. 46. 35. *See also Lady M. W. Montague*, Let. xxvi. [*1786*, but *1816* has omitted about one-half, containing further quotations from the *Moallakát*. See *The Moallakát, Or Seven Arabian Poems, Which Were Suspended On The Temple at Mecca* (1783), trans. William Jones, pp. 46-7, 35; and Lady Mary Wortley Montagu, *Letters . . . Written during her Travels in Europe, Asia and Africa* (1763), i. 158.]

(3) [*dislodged*. A disingenuous note in *1786*, omitted in *1816*, indicates Henley's difficulty in translating Beckford's French ('on . . .
dénicha'), which is disguised as a desire to express the supposed Arabic
original more accurately: 'Our language wants a verb, equivalent to
the French *denicher*; to convey, in this instance, the precise sense of
the author.']

Page 44. the locusts were heard from the thickets, on the plain of Catoul:
These insects are of the same species with the τεττιξ of the Greeks, and
the *cicada* of the Latins. The locusts are mentioned in Pliny, b. 11. 29.
They were so called from *loco usto*, because the havoc they made wherever they passed left behind the appearance of a place desolated by fire.
How could then the commentators of Vathek say that they are called
locusts, from their having been so denominated by the first English
settlers in America? [The first sentence derives from *1786*, but in *1816*
Beckford is in fact rejecting the remainder of Henley's note, which is
attributed vaguely to 'the commentators of Vathek'.]

Page 46. (1) *Vathek—with two little pages*: 'All the pages of the seraglio
are sons of Christians made slaves in time of war, in their most tender
age. The incursions of robbers in the confines of Circassia, afford the
means of supplying the seraglio, even in times of peace.' *Habesci's State
of the Ottoman Empire*, p. 157. That the pages here mentioned were
Circassians, appears from the description of their complexion:—*more
fair than the enamel of Franguistan*. [*1786*. The passage from Habesci
contains minor errors of transcription.]

(2) *Confectioners and cooks*: What their precise number might have
been in Vathek's establishment, it is not now easy to determine; but,
in the household of the present Grand Seignor, there are not fewer than
a hundred and ninety. *Habesci's State*, p. 145. [*1786*.]

Page 47. (1) *torches were lighted*, &c.: Mr. Marsden relates, in his
History of Sumatra, that tigers prove most fatal and destructive
enemies to the inhabitants, particularly in their journies; and adds,
that the numbers annually slain by those rapacious tyrants of the woods,
is almost incredible. As these tremendous enemies are alarmed at the
appearance of fire, it is usual for the natives to carry a splendid kind
of torch, chiefly to frighten them; and, also, to make a blaze with wood,
in different parts, round their villages, p. 149. [*1786*. The work cited
is William Marsden, *The History of Sumatra* (1783). But Beckford
was probably recalling a similar incident in Anthony Hamilton's *Fleur
d'Epine*, in which Pooh-Pooh disperses various dangerous animals in

a forest by lighting a faggot on a pole (*Fairy Tales and Romances*, 1849, pp. 375-6).]

(2) *One of the forests of cedar, that bordered their way, took fire*: Accidents of this kind, in Persia, are not unfrequent. 'It was an ancient practice with the kings and great men to set fire to large bunches of dry combustibles, fastened round wild beasts and birds, which being then let loose, naturally fled to the woods for shelter, and caused destructive conflagrations.' *Richardson's Dissertation*, p. 185. [*1786*, but *1816* has compressed the quotation from Richardson, which is more accurate in *1786*, and omits Biblical and classical parallels.]

(3) *hath seen some part of our bodies; and, what is worse, our very faces*: 'I was informed,' writes Dr. Cooke, 'that the Persian women, in general, would sooner expose to public view any part of their bodies than their faces.' *Voyages and Travels*, vol. II. p. 443. [*1786*. The reference is to John Cook, *Voyages and Travels Through The Russian Empire, Tartary, and Part of the Kingdom of Persia*, 2 vols., Edinburgh, 1770.]

Page 49. (1) *cakes baked in silver ovens for his royal mouth*: Portable ovens were a part of the furniture of eastern travellers. St. Jerom (on Lament. v. 10) hath particularly described them. The Caliph's were of the same kind, only substituting silver for brass. Dr. Pocock mentions his having been entertained in an Arabian camp with cakes baked for him. In what the peculiarity of the royal bread consisted, it is not easy to determine; but, in one of the Arabian Tales, a woman, to gratify her utmost desire, wishes to become the wife of the sultan's baker; assigning for the reason, that she might have her fill of that bread, which is called the sultan's. Vol. IV. p. 269. [*1786*. The first reference is apparently to Richard Pococke, *A Description of the East* (1743–5), i. 183.]

(2) [*manchets*: small loaves or rolls of the finest wheaten bread.]

(3) *vases of snow; and grapes from the banks of the Tigris*: It was customary in eastern climates, and especially in the sultry season, to carry, when journeying, supplies of snow. These *æstivæ nives* (as Mamertinus styles them) being put into separate vases, were, by that means, better kept from the air, as no more was opened at once than might suffice for immediate use. To preserve the whole from solution, the vessels that contained it were secured in packages of straw. Gesta Dei, p. 1098.—Vathek's ancestor, the CALIPH MAHADI, in the pilgrimage to Mecca, which he undertook from ostentation rather than devotion, loaded upon camels so prodigious a quantity as was not only

sufficient for himself and his attendants, amidst the burning sands of Arabia; but, also, to preserve, in their natural freshness, the various fruits he took with him, and to ice all their drink whilst he staid at Mecca: the greater part of whose inhabitants had never seen snow till then. *Anecdotes Arabes*, p. 326. [*1786*. The references are to *Gesta Dei Per Francos, Siue Orientalium Expeditionum, Et Regni Francorum Hierosolimitani* (Hanover, 1611), i. 1098; and J. F. de la Croix, *Anecdotes Arabes* (Paris, 1772).]

Page 50. (1) *horrible Kaf*: This mountain, which, in reality, is no other than Caucasus, was supposed to surround the earth, like a ring encompassing a finger. The sun was believed to rise from one of its eminences, (as over Oeta, by the Latin poets) and to set on the opposite; whence, *from Kaf to Kaf*, signified from one extremity of the earth to the other. The fabulous historians of the East affirm, that this mountain was founded upon a stone, called *sakhrat*, one grain of which, according to Lokman, would enable the possessor to work wonders. This stone is further described as the pivot of the earth; and said to be one vast emerald, from the refraction of whose beams, the heavens derive their azure. It is added, that whenever God would excite an earthquake, he commands the stone to move one of its fibres, (which supply in it the office of nerves) and, that being moved, the part of the earth connected with it, quakes, is convulsed, and sometimes expands. Such is the philosophy of the Koran!—

The Tarikh Tabari, written in Persian, analagous to the same tradition, relates, that, were it not for this emerald, the earth would be liable to perpetual commotions and unfit for the abode of mankind.

To arrive at the Kaf, a vast region,

> Far from the sun and summer-gale,

must be traversed. Over this dark and cheerless desart, the way is inextricable, without the direction of supernatural guidance. Here the dives or giants were confined after their defeat by the first heroes of the human race; and here, also, the peries, or faeries, are supposed in ordinary to reside. Sukrage, the giant, was King of Kaf, and had Rucail, one of the children of Adam, for his prime minister. The giant Argenk, likewise, from the time that Tahamurah made war upon him, reigned here, and reared a superb palace in the city of Aherman, with galleries, on whose walls were painted the creatures that inhabited the world prior to the formation of Adam. *D'Herbelot*, p. 230, &c. &c. [*1786*. The line of verse is from Thomas Gray, *The Progress of Poesy* (1757), l. 83.]

(2) *the simurgh*: That wonderful bird of the East, concerning which so many marvels are told, was not only endowed with reason, but possessed also the knowledge of every language. Hence it may be concluded to have been a dive in a borrowed form. This creature relates of itself that it had seen the great revolution of seven thousand years, twelve times commence and close; and that, in its duration, the world had been seven times void of inhabitants, and as often replenished. The simurgh is represented as a great friend to the race of Adam, and not less inimical to the dives. Tahamurath and Aherman were apprised by its predictions of all that was destined to befal them, and from it they obtained the promise of assistance in every undertaking. Armed with the buckler of Gian Ben Gian, Tahamurath was borne by it through the air, over the dark desart, to Kaf. From its bosom his helmet was crested with plumes, which the most renowned warriors have ever since worn. In every conflict the simurgh was invulnerable, and the heroes it favoured never failed of success. Though possessed of power sufficient to exterminate its foes, yet the exertion of that power was supposed to be forbidden.—Sadi, a serious author, gives it as an instance of the universality of Providence, that the simurgh, notwithstanding its immense bulk, is at no loss for sustenance on the mountain of Kaf. [*1786*, but *1816* has omitted a long sentence based on the *Tales from Inatulla* (1768), ii. 71-2, a parallel with Ariosto, a long footnote, and references to the sources of the note, d'Herbelot, pp. 1017, 810. Beckford had told Henley: 'I suppose you will prepare a tolerable long comment on the Simorgue. That most respectable bird deserves all you can say of her' (*The Collection . . . of Alfred Morrison, 2nd Series, 1882-93*, i. 197; dated 13 April 1786, but clearly written about a year earlier).]

(3) [*palampores*: a kind of chintz bed-cover. Henley wrote to Beckford on 12 April 1785 (Melville, p. 129): 'Several happy terms have occurred which I could wish to substitute in the place of others already inserted. Surely for instance Vathek mistaking the tattered awnings and chintzes for large flowers—would be better expressed by *palampores* instead of *chintzes* &c. &c.' *1786* has a long note on the word, omitted in *1816*.]

(4) *afrits*: These were a kind of Medusæ, or Lamiæ, supposed to be the most terrible and cruel of all the orders of the dives. *D'Herbelot*, p. 66. [*1786*.]

(5) *Tablets fraught with preternatural qualities*: Mr. Richardson

observes, 'that in the East, men of rank in general carried with them pocket astronomical tables, which they consulted on every affair of moment.' These tablets, however, were of the *magical* kind; and such as often occur in works of romance. Thus, in Boiardo, Orlando receives, from the father of the youth he had rescued, 'a book that would solve all doubts:' and, in Ariosto, Logistilla bestows upon Astolpho a similar directory. [*1786*, but *1816* has omitted the last sentence. The note refers, in addition to Richardson, p. 191, to Boiardo, *Orlando Innamorato*, I. v. 67, and Ariosto, *Orlando Furioso*, xv. xiv.]

Page 51. (1) *dwarfs*: Such unfortunate beings, as are thus 'curtailed of fair proportion,' have been, for ages, an appendage of Eastern grandeur. One part of their office consists in the instruction of the pages, but their principal duty is the amusement of their master. If a dwarf happen to be a mute, he is much esteemed; but if he be also an eunuch, he is regarded as a prodigy; and no pains or expense are spared to obtain him. Habesci's State of the Ottoman Empire, p. 164, &c. [*1786*. Beckford had already introduced dwarfs into *The Long Story*.]

(2) *A small spring supplies us with water for the abdest, and we daily repeat prayers, &c.*: Amongst the indispensable rules of the Mahometan faith, ablution is one of the chief. This rite is divided into three kinds. The first, performed before prayers, is called *abdest*. It begins with washing both hands, and repeating these words:—'Praised be Alla, who created clean water, and gave it the virtue to purify: he also hath rendered our faith conspicuous.' This done, water is taken in the right hand thrice, and the mouth being washed, the worshipper subjoins:—'I pray thee, O Lord, to let me taste of that water, which thou hast given to thy Prophet Mahomet in paradise, more fragrant than musk, whiter than milk, sweeter than honey: and which has the power to quench for ever, the thirst of him that drinks it.' This petition is accompanied with sniffing a little water into the nose; the face is then three times washed, and behind the ears; after which, water is taken with both hands, beginning with the right, and thrown to the elbow. The washing of the crown next follows, and the apertures of the ear with the thumbs: afterward the neck with all the fingers; and, finally, the feet. In this last operation, it is held sufficient to wet the sandal only. At each ceremonial a suitable petition is offered, and the whole concludes with this: 'Hold me up firmly, O Lord! and suffer not my foot to slip, that I may not fall from the bridge into hell.' Nothing can be more exemplary than the attention with which these rites are performed. If an

involuntary cough or sneeze interrupt them, the whole service is begun
anew, and that as often as it happens. *Habesci*, p. 91, &c. [*1786*.]

(3) [*Fakreddin*. Parreaux, p. 343, who describes the name as a common Arab surname meaning 'gloire de la religion', notes its appearance
in d'Herbelot, p. 330, and T. Gueulette's *Avantures de Fum Hoam*
(1723), ii. 1–2 (see Weber, *Tales of the East*, 1812, iii. 376). Beckford
had already used it in *The Long Story*.]

(4) *the bells of a cafila*: A cafila, or caravan, according to Pitts, is
divided into distinct companies, at the head of which an officer, or
person of distinction, is carried in a kind of horse litter, and followed
by a sumpter camel, loaded with his treasure. This camel hath a bell
fastened to either side, the sound of which may be heard at a considerable distance. Others have bells on their necks and their legs, to solace
them when drooping with heat and fatigue.—Inatulla also, in his tales,
hath a similar reference:—'the bells of the cafila may be rung in the
thirsty desert.' vol. II. p. 15. These small bells were known at Rome
from the earliest times, and called from their sounds *tintinnabulum*.
Phædrus gives us a lively description of the mule carrying the fiscal
monies; *clarumque collo jactans tintinnabulum*. Book II. fabl. vii. [*1786*,
but *1816* has added the last two sentences on Roman bells. The first
reference is to Joseph Pitts, *A True and Faithfull Account of the Religion
and Manners of the Mohammetans* (Exeter, 1704), p. 106. The reference
to *The Tales from Inatulla* (1768) should be to ii. 49.]

(5) *Deggial*: This word signifies properly a liar and impostor, but is
applied, by Mahometan writers, to their *Antichrist*. He is described as
having but one eye and eye-brow, and on his forehead the radicals of
cafer or *infidel* are said to be impressed. According to the traditions
of the faithful, his first appearance will be between Irak and Syria,
mounted on an ass. Seventy thousand Jews from Ispahan are expected
to follow him. His continuance on earth is to be forty days. All places
are to be destroyed by him and his emissaries, except *Mecca* or *Medina*;
which will be protected by angels from the general overthrow. At last,
however, he will be slain by Jesus, who is to encounter him at the gate
of Lud. *D'Herbelot*, p. 282. *Sale's Prelim. Disc.* p. 106. [*1786*.]

Page 52. (1) *sugar*: Dr. Pocock mentions the sugar-cane as a great
desert in Egypt; and adds, that, besides coarse loaf sugar and sugar
candy, it yields a third sort, remarkably fine, which is sent to the Grand
Seignor, and prepared only for himself. *Travels*, vol. I. p. 183. 204.
The jeweller's son, in the story of the third Calender, desires the prince

EXPLANATORY NOTES

to fetch some *melon* and *sugar*, that he might refresh himself with them. *Arab. Nights*, vol. I. p. 159. [*1786*. The reference is to Richard Pococke, *A Description of the East* (1743–5).]

(2) *red characters*: The laws of Draco are recorded by Plutarch, in his life of Solon, to have been written in blood. If more were meant by this expression, than that those laws were of a sanguinary nature, they will furnish the earliest instance of the use of *red characters*; which were afterwards considered as appropriate to supreme authority, and employed to denounce some requisition or threatening designed to strike terror. [*1786*, but *1816* has omitted the last sentence. The reference is to Plutarch's *Life of Solon*, xvii. 2.]

Page 53. (1) *thy body shall be spit upon*: There was no mark of contempt amongst the Easterns so ignominious as this. *Arab. Nights* vol. I. p. 115. Vol. IV. p. 275. [*1786*, but *1816* has omitted three sentences giving Biblical and classical parallels.]

(2) *bats will nestle in thy belly*: Bats, in those countries, were very abundant; and, both from their numbers and size, held in abhorrence. See what is related of them by Thevenot, Part I. p. 132, 3. *Egmont and Hayman*, vol. II. p. 87, and other travellers in the East. [*1786*. The references are to Jean de Thévenot, *Travels . . . Into The Levant. In Three Parts*, trans. A. Lovell, 1687; and J. Van Egmont and John Heyman, *Travels through Part of Europe, Asia Minor, The Islands of the Archipelago, Syria, Palestine, Egypt, Mount Sinai, &c.* (trans. from the Dutch), 2 vols., 1759.]

(3) *the Bismillah*: This word (which is prefixed to every chapter of the Koran, except the ninth) signifies, 'in the name of the most merciful God.'—It became not the initiatory formula of prayer, till the time of Moez the Fatimite. *D'Herbelot*, p. 326. [*1786*, but *1816* has omitted half of the note, including an explanation of 'Ablution' and parallels from the Psalms. In a letter to Beckford on 26 April 1785 (Melville, p. 130) Henley had suggested that mention of the Bismillah was anachronistic.]

Page 55. (1) *a magnificent tecth*. This kind of *moving throne*, though more common, at present, than in the days of Vathek, is still confined to persons of the highest rank. [*1786*.]

(2) *baths of rose water*: The use of perfumed waters for the purpose of bathing is of an early origin in the East, where every odoriferous plant breathes a richer fragrance than is known to our more humid climates. The rose which yields this lotion is, according to Hasselquist, of a

beautiful pale bluish colour, double, large as a man's fist, and more exquisite in scent than any other species. The quantities of this water distilled annually at Fajhum, and carried to distant countries, is immense. The mode of conveying it is in vessels of copper, coated with wax. *Voyag.* p. 248. [*1786*, but *1816* has omitted a parallel with Jonson. The reference is to Frederick Hasselquist, *Voyages and Travels in the Levant* (1766; trans. from the Swedish, Stockholm, 1757).]

(3) *lamb à la crème*: No dish amongst the Easterns was more generally admired. The Caliph Abdolmelek, at a splendid entertainment, to which whoever came was welcome, asked Amrou, the son of Hareth, what kind of meat he preferred to all others. The old man answered: 'An ass's neck, well seasoned and roasted.'—'But what say you,' replied the Caliph, 'to the leg or shoulder of a LAMB *à crème*?' and added,

> 'How sweetly we live if a shadow would last!'

M.S. Laud. Numb. 161. *A. Ockley's Hist. of the Saracens*, vol. II. p. 277. [*1786*. The reference to MS. Laud. derives from Simon Ockley, *The History of the Saracens* (3rd edn., 2 vols., Cambridge, 1757), which in fact reads: 'You do nothing, says *Abdolmélick*, what say you to a Leg or a Shoulder of sucking Lamb, well roasted and covered over with Butter and Milk?']

(4) *made the dwarfs dance, against their will*: Ali Chelebi al Moufti, in a treatise on the subject, held that dancing, after the example of the derviches, who made it a part of their devotion, was allowable. But in this opinion he was deemed to be heterodox; for Mahometans, in general, place dancing amongst the things that are forbidden. *D'Herbelot*, p. 98. [*1786*.]

Page 56. (1) *durst not refuse the commander of the faithful*: The mandates of Oriental potentates have ever been accounted irresistible. Hence the submission of these devotees to the will of the Caliph. *Esther* i. 19. *Daniel* vi. 8. *Ludeke Expos. brevis*, p. 60. [*1786*. The third reference is to Christoph Wilhelm Luedecke, *Expositio Brevis Locorum Scr. S. ad orientem sese referentium* etc. (Halle, 1777).]

(2) *properly lubricated with the balm of Mecca*: Unguents, for reasons sufficiently obvious, have been of general use in hot climates. According to Pliny, 'at the time of the Trojan war, they consisted of oils perfumed with the odours of flowers, and, chiefly, of ROSES.'—Hasselquist speaks of oil, impregnated with the tuberose and jessamine; but the unguent here mentioned was preferred to every other. Lady M. W.

Montagu, desirous to try its effects, seems to have suffered materially from having improperly applied it. [*1786*. The references are to Pliny, *Natural History*, XIII. i; Hasselquist, *Voyages and Travels* (1766), p. 267; and Lady Mary Wortley Montagu, *Letters* (1763), ii. 132-4.]

(3) *black eunuchs sabre in hand*: In this manner the apartments of the ladies were constantly guarded. Thus, in the story of the enchanted horse, Firouz Schah, traversing a strange palace by night, entered a room, 'and, by the light of a lanthorn, saw that the persons he had heard snoring, were black eunuchs with naked sabres by them; which was enough to inform him that this was the guard-chamber of some queen or princess.' *Arabian Nights*, vol. IV. p. 189. [*1786*. The quotation from the *Arabian Nights* has small inaccuracies.]

Page 57. (1) [*Nouronihar*. The name occurs in 'The Story of prince Ahmed, and the fairy Pari Banon' in the *Arabian Nights* (1783), iv. 214, where a note describes it as 'An Arabian word that signifies day-light'. Beckford had already used the name in *The Long Story*.]

(2) *to let down the great swing*: The swing was an exercise much used in the apartments of the Eastern ladies, and not only contributed to their amusement, but also to their health. *Tales of Inatulla*, vol. I. p. 259. [*1786*.]

Page 58. (1) [*my senses . . . your charms*: *1786* has a note, omitted in *1816*, in which Henley disingenuously cites a French phrase (Beckford's, in fact) to help him convey the meaning of his supposed Arabic original: 'or (to express an idiom for which we have no substitute)— *thy countenance*, RAYONNANTE DE BEAUTES ET DE GRACES'. Henley then gives parallels from 'Arabian Writers'.]

(2) *melodious Philomel, I am thy rose*: The passion of the nightingale for the rose is celebrated over all the East. Thus, Meshii [*sic*], as translated by Sir W. Jones:

> Come, charming maid, and hear thy poet sing,
> Thyself the rose, and he the bird of Spring:
> Love bids him sing, and Love will be obey'd,
> Be gay: too soon the flowers of Spring will
>   fade.

[*1786*. The quotation is of the last four lines of Jones's 'A Turkish Ode of Mesihi', *Poems* (1772), p. 113.]

Page 59. (1) *oil spilt in breaking the lamps*: It appears from Thevenot, that illuminations were usual on the arrival of a stranger, and he mentions, on an occasion of this sort, two hundred lamps being lighted. The quantity of oil, therefore, spilt on the margin of the bath, may be easily accounted for, from this custom. [*1786*. The reference is to Jean de Thévenot, *Travels* (1687), Pt. I, p. 160.]

(2) [*a jack-pudding*: 'a buffoon, clown, or merry-andrew, *esp.* one attending on a mountebank' (*OED*). The word translates Beckford's 'un Saltimbanque'.]

Page 60. (1) *calenders*: These were a sort of men amongst the Mahometans, who abandoned father and mother, wife and children, relations and possessions, to wander through the world, under a pretence of religion, entirely subsisting on the fortuitous bounty of those they had the address to dupe. *D'Herbelot, Suppl.* p. 204. [*1786*.]

(2) *santons*: A body of religionists who were also called *abdals*, and pretended to be inspired with the most enthusiastic raptures of divine love. They were regarded by the vulgar as *saints. Olearius*, tom. I. p. 971. *D'Herbelot*, p. 5. [*1786*. The reference is to Adam Olearius, *Voyages...faits en Moscovie, Tartarie et Perse...Traduits de l'Original & augmentez par le Sr. Wiquefort* (2 vols., Leyden, 1718).]

(3) *derviches*: The term *dervich* signifies a *poor man*, and is the general appellation by which a Mahometan monk is named. There are, however, discriminations that distinguish this class from the others already mentioned. They are bound by no vow of poverty, they abstained not from marriage, and, whenever disposed, they may relinquish both their blue shirt and profession. *D'Herbelot, Suppl.* 214.—It is observable that these different orders, though not established till the reign of Nasser al Samani, are notwithstanding mentioned by our author as coeval with Vathek, and by the author of the Arabian Nights, as existing in the days of Haroun al Raschid: so that the Arabian fabulists appear as inattentive to chronological exactness in points of this sort, as our immortal dramatist himself. [*1786*.]

(4) *Bramins*: These constitute the principal caste of the Indians, according to whose doctrine *Brahma*, from whom they are called, is the first of the three created beings, by whom the world was made. This Brahma is said to have communicated to the Indians four books, in which all the sciences and ceremonies of their religion are comprized. The word Brahma, in the Indian language, signifies *pervading all things*. The Brahmins lead a life of most rigid abstinence, refraining not only from the use, but even the touch, of animal food; and are equally exemplary for their contempt of pleasures and devotion to

philosophy and religion. *D'Herbelot*, p. 212. *Bruckeri Hist. Philosoph.* tom. I. p. 194. [*1786*. The reference is to Jacob Brucker, *Historia Critica Philosophiae A Mundi* (2nd edn., 6 vols., Leipzig, 1767).]

(5) *faquirs*: This sect are a kind of religious anchorets, who spend their whole lives in the severest austerities and mortification. It is almost impossible for the imagination to form an extravagance that has not been practised by some of them, to torment themselves. As their reputation for sanctity rises in proportion to their sufferings, those amongst them are reverenced the most, who are most ingenious in the invention of tortures, and persevering in enduring them. Hence some have persisted in sitting or standing for years together in one unvaried posture; supporting an almost intolerable burden; dragging the most cumbrous chains; exposing their naked bodies to the scorching sun, and hanging with the head downward before the fiercest fires. *Relig. Ceremon.* vol. III. p. 264, &c. *White's Sermons*, p. 504. [*1786*, but *1816* makes a small change in the first sentence. The second reference is to Joseph White, *Sermons Preached before the University of Oxford, In the Year 1784, At the Lecture founded by the Rev. John Bampton* (2nd edn. expanded, 1785). This passage resembles a description in Voltaire's *Bababec and the Fakirs* (1750), as well as Richard Owen Cambridge's 'Preface' to *The Fakeer: A Tale* (1756), pp. iii–v, where he gives as his own and Voltaire's source Louis Le Comte's *Memoirs and Remarks . . . on China* (1737), p. 335.]

(6) *some that cherished vermin*: In this attachment they were not singular. The Emperor Julian not only discovered the same partiality, but celebrated, with visible complacency, the shaggy and *populous* beard, which he fondly cherished; and even 'The Historian of the Roman Empire,' affirms 'that the little animal is a beast familiar to man, and signifies love.' Vol. II. p. 343. [*1786*. The reference is to Edward Gibbon, *The History of the Decline and Fall of the Roman Empire*, ii (1781), 343 and n.]

Page 61. (1) *Visnow and Ixhora*: Two deities of the Hindoos. The traditions of their votaries are, probably, allegorical; but without a key to disclose their mystic import, they are little better than senseless jargon; and, with the key, downright nonsense. [*1816*, a compressed and more derisive version of *1786*. Beckford may have had in mind the discussion of these deities, especially of the ten incarnations of Wistnou, in *Religious Ceremonies*, iii. 457–77.]

(2) *talapoins*: This order, which abounds in Siam, Laos, Pegu, and

other countries, consists of different classes, and both sexes, but chiefly of men. *Relig. Ceremon.* vol. IV. p. 62, &c. [*1786*. Henley wrote to Beckford on 19 June 1785 (Melville, p. 133), asking for help with the explanation of this term.]

(3) *objects of pity were sure to swarm around him*: Ludeke mentions the practice of bringing those who were suffering under any calamity, or had lost the use of their limbs, &c. into public, for the purpose of exciting compassion. On an occasion, therefore, of this sort, when Fakreddin, like a pious Mussulman, was publicly to distribute his alms, and the commander of the faithful to make his appearance, such an assemblage might well be expected. The Eastern custom of regaling a convention of this kind is of great antiquity, as is evident from the parable of the king, in the Gospels, who entertained the maimed, the lame, and the blind; nor was it discontinued when Dr. Pocock visited the East. Vol. I. p. 182. [*1786*. For Luedecke, see page 56, note 1 above. The second reference is to Richard Pococke, *Description of the East* (1743–5).]

Page 62. (1) *small plates of abominations*: The Koran hath established several distinctions relative to different kinds of food, in imitation of the Jewish prescriptions; and many Mahometans are so scrupulous as not to touch the flesh of any animal over which, *in articulo mortis*, the butcher had omitted to pronounce the *Bismillah. Relig. Cerem.* vol. VII. p. 110. [*1786*, but *1816* has added 'in imitation . . . prescriptions' and translates into Latin Henley's 'in the article of death'.]

(2) *Sinai*: This mountain is deemed by Mahometans the noblest of all others, and even regarded with the highest veneration, because the divine law was promulgated from it. *D'Herbelot*, p. 812. [*1786*.]

Page 63. (1) *Peries*: The word *Peri*, in the Persian language, signifies that beautiful race of creatures which constitutes the link between angels and men.—*See note [3] on page [4]*. [*1816* has retained only the first sentence of *1786* and has omitted the remaining seven-eighths, adding the cross-reference. For a full account, see d'Herbelot, pp. 701–2.]

(2) *butterflies of Cachemire*: The same insects are celebrated in an unpublished poem of Mesihi. Sir Anthony Shirley relates, that it was customary in Persia 'to hawke after butterflies with sparrows, made to that use, and stares.'—It is, perhaps, to this amusement that our Author alludes in the context. [*1786*, but *1816* has omitted Henley's description of Mesihi's poem as 'another of the MSS. mentioned in the Pre-

face' (i.e. of *1786*, where the MSS. are said to be in the 'Editor''s possession. Henley wrote to Beckford on 26 April 1785 (Melville, p. 130)
to ask 'what must be said' about these butterflies. Beckford replied
(see note (2) to page 50 above) that, 'The butterflies of Cachemire are
celebrated in a poem of Mesihi I slaved at with Zemir, the old Mahometan who assisted me in translating W. Montague's M.S., but they are
hardly worth a note.' See Sir Anthony Shirley, *His Relation of His
Travels into Persia* (1613), p. 78, although Henley does not quote this
source exactly.]

Page 64. (1) *Gulchenrouz*: The frame story of Gueullette's *Avantures
de Fum Hoam* (1723) concerns the love of the Sultan of China for the
Princess Gulchenraz, daughter of the King of Georgia (see *Chinese
Tales* in Weber, *Tales of the East*, iii. 355 ff.). But see also d'Herbelot,
p. 407: 'ᴳᵁᴸˢᶜᴴᴱᴺ Ráz, Le Rosier, ou le Jardin des secrets. Livre
Persien en vers sur la Metaphysique, & sur la Theologie mystique des
Sofis... Son Auteur est inconnu.']

(2) [*Sutlememe*: Taken by Beckford from Pétis de la Croix, *Les Mille
et un jours, Contes Persans* (1710), i. 7 (Weber, *Tales of the East*, ii. 308),
where it is the name of the nurse to the Princess of Casmire, the central
figure.]

Page 65. (1) *Megnoun and Leilah*: These personages are esteemed
amongst the Arabians as the most beautiful, chaste, and impassioned
of lovers; and their amours have been celebrated with all the charms
of verse in every Oriental language. The Mahometans regard them,
and the poetical records of their love, in the same light as the Bride-
groom and Spouse, and the Song of Songs are regarded by the Jews.
D'Herbelot, p. 573. [*1786*.]

(2) *dart the lance in the chace*: Throwing the lance was a favourite
pastime with the young Arabians; and so expert were they in this
practice (which prepared them for the mightier conflicts, both of the
chace and war) that they could bear off a ring on the points of their
javelins. *Richardson's Dissertat.* p. 198. 281. [*1786*, but *1816* has
omitted a reference to Virgil and a long footnote.]

(3) *The two brothers had mutually engaged their children to each other*:
Contracts of this nature were frequent amongst the Arabians. Another
instance occurs in the Story of Noureddin Ali and Benreddin Hassan.
[*1786*. The reference is to the *Arabian Nights*, i. 267.]

(4) *Nouronihar loved her cousin, more than her own beautiful eyes*:

This mode of expression not only occurs in the sacred writers, but also in the Greek and Roman. Thus Catullus says:

> Quem plus illa oculis suis amabat.

[*1786*, but *1816* has omitted a parallel from Moschus. The quotation is from Catullus, iii. 5.]

(5) *the same long languishing looks*: So Ariosto:

> ———negri occhi,———
> Pietosi a riguardare, a mover parchi.

[*1786*, but *1816* has omitted parallels from Spenser and Shakespeare. The quotation is from *Orlando Furioso*, VII. xii. 2–3.]

Page 66. *Shaddukian and Ambreabad*: These were two cities of the Peries, in the imaginary region of *Ginnistan*, the former signifies *pleasure* and *desire*, the latter *the city of Ambergris. See Richardson's Dissertat.* p. 169. [*1786*. Beckford wrote *c.* April 1785 (see the undated letter referred to in note 2 to page 50 above): 'I believe in most respects I have been exact in my costume. The Domes of Shadukian & Ambreabad you will find explained in Richardson.']

Page 67. [*Shaban*. This name occurs in 'The Story of Nourreddin Ali, and Bedreddin Hassan' in the *Arabian Nights*, i. 308, with the note: 'The Mahometans give this name generally to the black eunuchs.']

Page 68. *a spoon of cocknos*: The cocknos is a bird whose beak is much esteemed for its beautiful polish, and sometimes used as a spoon. Thus, in the History of Atalmulck and Zelica Begum, it was employed for a similar purpose:—'Zelica having called for refreshment, six old slaves instantly brought in and distributed *Mahramas*, and then served about in a great bason of Martabam, a salad *made of herbs of various kinds, citron juice, and the pith of cucumbers*. They served it first to the Princess in a *cocknos' beak*: she took a beak of the salad, eat it, and gave another to the next slave that sat by her on her right hand; which slave did as her mistress had done.' [*1786*. The quotation is from 'Histoire d'Atal-mulc, surnommé le Visir triste, et de la Princesse Zelica-Béghume', in Pétis de la Croix, *Les Mille et un jours, Contes Persans* (Paris, 1710–12), iii. 36–158 (Weber, *Tales of the East*, ii. 406). Henley had asked Beckford for help with this note on 26 April 1785 (Melville, p. 130) and Beckford's reply (see page 50, note 2 above) had referred him to the *Persian Tales* as above. The first sentence of Henley's note is taken direct from Beckford's letter.]

Page 70. (1) [*Dives*: see d'Herbelot, p. 298: 'DIV ou DIVE en langue Persienne signifie une creature qui n'est ni homme, ni Ange, ni diable, c'est un genie, un demon, comme les Grecs l'entendent, & un Geant qui n'est pas de l'espece des hommes', etc.]

(2) *Goules*: Goul, or *ghul*, in Arabic, signifies any terrifying object, which deprives people of the use of their senses. Hence it became the appellative of that species of monster which was supposed to haunt forests, cemeteries, and other lonely places; and believed not only to tear in pieces the living, but to dig up and devour the dead. *Richardson's Dissert.* p. 174. 274. [*1786*, but *1816* has omitted a second paragraph on insanity. *1787* and *1815* add: '*Voyez aussi* l'histoire d'Amine dans les Mille et une Nuits [*Arabian Nights*, i. 199–201].']

Page 71. (1) *feathers of the heron, all sparkling with carbuncles*: Panaches of this kind are amongst the attributes of Eastern royalty. *Tales of Inatulla*, vol. ii. p. 205. [*1786*.]

(2) [Once again *1816* omits the disingenuous note in *1786*: 'The original, in this instance, as in the others already noticed, is more analagous to the French, than the English idiom: — *dont l'oeil pénétre jusqu'à la moelle des jeunes filles*.' See page 43 note 3 and page 58 note 1 above.]

(3) *the carbuncle of Giamschid*: This mighty potentate was the fourth sovereign of the dynasty of the Pischadians, and brother or nephew to Tahamurath. His proper name was *giam* or *gem*, and *sched*, which in the language of the ancient Persians denominated the sun: an addition, ascribed by some to the majesty of his person, and by others to the splendour of his actions. One of the most magnificent monuments of his reign was the city of Istakhar, of which Tahamurath had laid the foundations. This city, at present called *Gihil-*, or *Tchil-minar*, from the forty columns reared in it by Homai, or (according to our author and others) by Soliman Ben Daoud, was known to the Greeks by the name of Persepolis: and there is still extant in the East a tradition, that, when Alexander burnt the edifices of the Persian kings, seven stupendous structures of Giamschid were consumed with his palace. [*1786*, but *1816* has omitted a footnote and three further paragraphs citing Strabo and Milton. The source of the note is in fact d'Herbelot, p. 395.]

(4) *the torches were extinguished*: To the union here prefigured, the following lines may be applied:

> Non *Hymenaeus* adest illi, non gratia lecto;
> Eumenides tenuere faces de funere raptas:
> Eumenides stravere torum.

[*1786*, but *1816* has omitted about four-fifths, containing many parallels. The lines quoted are from Ovid, *Metamorphoses*, vi. 429-31.]

(5) *She clapped her hands*: This was the ordinary method in the East of calling the attendants in waiting. See *Arabian Nights*, vol. I. p. 5. 106. 193, &c. [*1786*.]

Page 74. [*the rights of hospitality*: *1816* omits *1786*'s citation of Richardson, *Dissertation*, p. 219, which is worth quoting: 'The wretch, who had betrayed the man, whose bread he had eaten, was justly stamped with the deepest infamy: a *Bread and Salt Traitor* being one of the most opprobious epithets by which one Asiatic could express his detestation of another.']

Page 75. [The use of narcotics to give the appearance of death is a fairly common device in the *Arabian Nights* and their imitators.]

Page 76. *Funeral vestments were prepared; their bodies washed, &c.*: The rites here practised had obtained from the earliest ages. Most of them may be found in Homer and the other poets of Greece. Lucian describes the dead in his time as washed, perfumed, vested, and crowned, with the flowers most in season; or, according to other writers, those in particular which the deceased were wont to prefer. [*1786*, but *1816* has omitted a Greek phrase, the last sentence of the paragraph and a second paragraph on classical burial dress. The reference is to Lucian, *On Funerals* (ed. A. M. Harmon, 1925, iv. 119).]

Page 77. (1) *all instruments of music were broken*: Thus, in the Arabian Nights: 'Haroun al Raschid wept over Schemselnihar, and, before he left the room, ordered all the musical instruments to be broken.' Vol. II. p. 196. [*1786*.]

(2) *Imans began to recite their prayers*: An iman is the principal priest of a mosque. It was the office of the imans to precede the bier, praying as the procession moved on. *Relig. Cerem.* vol. VII. p. 117. [*1786*.]

(3) [*'La Ilah illa Alla!'*: The note in *1786*, omitted in *1816* but retained in reduced form in *1787* and *1815*, began: 'This exclamation, which contains the leading principle of Mahometan belief, and signifies *there is no God but God*; was commonly uttered under some violent emotion of mind.' Cf. Voltaire, *Travels of Scarmentado* (*Zadig and Other Tales*, trans. R. B. Boswell, 1891, p. 203): '"Allah! Illah! Allah!" These are the words in which Turks solemnly profess their faith: but I imagined them to be expressions of love, and responded in the tenderest accents . . .'.]

Page 79. (1) *the angel of death had opened the portal of some other world*: The name of this exterminating angel is *Azrael*, and his office is to conduct the dead to the abode assigned them; which is said by some to be near the place of their interment. Such was the office of Mercury in the Grecian Mythology. *Sale's Prelim. Disc.* p. 101. *Hyde in notis ad Bobov.* p. 19. *R. Elias, in Tishbi. Buxtorf Synag. Jud. et Lexic. Talmud. Homer. Odyss.* [*1786*, but *1816* has added the references to Mercury and the *Odyssey*. The references to Bobovius, R. Elias, and Buxtorfius derive directly from Sale: see Johannes Buxtorfius, *Synagoga Judaica* (1603) and *Lexicon Chaldaicum Talmudicum et Rabbinicum* (1639) and Thomas Hyde's notes to Albertus Bobovius' *Tractatus . . . De Turcarum Liturgia* (Oxford, 1690).]

(2) *Monker and Nekir*: These are two black angels of a tremendous appearance, who examine the departed on the subject of his faith: by whom, if he give not a satisfactory account, he is sure to be cudgelled with maces of red-hot iron, and tormented more variously than words can describe. *Relig. Ceremon.* vol. VII. p. 59. 68. 118. vol. V. p. 290. *Sale's Prelim. Disc.* p. 101. [*1786*, but *1816* has omitted another reference to the unpublished MSS. mentioned in Henley's Preface. Henley asked Beckford for advice about this note on 19 June 1785 (Melville, p. 133). In addition to sources given, Monker and Nekir are mentioned in d'Herbelot, p. 58.]

(3) *the fatal bridge*: This bridge, called in Arabick *al Siral*, and said to extend over the infernal gulph, is represented as narrower than a spider's web, and sharper than the edge of a sword. Yet the paradise of Mahomet can be entered by no other avenue. Those indeed who have behaved well need not be alarmed; mixed characters will find it difficult; but the wicked soon miss their standing, and plunge headlong into the abyss. *Pocock in Port. Mos.* p. 282, &c. [*1786*, but *1816* has omitted half, containing English parallels, and misreads *al Sirat* as *al Siral*. The reference to Edward Pococke, *Porta Mosis sive dissertationes aliquot a . . . Mose Maimonide* (Oxford, 1655) is presumably to the 'Appendix Notarum Miscellanea' (dated 1654), p. 288 (not 282). The reference derives from Sale's *Preliminary Discourse*, sect. iv., p. 121.]

Page 80. (1) *a certain series of years*: According to the tradition from the Prophet, not less than nine hundred, nor more than seven thousand. [*1786*.]

(2) *the sacred camel*: It was an article of the Mahometan creed, that

all animals would be raised again, and some of them admitted into paradise. The animal here mentioned appears to have been one of those *white-winged* CAMELS *caparisoned with gold*, which Ali affirmed would be provided to convey the faithful. *Relig. Cer.* vol. VII. p. 70. *Sale's Prelim. Disc.* p. 112. *Al Janheri. Ebno'l Athir*, &c. [*1786*, but *1816* omits a footnote and reads '*Al Janheri*' for '*Al Jauheri*'. Henley's references to '*Al Jauheri. Ebno'l Athir*' may merely derive from Sale's *Preliminary Discourse*, sect. v, p. 172, where 'Al Jawhari. Ebn al Athir' are cited on the camel. But the spelling suggests that Henley may have looked at Sale's source, Edward Pococke, *Specimen Historiae Arabum* (Oxford, 1650), where Al Jauhar and Ebnol Athir are frequently cited.]

Page 81. the Caliph presented himself to the emir in a new light: The propensity of a vicious person, in affliction, to seek consolation from the ceremonies of religion, is an exquisite trait in the character of Vathek. [*1786*.]

Page 88. (1) *wine hoarded up in bottles, prior to the birth of Mahomet*: The prohibition of wine by the Prophet materially diminished its consumption, within the limits of his own dominions. Hence a reserve of it might be expected, of the age here specified. The custom of hoarding wine was not unknown to the Persians, though not so often practised by them, as by the Greeks and the Romans.

'I purchase' (says Lebeid) 'the old liquor, at a dear rate, in dark leathern bottles, long reposited; or in casks black with pitch, whose seals I break, and then fill the cheerful goblet.' *Moallakat*, p. 53. [*1786*. The quotation is from 'The Poem of Lebeid' in Sir William Jones's translation of *The Moallakát* (1783), p. 53.]

(2) *excavated ovens in the rock*: As substitutes for the portable ovens, which were lost. [*1786*.]

(3) [*Dilara*: The name of a beautiful young woman in Pétis de la Croix, *Les Mille et un jours* (1710), i. 302 (Weber, *Tales of the East*, ii. 345 ff., 'The History of Couloufe and of the beautiful Dilara').]

Page 90. [*Nerkes . . . Cafour*: The names are taken from d'Herbelot, p. 669, where it is stated that they are often given 'à des Esclaves Noirs, qui sont fort estimez dans tout l'Orient'.]

Page 91. the confines of some cemetery: Places of interment in the East were commonly situated in scenes of solitude. We read of one in the history of the first calender, abounding with so many monuments, that four days were successively spent in it without the inquirer being able to find the tomb he looked for: and, from the story of Ganem, it appears that the doors of these cemeteries were often left open. *Arabian Nights*, vol. II. p. 112. [*1786*. The reference should be to the *Arabian Nights*, i. 112; the passage from the story of Ganem is in the *Arabian Nights*, iii. 134-5.]

Page 94. a Myrabolan comfit: The invention of this confection is attributed by M. Cardonne to Avicenna, but there is abundant reason, exclusive of our author's authority, to suppose it of a much earlier origin. Both the Latins and Greeks were acquainted with the balsam, and the tree that produced it was indigenous in various parts of Arabia. [*1786*. The reference is to Denis Cardonne, *A Miscellany of Eastern Learning* (2 vols., 1771), ii. 143: 'Medicine is indebted to [Avicenna] for the discovery of cassia, rhubarb, mirabillons, and tamarinds'.]

Page 95. blue fishes: Fishes of the same colour are mentioned in the Arabian Nights; and, like these, were endowed with the gift of speech. [*1786*. See the *Arabian Nights*, i. 63, 65.]

Page 98. astrolabes: The mention of the astrolabe may be deemed incompatible, at first view, with chronological exactness, as there is no instance of any being constructed by a Mussulman, till after the time of Vathek. It may, however, be remarked, to go no higher, that Sinesius, bishop of Ptolemais, invented one in the fifth century; and that Carathis was not only herself a Greek, but also cultivated those sciences which the good Mussulmans of her time all held in abhorrence. *Bailly*, *Hist. de l'Astronom. Moderne*, tom. I. p. 563. 573. [*1786*. The reference is to J. S. Bailly, *Histoire de l'Astronomie Moderne depuis la fondation de l'école d'Alexandre* (3 vols., Paris, 1779-82).]

Page 99. [Motavakel: For a full account of Vathek's brother and successor, see d'Herbelot, pp. 640-2. This revolt is Beckford's invention.]

Page 100. On the banks of the stream, hives and oratories: The bee is an insect held in high veneration amongst the Mahometans, it being pointed out in the Koran, 'for a sign unto the people that understand'. It has been said, in the same sense: 'Go to the ant, thou sluggard,' *Prov.* vi. 6. The santons, therefore, who inhabit the fertile banks of Rocnabad, are not less famous for their hives than their oratories. *D'Herbelot*, p. 717. [*1786*. See the *Koran*, ch. 16, ed. Sale, ii. 84.]

Page 102. (1) Shieks, cadis: Shieks are the chiefs of the societies of derviches: cadis are the magistrates of a town or city. [*1786*.]

(2) *Asses in bridles of riband inscribed from the Koran*: As the judges of Israel in ancient days rode on white asses, so amongst the Mahometans, those that affect an extraordinary sanctity, use the same animal in preference to the horse. Sir John Chardin observed in various parts of the East, that their reins, as here represented, were of silk, with the name of God, or other inscriptions upon them. *Ludeke Expos. brevis*, p. 49. *Chardin's MS*. cited by Harmer. [*1786*. The references are to C. W. Luedecke, *Expositio Brevis* (1777) (see page 56, note 1); and Thomas Harmer, *Observations on Divers Passages of Scripture* (2nd edn., 1776) i. 470-1, which printed some of Chardin's MSS.]

Page 103. (1) [*Sheddad*: See d'Herbelot, p. 780, 'SCHEDAD': 'Ce Personnage fabuleux vivoit & regnoit en Arabie, selon les anciennes Histoires de l'Orient, du temps de Giamschid Roy de Perse de la première Dynastie... Schedad bâtit dans la Syrie une Ville qu'il nomma, Gennet, Paradis....']

(2) [*One of these*, etc.: This episode seems to derive from Addison's 'Vision of Mirzah', in *Spectator* No. 159 (1 Sept. 1711), which describes the 'inexpressibly melodious' tunes played by a shepherd: 'They put me in mind of those heavenly Airs that are played to the departed Souls of good Men upon their first Arrival in Paradise, to wear out the Impressions of their last Agonies, and qualify them for the Pleasures of that happy Place. My Heart melted away in secret Raptures.']

Page 104. (1) [*energetic*: powerfully effective.]

(2) *Eblis*: D'Herbelot supposes this title to have been a corruption of the Greek Διαβολος *diabolos*. It was the appellation conferred by the Arabians upon the prince of the apostate angels, and appears more likely to originate from the Hebrew הבל, *hebel*, vanity, pride.—*See below the note* [3 to page 111], '*creatures of clay*'. [*1786*, but *1816* has rephrased and recast it, adding the Hebrew etymology. See d'Herbelot, p. 307.]

Page 105. *compensate for thy impieties by an exemplary life*: It is an established article of the Mussulman creed, that the actions of mankind are all weighed in a vast unerring balance, and the future condition of the agents determined according to the preponderance of evil or good. This fiction, which seems to have been borrowed from the Jews, had probably its origin in the figurative language of scripture. Thus, Psalm lxii. 9. Surely men of low degree are vanity, and men of high degree are a lie: to be laid in the balance, they are altogether lighter than vanity:—and, in Daniel, the sentence against the King of Babylon, inscribed on the wall: Thou art weighed in the balance, and found wanting. [*1786*. See Daniel 5: 27.]

Page 106. (1) *Balkis*: This was the Arabian name of the Queen of Sheba, who went from the south to hear the wisdom and admire the glory of Solomon. The Koran represents her as a worshipper of fire. Solomon is said not only to have entertained her with the greatest magnificence, but also to have raised her to his bed and his throne. *Al Koran*, ch. XXVII. and *Sale's notes. D'Herbelot*, p. 182. [*1786*.]

(2) [*Istakar*: The main source for Beckford's description of Istakhar, the ancient Persepolis, seems to have been the detailed account in Jean Chardin's *Voyages . . . en Perse, et autres Lieux de l'Orient* (Amsterdam, 1711), iii. 99–139, especially the opening pages and the numerous engravings. Beckford may also have been influenced by illustrations in Corneille Le Brun, *Voyages . . . par la Moscovie, en Perse, et aux Index Orientales* (2 vols., Amsterdam, 1718; English translation, 2 vols., 1737). In Chardin Beckford would find the two rocks forming the portal to the valley of Istakhar, the royal mausoleums on the mountainside, the terrace of black marble, the staircase, the watchtowers, the lofty columns, the walls embossed with figures and the animals depicted on pillars. Chardin also mentions the appearance of the temple by moonlight and the legends of concealed treasures in the subterranean tombs.]

Page 108. [*The rock yawned*, etc.: Suggested parallels with the subterranean palace of Eblis described in J. P. Bignon, *Avantures d'Abdalla* (1712; English trans. by W. Hatchett, 1729) have been over-emphasized, but some resemblances are of interest. See 'The History of Dilsenguin, the Restorer of Magic; and of the Princess Perifirime, Foundress of the Fairies', in Weber, *Tales of the East*, iii. 661–2.]

Page 111. (1) [*Eblis*: Cf. Milton's description of Satan, *Paradise Lost*, i. 591–6, 600–4.]

(2) *Ouranbad*: This monster is represented as a fierce flying hydra, and belongs to the same class with the *rakshe* whose ordinary food was serpents and dragons; the *soham*, which had the head of a horse, with four eyes, and the body of a flame-coloured dragon; the *syl*, a basilisk with a face resembling the human, but so tremendous that no mortal could bear to behold it; the *ejder*, and others. See these respective titles in Richardson's Persian, Arabic, and English Dictionary. [*1786*. The reference is to John Richardson, *A Dictionary, Persian, Arabic, and English* (2 vols., Oxford, 1777–80). See also d'Herbelot, p. 71.]

(3) *Creatures of clay*: Nothing could have been more appositely

imagined than this compellation. Eblis, according to Arabian mythology, had suffered a degradation from his primeval rank, and was
consigned to these regions, for having refused to worship Adam, in
obedience to the supreme command: alledging in justification of his
refusal, that himself had been formed of etherial fire, whilst Adam was
only a creature of clay. *Al Koran*, c. 55, &c. [*1786*. See also d'Herbelot,
pp. 55, 298, 307, 396.]

(4) *the fortress of Aherman*: In the mythology of the easterns, Aherman was accounted *the Demon of Discord*. The ancient Persian romances abound in descriptions of this fortress, in which the inferior demons
assemble to receive the behests of their prince; and from whom they
proceed to exercise their malice in every part of the world. *D'Herbelot*,
p. 71. [*1786*.]

(5) *the halls of Argenk*: The halls of this mighty dive, who reigned in
the mountains of Kaf, contained the statues of the seventy-two Solimans, and the portraits of the various creatures subject to them; not
one of which bore the slightest similitude to man. Some had many
heads; others, many arms; and some consisted of many bodies. Their
heads were all very extraordinary, some resembling the elephant's,
the buffalo's and the boar's; whilst others were still more monstrous.
D'Herbelot, p. 820. Some of the idols worshipped to this day in the
Hindostan answer to this description.

Ariosto, who owes more to Arabian fable than his commentators
have hitherto supposed, seems to have been no stranger to the halls of
Argenk, when he described one of the fountains of Merlin:—

> Era una delle fonti di Merlino
> Dello quattro di Francia da lui fatte;
> D'intorno cinta di bel marmo fino,
> Lucido, e terso, e bianco più che latte.
> Quivi d' intaglio con lavor divino
> Avea Merlino immagini ritratte.
> Direste che spiravano, e se prive
> Non fossero di voce, ch' eran vive.
>
> Quivi una Bestia uscir della foresta
> Parea di crudel vista, odiosa, e brutta,
> Che avea le orecchie d'asino, e la testa
> Di lupo, e i denti, e per gran fame asciutta;
> Branche avea di leon; l'altro, che resta,
> Tutto era volpe.

[*1786*, but *1816* has added the sentence at the end of the first paragraph. The quotation is from *Orlando Furioso*, XXVI. xxx–xxxi.]

Page 112. (1) *holding his right hand motionless on his heart*: Sandys observes, that the application of the right hand to the heart is the customary mode of eastern salutation; but the perseverance of the votaries of Eblis in this attitude, was intended to express their devotion to him both heart and hand. [*1786*. The reference is to George Sandys, *A Relation of a Journey began An: Dom: 1610* (1615), p. 64.]

(2) [*Soliman Daki . . . Gian Ben Gian*: Beckford wrote to Henley, *c*. April 1785 (for this misdated letter, see page 50, note 2): 'Soliman raad, Soliman Daki (not Dawmins for God's sake) & Soliman surnamed Gian-ben-Gian will furnish ample food for a display of oriental erudition.' 'Soliman Raad' is listed in *1786* and all the French editions, but is omitted, perhaps in error, in *1816* (see Textual Notes). Henley for once was not tempted to display his 'oriental erudition' in a note on this subject.]

Page 113. *In my life-time, I filled, &c.*: This recital agrees perfectly with those in the Koran, and other Arabian legends. [*1786*. The 'recital' is in fact translated with little alteration from d'Herbelot, p. 819.]

Page 114. [*his heart enveloped in flames*: A definite source for this striking episode seems to be Thomas Gueullette's *Les Sultanes de Guzurate ou les Songes des hommes eveillés*, *Contes Mogols* (1732), trans. into English as *Mogul Tales, Or, The Dreams of Men Awake* (2 vols., 1736). The following quotations are from 'The History of the Blind-Man of Chitor, whose Name was Aboul-Assam' in this translation, i. 173–7 (Weber, *Tales of the East*, iii. 57–9). After a career of crime, Aboul-Assam decides to visit Persepolis and the temple built there by Solomon for his queen, who was 'of the Religion of the *Gubres*, i.e. *Persees* or *Worshippers of Fire*'. He is led into a 'subteraneous Passage' in the side of the mountain: 'at last we travers'd a long Alley of black Marble, but so finely polish'd, that it had the Appearance of a Looking-Glass . . . we reach'd a large Hall, where we found three Men standing Mute, and in Postures of Sorrow'. They were awaiting the 'just Judgement of God': 'Alas, cry'd the third, we are continually tortured for the evil Actions we have done, see what a wretched State we are in; then they unbutton'd their Wastcoats, and through their Skin, which appear'd like Chrystal, I saw their Heart compass'd with Fire, by which, tho' they were burnt without ceasing, yet they were never consumed.'

Seeing their evil actions portrayed on a 'large Table', Aboul-Assam condemns them, whereupon his own misdeeds are depicted. He is then punished, but only temporarily.]

Page 116. (1) [*Each person proceeded in order*, etc.: These stories are the so-called 'Episodes' to *Vathek*, on which Beckford worked from 1782 or 1783 to 1786 and which, until Henley disobediently published his English translation of *Vathek*, he intended should be published with the main tale as a kind of *Suite des Contes Arabes*. *Lausanne* lists four stories as follows:

Histoire des deux princes amis, *Alasi* & *Jironz*, enfermés dans le palais souterrain.

Histoire du prince *Kalilah* & de la princesse *Zulkais*, sa soeur, enfermés dans le palais souterrain.

Histoire du prince *Berkiarekh* enfermé dans le palais souter rain.

Histoire du prince ...... enfermé dans le palais souterrain.

1786, without giving their titles, also refers to four tales, but only the first three are listed in *1787* and *1815*, and the first issue of *1816*, which follows the French editions in specifying the titles (see Textual Note). *Zulkais et Kalilah* is incomplete and there is evidence to suggest that the later part was suppressed by Beckford. The fourth 'Episode', perhaps the *Histoire de Motassem* which Beckford did not finish until 1815, may have met the same fate. Beckford played with the possibility of publishing the 'Episodes' almost to the end of his life. The prefatory note to *1815* states: 'J'ai preparé quelques Episodes; ils sont indiqués, à la page 200, comme faisant suite a Vathek — peut-être paroitront-ils un jour.' He also wrote in 1815 an unpublished preface intended for an edition of the 'Episodes' and another 'Avertissement', probably written during the 1830s, when he entered into abortive negotiations for their publication. Samuel Rogers heard part of them read at Font-hill in 1817 and his account of these somewhat lurid tales excited in Byron an unsuccessful desire to borrow them. For a full discussion of the 'Episodes' and the problems connected with them, see Parreaux, pp. 411–43. Two of the three 'Episodes' were first published in the *English Review* (Dec. 1909; Aug. and Sept. 1910) in French, and all three were published in an English translation by Sir Frank T. Marzials in 1912. Three editions of *Vathek* reunite it with the 'Episodes', all giving the French texts only: ed. Guy Chapman (2 vols., Cambridge,

1929); ed. J. B. Brunius (Paris [1948]); and ed. E. Giddey (Lausanne, 1962).]

(2) *Carathis on the back of an afrit*: The expedition of the afrit in fetching Carathis, is characteristic of this order of dives. We read in the Koran that another of the fraternity offered to bring the Queen of Saba's throne to Solomon, before he could rise from his place, c. 27. [*1786*.]

Page 119. (1) *Glanced off in a whirl that rendered her invisible*: It was extremely proper to punish Carathis by a rite, and one of the principal characteristics of that science in which she so much delighted, and which was the primary cause of Vathek's perdition and of her own. The circle, the emblem of eternity, and the symbol of the sun, was held sacred in the most ancient ceremonies of incantations; and the whirling round deemed as a necessary operation in magical mysteries. Was not the name of the greatest enchantress in fabulous antiquity, Circe, derived from Κίρκος, a circle, on account of her magical revolutions and of the circular appearance and motion of the sun her father? The fairies and elves used to arrange themselves in a ring on the grass; and even the augur, in the liturgy of the Romans, whirled round to encompass the four cardinal points of the world. It is remarkable, that a derivative of the Arabic word (which corresponds to the Hebrew סהר, and is interpreted *scindere secare se in orbem, inde notio circinandi, mox gyrandi et hinc à motu versatili, fascinavit, incantavit*) signifies, in the Koran, *the glimmering of twilight*; a sense deducible from the shapeless glimpses of objects, when hurried round with the velocity here described, and very applicable to the sudden disappearance of Carathis, who, like the stone in a sling, by the progressive and rapid increase of the circular motion, soon ceased to be perceptible. Nothing can impress a greater awe upon the mind than does this passage in the original. [*1816* is three times as long as *1786*. The basis of *1786* is retained in the first sentence and the sentence beginning 'It is remarkable' to 'the velocity here described'. Henley and Beckford corresponded about the punishment of Carathis during April 1785. Henley suggested on 12 April that she deserved 'a different and more conspicuous punishment than the rest—perhaps Vathek's and Nouronihar's should have been also diversified' (Melville, p. 129). On 23 April Beckford admitted that Nouronihar was 'too severely punished' and wondered how to 'add a crime or two to her share' (Melville, p. 130). On 26 April Henley suggested that this passage should read: ' and execrating the hour in which she was begotten, and the womb that had borne her, started at once into a whirl so rapid as rendered her form altogether indistinct. Thus, with every energy of her soul intensely occupied on her immediate perceptions, was she doomed to wander in eccentric revolutions, without pause or remission'. Henley went on to discuss ways of discriminating the punishments of Nouronihar and Vathek and suggested the omission of the final reference to Gulchenrouz (Melville, p. 131). Beckford replied (for this misdated letter see page 50, note 2 above): 'The catastrophe of Carathis had better remain as you first intended. I am perfectly at a loss how to deepen Vathec's damnation, &, as to the end where mention was made of Gul[chenrouz], be assured we cannot improve it. The period runs admirably, & for my part I think the contrast between the boisterous Caliph & the peacable innocent Gul[chenrouz] not ill imagined.']

(2) *they, at once, lost the most precious gift of heaven*:—HOPE: It is a soothing reflection to the bulk of mankind, that the commonness of any blessing is the true test of its value. Hence, Hope is justly styled 'the most precious of the gifts of heaven,' because, as Thales long since observed—όις αλλο μηδεν, αυτη παρεσιν—it abides with those who are destitute of every other. Dante's inscription over the gate of hell was written in the same sense, and perhaps in allusion to the saying of the Grecian sage:—

> Per me si va nella città dolente:
>   Per me si va nell' eterno dolore:
>   Per me si va tra la perduta gente.
> Giustizia mosse 'l mio alto fattore:
>   Fecemi la divina potestate,
>   La somma sapienza, e 'l primo amore.
> Dinanzi a me non fur cose create,
>   Se non eterne, ed io eterno duro:
>   Lasciate ogni speranza, voi che 'ntrate.

CANTO III.

Strongly impressed with this idea, and in order to complete his description of the infernal dungeon, Milton says,

> ———— where ————
> ———————— hope never comes
> That comes to all.

Paradise L. 1. 66.

[*1816* has transferred the parallel with Dante, *Inferno*, iii. 1 ff., which was placed in an earlier note in *1786*, to this point, and adds the parallel with Milton, *Paradise Lost*, i. 65–7. Beckford had quoted the lines from Dante in a letter written in [? 1778] and asked: 'What can be more dire than the beginning of the Canto' (Melville, pp. 43–4).]

APPENDIX I

PREFACES TO *VATHEK*

Henley's English translation, 1786

PREFACE

THE Original of the following Story, with some others of a similar kind, collected in the East by a Man of letters, was communicated to the Editor above three years ago. The pleasure he received from the perusal of it, induced him at that time to transcribe, and since to translate it. How far the copy may be a just representation, it becomes not him to determine. He presumes, however, to hope that, if the difficulty of accommodating our English idioms to the Arabick, preserving the correspondent tones of a diversified narration, and discriminating the nicer touches of character through the shades of foreign manners, be duly considered; a failure in some points, will not preclude him from all claim to indulgence: especially, if those images, sentiments, and passions, which, being independant of local peculiarities, may be expressed in every language, shall be found to retain their native energy in our own.

The French edition published at Lausanne, 1786

AVIS

L'OUVRAGE que nous présentons au public a été composé en François, par M. BECKFORD. L'indiscrétion d'un homme de Lettres à qui le manuscrit avoit été confié, il y a trois ans, en a fait connoître la traduction angloise avant la publication de l'original. Le Traducteur a même pris sur lui d'avancer, dans sa Préface, que Vathek étoit traduit de l'Arabe. L'Auteur s'inscrit en faux contre cette assertion, & s'engage à ne point en imposer au public sur d'autres ouvrages de ce genre qu'il se propose de faire connoître; il les puisera dans la collection précieuse de manuscrits orientaux laissés par feu M. Worthley Montague, & dont les originaux se trouvent à Londres chez M. Palmer, Régisseur de Duc de Bedford.

The French edition published in London, *1815*

LES editions de Paris et de Lausanne, etant devenu extrémement rares, j'ai consenti enfin a ce que l'on republiât à Londres ce petit ouvrage tel que je l'ai composé.

La traduction, comme on sçait, a paru avant l'original; il est fort aisé de croire que ce n'etoit pas mon intention—des circonstances, peu interessantes pour le public, en ont été la cause.

J'ai preparé quelques Episodes; ils sont indiqués, à la page 200, comme faisant suite a Vathek—peut-être paroitront-ils un jour.

W. BECKFORD

1 Juin, 1815

Draft 'Avertissement pour l'édition de Vathek avec Les Épisodes' (*printed in* The Episodes of Vathek, *translated by Sir Frank T. Marzials, 1912, p. xxix*)

DEPUIS quelque tems nous avançons à pas précipités vers la tolérance universelle. Le fameux drame d'Horace Walpole, fondé sur l'inceste le plus révoltant, se public enfin sans scrupule. On dévore 'Don Juan,' on se jette à corps perdu sur les romans de Madame du Devant et de Victor Hugo, on ne tombe pas mort de surprise et d'indignation en lisant les rapsodies blasphématoires d'Edgar Quinet. Je ne prétend pas avoisiner même l'effervescente luxure de ces énergiques ouvrages, mais comme dans le siècle d'or de la compagnie de Jésus tout parôissoit licite à ces doctes personnages pour atteindre une heureuse fin, j'ose me flatter qu'au moins *la morale* de mes contes est assez évidente pour produire des réflexions salutaires. Qu'on les parcoure donc avec confiance en se pénétrant d'une vérité que la religion même nous démontre, et se disant au fond de sa conscience : Ceux qui, à l'instar du Calife Vathek et de ses malheureux compagnons, se livrent aux passions criminelles, et aux actions atroces, termineront leur carrière, par une rétribution terrible, mais juste, dans le séjour de l'eternelle vengeance.

APPENDIX II

Account of Vathek from d'Herbelot's *Bibliothèque Orientale* (1697), pp. 911–12

VATHEK Billah. C'est le nom du neuviéme Khalife de la Race des Abbassides. Il étoit fils de Motâssem, & petit fils de Haroun Al Raschid; c'est-pourquoy, il avoit pour Nom propre, celuy de, Haroun. Sa Mere qui se nommoit, Carathis, étoit Grecque de Nation, & il succeda à Motâssem son pere, l'an 227. de l'hegire.

Ce Prince étoit fort attaché à la Secte des Motazales & favorisoit beaucoup tous ceux qui étoient de la Famille d'Ali. Il persecuta sur tout, tous ceux qui refusoient de croire, & de declarér que l'Alcoran fut créé. Car, c'étoit-là la question du temps.

Ahmed fils de Nasser, fils de Malek, surnommé, Al Khoraï, un des plus celebres Docteurs entre ceux qui portent le titre de, Hafedh, ou Hofadh au plurier; c'est-à-dire, de Conservateurs des Traditions Prophetiques, gagna plusieurs de ses Collegues, & s'accosta des principaux Seigneurs de la Ville de Bagdet.

Tous ces Docteurs joints ensemble resolurent avec ces Seigneurs de déposseder Vathek du Khalifat, & ils étoient déja convenus du jour auquel cette resolution devoit être executée, & auquel on devoit mettre Ahmed sur le Thrône du Khalifat. Mais, il arriva que quelques-uns de ces Conjurez ayant voulu precipiter la chose, ne furent pas suivis des autres qui attendoient le jour prefixe duquel on étoit convenu.

Sur ces entrefaites le Gouverneur de la Ville de Bagdet eut

quelque vent de cette Conspiration. Le soupçon luy fit appro-
fondir la chose, & il en fut enfin entiérement éclairci. Il envoya
aussi tost arrester Ahmed dans son logis, luy fit mettre ensuite
les fers aux pieds, & le fit transporter en la Ville de Samarah,
qui étoit alors le siege Royal, & la demeure ordinaire des
Khalifes.

Vathek ayant fait venir Ahmed en sa presence, ne luy dit pas
un mot de la Conjuration. Il le pressa seulement sur le fait de
la Religion, & particuliérement sur la question dont il étoit alors
furieusement entêté. Mais, le Docteur Ahmed persistant toû-
jours dans le sentiment ordinaire des Musulmans Orthodoxes,
& refusant d'admettre la Création de l'Alcoran, le Khalife irrité
de ce refus, mit la main à l'épée, & luy coupa la teste de sa propre
main.

Ce Khalife Vathek prenoit à cœur d'imiter le Khalife
Mamoun son oncle en toutes choses. Car, il s'affectionna à
l'étude des sciences, & il carressoit beaucoup les Gens de lettres.
Il étoit aussi fort liberal & charitable, ayant grand soin qu'on
ne vit aucun mendiant dans ses Etats, de sorte que sous son
regne, on n'en vit jamais aucun, ni à la Mecque, ni à Medine.
Il s'étoit addonné particulierement à l'Astrologie, & ses Maîtres
en cette science ayant dressé son Horoscope, luy promirent
cinquante ans de vie. Mais, il ne passa pas néanmoins le dix-
iéme jour depuis cette prediction, & il mourut d'hydropysie,
l'an de l'hegire 232. n'ayant atteint que la trente-sixiéme année
de son âge. Quelques Auteurs ne luy en donnent même que
trente-deux. Motavakkel son frere luy succeda. *Khondemir*.

On ne trouve point pendant le regne de ce Khalife d'autre
expedition militaire que celle de Sicile, les Musulmans ayant
assiegé la Ville de Messine dans l'an 228. de l'hegire. Cette
Ville se rendit à eux, & sa perte fut suivie de celle de l'Isle
entiére, selon le rapport de Novaïri.

L'Auteur du Giamê alhekaïat, rapporte qu'Ahmed Ben
Nezir ayant été emprisonné au sujet de la question sur l'Alcoran,
de laquelle on a déja parlé, trouva si bonne compagnie dans
la prison, qu'il fut tout consolé dans une si triste demeure. Car,

A'bdalmalek Zaiiat Vizir du Khalife, homme fort emporté, persecutoit cruellement les plus honnestes gens de la Ville, & en remplissoit les prisons.

Parmy tous ces gens-là, Ahmed Ben Israïl, grand Astrologue se trouva du nombre, & Ahmed Ben Nezir luy raconta aussi bien qu'aux autres, que la nuit précedente un Phantôme luy avoit apparu en songe, & luy avoit dit, que dans un mois, le Khalife ne seroit pas en vie, sur quoy il pria cet Astrologue de faire son calcul, & de verifier cette direction. Mais, l'Astrologue refusa de se hazarder à cette entreprise, & le mois s'étant écoulé jusqu'au dernier jour, il dit à Ahmed Ben Nezir: Où est la promesse de vôtre Phantôme? Car nous voicy arrivé au terme qu'il vous avoit marqué. Ahmed luy ayant répondu, qu'il pouvoit encore se passer bien des choses avant que la nuit fust finie, il arriva qu'à la seconde garde de la méme nuit, une Troupe de gens qui vinrent à la prison, donnerent avis de la mort de Vathek.

L'Auteur du Nighiaristan qui cite les Auteurs du Raoudhat alsafa, & du Habib alseïr, dit que le Khalife Vathek mangeoit & beuvoit avec excès, & le plus souvent sans appetit, ce qui joint aux plaisirs qu'il prenoit sans discretion avec les femmes, luy causa une hydropisie. Il avoir pour lors un tréssçavant Medecin de la Ville de Nischabour qui entreprit de le guerir, & le mit pour cet effet dans un four à chaux, aprés que la pierre en avoit été tirée, ne luy donnant pendant quelque temps que des viandes convenables à son mal à certaines heures reglées. Cette Cure luy réussit si bien, que Vathek retourna en parfaite santé. Mais, il n'observa pas l'avis que le Medecin luy donna, de ne plus retomber dans cette vie dereglée qu'il avoit menée jusques lors, d'autant que s'il retomboit dans le même mal, le même remede qu'il avoit pratiqué luy seroit inutile, & que son hydropysie alors deviendroit incurable. Le prognostic du Medecin se verifia dans sa personne. Car, ayant repris son premier train de vie, il finit bientost ses jours, comme l'on a déja vû.

Le même Auteur remarque, que le Khalife Vathek avoit l'œil si terrible, qu'ayant jetté un peu avant sa mort, une œillade

de colere sur un de ses Domestiques qui avoit fait quelque
manquement, cet homme en perdit contenance, & se renversa
sur un autre qui étoit proche de luy. Et par un accident assez
extraordinaire, il arriva que le même étant expiré, & son visage
couvert d'un linge, une fouine se glissa par dessous, & luy
arracha ce même œil dont les regards étoient si redoutables.

Ce fut sous le regne de Vathek, que Thaher second du nom,
quatriéme Sultan de la Dynastie des Thaheriens, reçut la
Patente & l'Etendart que les Khalifes avoient accoûtumé
d'envoyer aux Princes leurs Vassaux, qui vouloient bien recon-
noistre encore leur autorité, quoyqu'ils fussent d'ailleurs absolus
dans leurs Etats.

THE WORLD'S CLASSICS

A Select List

ANN RADCLIFFE: The Mysteries of Udolpho
Edited by Bonamy Dobrée

The Italian
Edited by Frederick Garber

TOBIAS SMOLLETT: Roderick Random
Edited by Paul-Gabriel Boucé

Travels through France and Italy
Edited by Frank Felsenstein

SIR WALTER SCOTT: The Heart of Midlothian
Edited by Clare Lamont

MARY WOLLSTONECRAFT:
Mary *and* The Wrongs of Woman
Edited by Gary Kelly

A complete list of Oxford Paperbacks, including books in The World's Classics, Past Masters, and OPUS Series, can be obtained from the General Publicity Department, Oxford University Press, Walton Street, Oxford OX2 6DP.

nugatory (9) →